DANGEROUS SECRETS

THE STORY OF IDUNA AND AGNARR

Inspired by

Disnep

FROZEN II

DANGEROUS
SECRETS

THE STORY OF IDUNA AND AGNARR

AN ORIGINAL TALE BY

MARI MANCUSI

Disnep PRESS

Los Angeles · New York

To my amazing Avalon.
Be fearless. Be kind.
And always do the next right thing.

—M.M.

Only Ahtohallan knows. . . .

The Dark Sea

THE STORM IS GETTING WORSE.

Lightning slashes across an angry black sky, soon followed by the crash of thunder. Waves pound against the ship's hull as I grip the wooden rail with white knuckles. Fierce gusts of wind tug my hair free from its braid, and damp brown strands whip at my face. I don't dare let go to brush them away.

Instead, I keep my eyes on the sea. Looking for *her*.

In some ways, I've spent my entire life looking for her. And tonight, my journey may finally come to an end. Unfinished. Unfound.

Ahtohallan. Please! I need you!

Perhaps she never existed at all. Perhaps she was simply a myth. A silly song to lull children to sleep. To make them feel safe and secure in a world that's anything but. Perhaps I was a fool to think we could simply go and seek her out. Learn the mother's secrets.

I do know something about a mother's secrets.

Another wave sweeps in, bashing against the ship's hull, sending a spray of icy seawater splashing at my face. I stumble backward, momentarily blinded by the salt stinging my eyes. A strong pair of hands clamps down on my hips; a solid chest at my back keeps me upright.

I turn, already knowing whom I'll find standing tall behind me. The man who has been with me almost my entire life. The man who has made me laugh—and cry—more than anyone else in the world. My husband. The father of my daughters. My enemy. My friend.

My love.

Agnarr, king of Arendelle.

"Come, Iduna," he says, pulling me around to face him. He reaches out, clasping my hands in his. They are as warm and strong as mine are cold and trembling.

I look up, taking in the sharp line of his jaw. The fierceness in his leaf-green eyes. If he's frightened, he's not showing it. "We need to go below deck," he says, shouting to be heard over the furious wind. "Captain's orders. It's not safe up here. One rogue wave could knock you overboard."

I feel a sob rise to my throat. I want to lash out, protest the orders. *I'm fine. I can take care of myself. I'm not some silly girl frightened by the elements.*

But what I really want to say is, *I can't leave. I haven't found her yet.*

If I go below, I may never find her.

And if I don't . . .

Elsa. My sweet Elsa . . . My dear Anna . . .

Agnarr gives me a pointed look. I sigh, untangling my hands from his, and begin stumbling toward the stairs that lead to our cabin below, on legs unaccustomed to rough seas. I'm almost there when the ship suddenly pitches hard to the left and I lose my footing, grabbing on to the railing to save myself. I can feel a few of the crew watching me with concern, but I push forward, keeping my head held high. I am a queen, after all. There are certain expectations.

Once below, I push open our cabin door and move inside, letting it bang shut behind me. The captain has given us his cabin for the journey, which I insisted wasn't necessary, but I was overruled. *It's the only cabin suited for a fine lady,* he protested. Because that's how he sees me. That's how they all see me now. A fine lady. A perfectly poised Arendellian queen.

But now, at last, Agnarr knows the truth.

I ease myself down on the bed, reaching to grab my knitting needles and my half-finished project. An inappropriate task under the circumstances, but perhaps the only thing that might steady my hands—my pounding heart. I can hear Agnarr push open the door, his strong, solid presence filling the room. But I don't look up. Instead, I start to knit as the ship rocks beneath my feet. It's dark down below, too dark to really see the delicate yarn, but my hands are sure and true, the repetitive motions as natural and familiar to me as taking in air. Yelana would be proud.

Yelana. Is she still out there, in the Enchanted Forest, still locked in the mist?

Only Ahtohallan knows.

Suddenly, I want to throw my needles across the room. Or collapse on the bed in tears. But I do neither, keeping my attention on the unfinished shawl. Forcing myself to let each stitch lull me into something resembling comfort.

Agnarr pulls out a wooden stool from the captain's desk, sitting down across from me. He picks up a corner of the unfinished shawl, running his large fingers across the tiny stitches. I dare to sneak a peek at him, realizing his eyes have become soft and faraway.

"This is the same pattern," he says slowly. And I know what he means without asking. Because of course it is. I hadn't even realized it when I started, but of course it is.

The same pattern as the shawl my mother knitted me when I was a baby.

The shawl that saved his life.

"It's an old Northuldra pattern," I explain, surprised how easily the words leave my mouth now that the truth is known. "Belonging to my family." I pick up his hand and place it on each symbol in turn. "Earth, fire, water, wind." I pause on the wind symbol, thinking back to Gale. "It was the Wind Spirit who helped me save your life that day in the forest."

He gives a low whistle. "A wind spirit! If only I'd known," he says, reaching up to brush his thumb gently across my cheek. Even after all these years, his touch still sparks a longing ache deep inside, and it's an imperative, not an option, to drop my needles to return the gesture. To run my fingers against the light stubble of his jaw. "It would have made my stories to the girls so much more interesting."

I smile at this. I can't help it. He has always found a way to help me find sunshine amidst the gloomiest of days. It's strange, though, to realize he knows everything now. After a lifetime overshadowed with secrets, it should feel freeing.

But in truth, it still scares me a little, and I find myself glancing at him when he doesn't know I'm looking. Trying to see, trying to know whether the truth has changed his feelings toward me. Does he resent me for keeping so much from him for so long? Or does he truly understand why I did it? If we survive this night, how will things change between us? Will the truth bring us closer together? Or tear us apart?

Only Ahtohallan knows. . . .

I reach out and take Agnarr's hands in mine, meeting his deep green eyes with my blue ones. I swallow down the lump in my throat that threatens to choke me, and force another smile.

"I will never forget that day," I start with a whisper, not sure he can even hear me over the tempest outside. "That horrible, wonderful day."

"Tell me," he whispers back, leaning in close. I can feel his breath on my lips. Our faces are inches away. "Tell me everything."

I swallow all the words that threaten to jump out of my throat in a hurried rush, throwing myself back on the bed, staring up at the wooden-beamed ceiling. After I breathe calmly, I say, "That might take all night."

He crawls onto the bed, lying down next to me. He reaches out and curls his hand into mine. "For you, I've got forever."

I swallow hard, tears welling in my eyes. I want to protest: we don't have forever. Or even all night. We may not have an hour, judging from the way the wooden beams of the ship are creaking and cracking. But at the same time, it doesn't matter. It's time. It's long past time. He deserves to know everything.

I swipe the tears away, rolling to my side and propping my head up with my elbow. "You have to tell your part, too," I say. "This story isn't only mine, you know."

His arm curls around my waist, his hand settling at the small of my back as he tugs me closer to him. He's so warm. How is it possible that he's still so warm? "I think I can manage that," he says with a small smile. "But you must start. It all began with you, after all."

"All right," I say, resting my head on his chest, his steady heartbeat against my ear. I close my eyes, trying to decide where to begin. So much has happened over the years. But there is that one day. One fateful day that changed the course of both our lives forever.

I open my eyes. "It all starts with the wind," I say. "My dear friend Gale."

As I speak, the words begin to course through me

like the forbidding waters roiling outside. And like the waters, I will finally make myself heard.

Agnarr will listen.

He's always been the storyteller in our family. But not this time. Now it's my turn to tell the tale.

CHAPTER ONE

Iduna
Twenty-Six Years Earlier

"STOP IT! YOU'RE TICKLING ME!"

I squealed in protest as the wind swirled around me, twirling me off my feet.

Gale, the Wind Spirit, seemed particularly, well, *spirited* this morning, tossing me playfully toward the sky, then catching me in a soft cushion of air as I fell back to the earth. My stomach dipped and rolled with each up and down motion as I tried to wrestle my way back to the ground. But I didn't put up too much of a fight. After all, this was the closest I, a human girl, could come to flying.

And who didn't want to fly?

"Where have you gone to, Iduna?" Yelana's voice cut through the forest. "Come back here and finish your knitting!"

Uh-oh. Gale dropped me unceremoniously onto my butt, swirling away quickly to hide behind a nearby oak. The Wind Spirit knew better than to mess with Yelana when she came calling. I groaned and rolled my eyes as I scrambled to my feet.

"Coward," I scolded.

Gale swept up a small pile of leaves, creating an overly exaggerated Yelana-shaped leaf monster, complete with scolding finger. I couldn't help a small laugh. "Yes, yes, I know. She can be scary. But still! You're the Wind Spirit!"

I turned my gaze toward the direction of our camp, where Yelana was probably sitting near the fire with the rest of the women. *Knitting.* Who could sit around and knit on a day like that? The sky was awake! Brilliant sunlight streamed through the canopy of trees above. It was the perfect backdrop for the day's impending celebration: the completion of the pact between us, the Northuldra, and the Arendellians, who lived in a stone city on the banks of the fjord.

They'd come to us years ago with an offer of peace and goodwill, promising to build a mighty dam to help us water our reindeer and keep our land fertile and fresh. I didn't really understand the whole thing, and I wasn't sure our elders were completely sold on the idea at first. But in the end, they came to an agreement and the dam was built. That day we would feast together to mark this new alliance between our people and theirs.

It was a day to dance and sing and celebrate the beauty of the forest.

Not sit around and knit.

Besides, I was only twelve years old. Which meant I literally had ages to learn boring grown-up things like knitting. Not to mention I already had a perfectly good knitted shawl to keep me warm. I hugged it to my chest, running my fingertips along the intricate patterns depicting the four spirits. My mother had made it for me when I was a baby, and I'd worn it ever since. I remembered her now, cuddling my five-year-old self close as I breathed in her warm, earthy scent. Listening to her sing sweet songs about a river of memories.

Memories were all I had left of my mother now. My father, too.

I shook the memories away, turning back to Gale, who was busy stirring up a pile of brown leaves into a small whirlwind. I bowed playfully to the spirit as I moved farther away from Yelana and her call to return to knitting.

"May I have this dance, fine sir?"

"But of course, my fair lady!" I replied in my best approximation of a wind spirit's voice. Gale couldn't talk like normal people could. But sometimes I swore I could hear the spirit sing. Sweet, high notes so heartbreakingly beautiful I felt as if I could get lost in them.

Gale picked me up again, with more force this time, twirling me back into the air. This time I didn't bother to fight it. "Higher!" I begged instead. "Higher than the treetops! I want to see the entire world!"

"Anything you wish, Princess!" I made the wind respond as it pulled me higher and higher until we rose above the trees and into open blue sky.

I wasn't really a princess, of course. We didn't even

have royalty here in the forest. Instead, we had a council of elders, which was basically a bunch of wise old people who liked to sit around and give advice. Other voices should be invited to the conversation, even if they didn't always agree with each other. For one person to rule over all, the elders would say, wasn't good.

But in the books the Arendellians brought to our villages as gifts while building the dam, there were often princesses. And princes and kings and queens, too, who were breathtakingly beautiful and wore fine clothes and jewels and lived in mighty castles like the one down on the fjord. Some were good and helped their people prosper while keeping the peace. Others were evil and did not appreciate all that was given to them. They would scorch the earth for their own selfish gain, not caring who got hurt in the process.

If I ever became a princess, I'd be one of the good ones for sure.

"Whoa! Who's that? Hey, come here, little fellow."

I almost fell out of the wind's embrace as I whirled around, my eyes locking on a strange boy far below me, trudging down the reindeer path. He didn't look much older than me, with thick blond hair and a strange fitted green jacket and a shirt as red as the autumn leaves underneath his feet. As I watched from above, he knelt to the ground, reaching out to try to pet a small rabbit that was sniffing the grass nearby. The rabbit, of course, was having none of this and quickly hopped away. The boy got to his feet just in time to find himself inches away from the daily reindeer parade to the watering hole, and, with a startled look, he leapt backward. I rolled my eyes. Hadn't he ever seen reindeer before?

One of the baby reindeer lagged behind the rest, going up to him and sniffing him curiously. The boy's face brightened and he dropped to his knees, pulling the creature into his arms and cuddling it as if it were the most precious treasure in the world. It made me smile.

I was about to tell Gale to set me down so I could introduce myself when I heard an angry voice cut through the trees.

"Agnarr! Where are you?"

The baby reindeer froze. It squirmed out of the boy's—Agnarr's—arms and raced in the direction of the herd. Agnarr watched it go, a sad expression taking over his face. The voice came again. Louder this time. More impatient. His shoulders slumped and he ran toward it, disappearing from view.

It was then that it all started to come together. He must be one of the Arendellians!

"Come on, Gale! Let's follow him!" I cried, any thought of adhering to Yelana's impatient call forgotten. "I want to see their camp!"

Gale obliged, whisking me in the direction Agnarr had gone, opposite the path of the reindeer herd. A few moments later, a small camp came into view. There were tents set up around a central firepit, though they were much different from the huts we used, which consisted of a tripod of poles covered by flat wooden slats. These tents were more like little houses made of brightly colored fabrics and topped with tiny flags fluttering gaily in the breeze. In the center, plopped down on the firepit, was a huge black cauldron, bubbling over with a delicious-smelling stew.

"Put me down," I whispered to Gale. "I want to get a better look."

The Wind Spirit lowered me gently. Once on the ground, I crept closer to the camp, using the trees for cover. The place was bustling with activity. Men and women of varying hair and skin colors stood at attention, dressed in identical green outfits, long sheathed swords hanging from their belts, burnished metal shields held at the ready. Soldiers, I supposed. There were also everyday citizens dressed in colorful embroidered vests and dresses. The cloth was so fine, I wanted to walk up and run it through my fingers to see what it would feel like.

It was then that I noticed the red cloak hanging from a rope stretched across two trees, alongside other clothes, probably hung out to dry. The need to run my hands over the bright, colorful cloth washed over me and, before I thought it through, I motioned for Gale to grab it and bring it to me. A moment later, the spirit dropped the cloak into my arms. I ran my hand against the finely woven fabric, watching as it slipped through my fingers like gossamer. How did they make it this soft?

Inspired, I slipped the cloak onto my shoulders, pulling the hood low over my face. Then I glanced at my reflection in a nearby stream. I looked like one of them now. A sudden idea took hold, and stuffing my shawl into a knothole in a nearby old oak, I grinned conspiratorially at Gale.

Time to explore.

I slipped into the camp, feeling as if I'd stepped into another world. The fancy tents were even more elaborate up close—gigantic pavilions with massive rooms containing actual beds and tables and chairs that looked to be hewn of the finest oaks. How had they carried all this up through the forest? And more important, why would they bother?

I shook my head, confounded as I continued to explore the camp. Suddenly I came across a group of women in simple homespun dresses and aprons, chattering as they carried baskets full of fruits and vegetables over to a long row table.

"I can't believe we're really here!" I heard one of them say. "It's so magical!"

"Magical?" scoffed another. "This forest is filthy! Get me back to civilization as soon as possible!"

"You just want to get back to Stephen," teased another. "The two of you complain endlessly when you're apart."

The second woman grinned. "All I can say is he'd better be working on our love spoon! I'm not planning to wait forever, you know!"

The trio broke out into giggles as they set the baskets on the table, then turned around for another batch. I ducked to keep out of sight, popping into a nearby vacant tent.

Empty of people. But full of food.

I stared wide-eyed at the feast piled high on the table. The smells surrounded me even as I feasted on the sight with my eyes. Puffy loaves of steaming dark brown bread, plates of rich meat soaked in gravy, smoky chunks and slices of various fish, earthy potatoes, roasted vegetables, and . . .

What were those dark brown blocks near the desserts at the very end?

Unable to resist, I snuck a delectable chunk and shoved it in my mouth. The sweetness practically exploded on my tongue as I closed my eyes in rapture.

Suddenly, I heard voices outside the tent. I froze.

"There you are, Agnarr," someone barked. "What did I tell you about running off like that?"

I froze. Agnarr? The boy from earlier? I dared peek outside the tent to get a better look. Sure enough, there he was, still dressed in his bright green suit. But he was no longer smiling. Instead, he was hanging his head, appearing ashamed. A tall, robust-looking man with a big blond mustache towered over him.

"I'm sorry, Papa," Agnarr murmured, shuffling his feet. "I just . . . wanted to look around a little. It feels so . . . magical here."

His father's face grew beet red. "Magic," he spat. "Agnarr, what have I told you about magic? Nothing good comes from magic. It is to be feared, not admired."

"I'm sorry, Papa," Agnarr murmured, still not looking his father in the eye. "I just—"

But his father waved him off, dismissing him without so much as a goodbye. Instead, he stormed over to the soldiers gathered at the head of the camp. "Are you ready?" he asked. "For the . . . festivities?" He laughed at this, but somehow the laughter didn't sound real. It was harsh. Bitter. Almost threatening in tone. I frowned, a strange feeling worming through my stomach. What he said hadn't been wrong. But there was something about the *way* he said it. . . .

I turned my attention back to Agnarr. He was watching his father with a look of unhappiness. And maybe a little . . . loneliness?

My heart tugged at the sight. I knew all too well what it was like to feel alone. Even when surrounded by so many others.

I watched as a new man approached. This one was wearing the same uniform as the other soldiers and had dark skin and kind eyes. Agnarr looked up at him and I saw his face brighten. Whoever this man was, he was a friend. I couldn't catch what they were saying, but I could tell they were joking around; the somber mood was lifting.

The call of horns broke through the air, announcing the official start of the feast. Everyone in the camp erupted into excited chatter and rushed toward the sound, arms laden with trays of food and other baskets and boxes, presumably gifts of some kind.

Now no longer nearby the others, I was able to sneak

out of the tent—after taking a second helping of the sweet brown blocks, obviously—and head in the direction of the celebration.

I was halfway there when I realized I'd left my shawl in the tree and was still wearing the borrowed Arendellian cape. I slipped the cape off my shoulders and hung it on a nearby tree branch; if the elders caught me wearing something so unfamiliar, they might question why. I considered going back to get my shawl, but in the end decided against it. It would still be there when I returned later, and I didn't want to be late for the feast.

"Gale, take me to the celebration," I whispered. In a moment I was up in the air, swirling in the gusts, twirling among the leaves. The air tickled my flushed cheeks and I couldn't help laughing out loud. And who could blame me? It was a glorious thing, dancing with the wind.

Suddenly, I got the sense I was being watched. Had Yelana finally become impatient with my absence and tracked me down? Well, when I looked below, it wasn't her at all, but rather Agnarr himself, looking up at me with the most fascinated eyes. I realized he probably thought it was magic, what his father had been talking about before. That I was some creature of nature, able to spread my hands and fly of my own accord.

The thought tickled me even more than Gale's breeze, and I burst into laughter as the Wind Spirit spun me higher and higher until I was breathless and dizzy. I could feel Agnarr still watching me. But I didn't mind.

Instead, I tucked my knees to my chest and launched into a perfect double-barrel roll. Might as well give him something to see.

But just as I was about to have Gale set me down so I could meet Agnarr at last, the laughter and happy sounds emanating from the feast suddenly grew quiet.

Too quiet.

CHAPTER TWO

Iduna

MY HEART POUNDED WITH FRIGHT AS A heightened pitch of angry voices suddenly reached my ears. What was going on? Gale seemed to sense my unease, setting me down before I could ask. By the time my feet had touched the earth, Agnarr was long gone and the angry shouting had transformed into screams of terror. A herd of spooked reindeer bolted past, almost trampling me.

It was then that I smelled it. The stench of smoke. I looked up, shocked to see flames of a purplish hue emanating from the angry Fire Spirit leaping from tree to tree, setting everything aflame, black smoke rising skyward. The ground suddenly rocked under my feet and my heart leapt to my throat as my ears caught an all-too-familiar sound.

It was the roar of the Earth Giants! The earth trembled with every pounding step. Had our celebration awoken them from their slumber by the river?

A shiver of fear tripped down my spine. I needed to find my family. Now.

I raced through the forest, the smoke getting thicker as I got closer to our camp, until it was nearly impossible to see. My eyes stung and watered, and my breath heaved down my throat in short gasps. It was then that I realized something else was going on amid the chaos. Something worse than the raging spirits themselves.

The Arendellians and Northuldra were attacking one another.

My ears picked up the sound of swords violently clanging against each other. The shouts of anger, then agony, rising above the crackle of flame and the roar of wind. Through the thick smoke I could barely make out shadows darting and swooping in combat, though what had begun the battle was unclear. All I knew was that the situation was very bad, and seemed to be getting worse by the minute.

I didn't know where to go. What to do. Was there anywhere safe to retreat until this was over?

My mother's shawl! I had to get it now, since the trees were on fire. It was the only thing I had left of her and I couldn't let it burn.

I changed directions, sprinting back toward the tree. My throat was raw from inhaling smoke and my lungs ached. As I ran, my mind raced with troubled thoughts. The spirits were clearly angry, lashing out at everyone in the forest. Was their rage caused by the battle? Or had they started it?

Finally, I reached the tree outside the completely deserted Arendellian camp. Upon plucking the shawl from the hollow, I wrapped it around my shoulders. Hugging the fringe to my chest in relief, I looked all over. The fire was still raging, the earth still shaking. Even the wind had risen up into a monstrous gale. I'd never seen anything like it.

I was on the verge of leaving when I heard a weak cry. Whirling around, my eyes widened as I spotted a crumpled figure splayed out against a large boulder. Blood seeped from a cut in the person's head, pouring down the rock, darkening the earth below. There was so much blood that it took me a moment to recognize him. But when I did, I gasped.

It was the boy. Agnarr. And he was badly hurt.

I glanced back at my forest. I knew I needed to return there, to our side, to find my family. To shelter in safety with them until the spirits were appeased and the battle had ceased. But what if I abandoned Agnarr and no one came for him? The crackling of the flames roared louder; the heat curled the hair on my arms. The air was filled with thick smoke. And he was in no shape to get to safety on his own.

Suddenly I heard voices calling my name from somewhere within the forest. My family was looking for me, I realized. They sounded worried. I needed to get to them, let them know I was all right. Let them lead me to where it was safe.

But then Agnarr would die.

I stared down at him, paralyzed by indecision. He looked pale as death, but I could see his chest rise and fall with shallow breaths. He was alive, but for how long? There were no Arendellians around. Even if they were looking for him, they might not find him before he lost too much blood. Before his lungs filled with smoke and he couldn't breathe.

But—just maybe—I could save him.

My mind raced; I was torn. I thought back to the forest. The fighting between his people and mine. That made him an enemy, even if I didn't know why.

I looked down at his drained face. And yet . . . he was also just a boy.

An injured boy who would die if I didn't do something.

A tree behind me creaked, fire snapping at its limbs. A branch broke, crashing from above. On instinct, I threw myself at Agnarr, rolling him to the side just in time to avoid the fiery brand. It hit the ground where he'd been lying only seconds before, and the dry brush around it flared up.

I inhaled deeply, making my decision. Lifting my raw voice to the sky, I sang for Gale, calling for the Wind Spirit the same way I always did. *"Ah ah ah ah!"*

For a moment, I heard nothing, and I began to worry the spirit was too wrapped up in whatever was happening to answer my call. But at last there was a rush of wind and a breeze that floated around me questioningly. I let out a breath of relief.

"Help us, Gale," I begged.

The Wind Spirit obeyed, scooping both of us up into its embrace and sweeping us across the forest in a fierce rush. For a moment the boy's eyes fluttered and I wondered if he would regain consciousness. He muttered something softly that I couldn't quite hear, then passed out again.

"Come on," I said to the wind, my heart beating fast in my chest. "We have to hurry."

Gale picked up the pace, rushing us faster away from danger. As we flew, my eyes darted around the woods, desperate to find someone—anyone—who could help us.

It was then that I saw the group of Arendellian horses and wagons, piled high with injured people hacking and sputtering, rubbing their eyes, their skin caked with soot. It appeared they were about to evacuate the area.

"There!" I pointed for Gale. "Put him down in that wagon."

The Wind Spirit obliged, sweeping us forward and dropping us gently onto the wagon. As Agnarr's back settled against the cart's wood, he murmured something again. I leaned over him, trying to hear what he had to say.

Suddenly, everything went dark.

I reached up, surprised to find an Arendellian cloak over my head, covering almost my entire body. Gale must have thrown it over me. But why?

Danger was approaching.

My ears pricked at the sounds of footsteps, loud, and

of more than one person approaching. I held my breath, my heart pounding so hard I wondered if I'd crack a rib. The wagon rocked, as if someone had stepped onto the front of it. Then, to my horror, it began to move.

I struggled to peek out from under the cloak. I needed to jump out of the wagon while I still could. Run back to the safety of the forest. But there, riding behind the wagon, were three Arendellian soldiers armed with sharp swords.

"Do you see any of those traitors?" one of them asked the others, his eyes darting suspiciously in all directions, his voice rough from inhaling smoke.

"If I did, I wouldn't be standing here talking to you," stated the middle one, with dark hair in total disarray. "I'd slash them all down where they stood."

"I can't believe it! We came in peace! We built them a dam! And this is how they repay us? With sorcery? Trickery?" the third shouted, his horse dancing under him as it felt his tension.

My heart panged in horror, refusing to believe the soldiers' hateful words. We were a peaceful people. We'd welcomed the Arendellians to our land. Accepted their gift of the dam. Why would we rise up against them now?

As for magic or sorcery—we didn't have any. We used only the gifts given to us from the spirits. The elders had been very clear on that from the first day we met the Arendellians.

At that moment there was another gust of wind. At first I thought it was Gale, maybe rushing in to save me from my fate. Instead, a thick, heavy mist seemed to drop from the sky, settling down onto the earth like a giant wall behind us. It blocked out the forest, from sky to ground, as far as my eyes could see.

The wagons ground to a halt. The soldiers called out in alarm, staring at the shimmering gray fog in dismay.

"More black magic!" one of them muttered, making strange patterns with his hands, as if to ward off whatever it was. "Evil sorcery!"

"Let's get out of here," the other barked. "Before it comes for us, too!"

My heart lurched. What was happening? My home! My family! Trapped behind some kind of wall—and I was on the wrong side. I had to return before it was too late.

Or was it already too late?

If I showed myself now, the soldiers might declare me a traitor. But if I didn't, I might lose my entire world. Panic flared inside me. What should I do?

Suddenly, I felt a flutter of movement beside me. I glanced over. Agnarr had woken—though maybe not completely. He blinked, looking at me with sleepy green eyes. For a moment our gazes locked. My heart thudded. I shook my head, glancing back at the growing mist and letting out a small moan.

Agnarr took my trembling hand in his and squeezed so lightly I could barely feel it. Yet at the same time, it was as if I could feel nothing else in the world.

"It's going to be okay," he whispered. With his free hand, he reached into his pocket and pulled out a small wrapped square. I opened the paper tentatively, revealing a tiny block of that brown stuff I'd tasted in the tents. Shocked, I returned my gaze to Agnarr, who smiled.

"Chocolate makes everything better," he whispered.

Then his eyes closed again and his breathing slowed. He'd fallen back asleep. But his hand remained in my own as the wagons rolled on, away from the mist. Resigned, I settled down under my cloak, slipping the block of chocolate into my mouth. Its sweetness could only be rivaled by the warmth of Agnarr's hand.

Like it or not, I was going to Arendelle.

But as to whether it would be okay?

Only Ahtohallan knows.

CHAPTER THREE

Iduna

"THERE'S SOMEONE ELSE IN THE WAGON!"

I woke in confusion as the Arendellian cloak was ripped from my head and body, the sudden burst of sunlight nearly blinding me after a night spent in darkness. I blinked rapidly, trying to gain my bearings as my heart thudded with rising panic. Where was I? Why did I ache so much? And who were these large, strangely dressed men leaning over me with confused looks on their bearded faces? I pulled the cloak back over my shoulders, huddling in fear.

It came back to me in a rush. The celebration. The battle. The boy I'd saved. The trap I'd somehow found myself in. The mist falling over the forest. I struggled to sit up, fear raging through me like wildfire. Where was Agnarr? Had I really slept through them taking him out of the wagon? I thought back to his hand clasping mine, to his promise that everything would be okay.

But now he was gone. And I was with men who would rather see me dead.

I tried to dart away, leaping from the wagon. But I landed wrong, on legs that had moments before been fast asleep. A jarring pain shot through my ankle and up my calf, and I dropped to the ground with a small cry. The men quickly surrounded me, now with suspicious looks on their bearded faces.

I bit my lip, realizing I'd made a huge mistake.

"Who are you, girl?" one man demanded. "Why were you trying to run?"

I blinked up at them, terror making it impossible to speak. My mind flashed back to the soldier's words the day before.

I'd slash them all down.

"You don't think she's one of *them*, do you?" another man added, squinting at me with cold gray eyes. "A little stowaway from the forest?"

The first man spit on the ground, then grabbed me roughly by the arm, pulling me to my feet. I winced as pain shot up my leg all over again, but gritted my teeth, refusing to let them see me cry. The man clasped his meaty hands on my face, turning me left, then right. "Well, speak up, girl!"

I withdrew into myself, hunching my shoulders and dropping my chin. My whole body was shaking with fear. I tried to tell myself that maybe this was simply a dream, that I'd wake up any second back in the forest, cuddled under a pile of reindeer hides.

But truth be told, it didn't feel like a dream. It felt more like a nightmare.

I opened my mouth and attempted to speak, though I had no idea what I could say to save myself. Why, oh, why had I fallen asleep in the wagon? If I had been awake when they stopped, I could have snuck away somehow. But now I was in the center of their city, stone buildings rising up in all directions, blocking my path. And with my injured ankle? There was no escaping my fate.

Where was Gale? If Gale were here, just maybe it would distract them—give me a chance to slip away. I whispered our song under my breath, but the air remained dead as that on a hot summer's day, not even a hint of a breeze in this strange town's center.

I saw no sign of any rescue from my spirit friend.

"All right now, what's the meaning of this?" demanded someone new who had suddenly burst onto the scene. A man with a full head of dark hair pushed his way through the others. He was wearing a fancy suit the color of lingonberries; the way the others quickly scattered as he approached told me he was in charge.

"This girl, sir. We found her in the wagon. But all the children who traveled to the dam with us have already been accounted for. And she refuses to say who she is."

When he reached me, he stared down, searching my face with eyes the color of the brown blocks Agnarr had called chocolate. I let out an involuntary whimper, the fear inside me so strong I was afraid I would throw up on his shoes.

"Please," I whispered, my voice hoarse from the smoke I'd inhaled. Though I hardly knew what I was asking for. Mercy? Why would they grant me mercy when they believed my family had slaughtered their people in cold blood? To them, I was a monster. A sorceress. I was—

"A child!" the man exclaimed, his voice filled with wonder. "Why, you're just a little girl."

"I'm twelve," I blurted out before I could stop myself. "I am nearly a woman." My voice, which I wanted to sound strong, came out more like a squeak.

To my surprise, he laughed, laying a kind hand on my shoulder. "My mistake," he told me. "Of course. And you are quite the fine lady at that."

I swallowed hard, dropping my gaze to the ground. The cloak I still wore slid off my shoulders, revealing my mother's shawl tied around my neck. The man's eyes widened as they took in the shawl. Then he quickly grabbed the cloak and dropped to his knees in front of me to settle it back on my shoulders.

"What is your name?" he whispered, his face inches from mine. I was surprised at the sudden gravity of his voice.

"Iduna," I whispered back, glancing worriedly at the men on either side, who were still giving me suspicious looks.

The man in charge slapped his hand on his forehead. "Iduna! Of course!" he cried, his voice suddenly loud as he rose back to his feet. "Daughter of Greta and Torra, the brave shield-maiden and soldier who were with us at the dam."

I opened my mouth to protest. *Greta? Torra?* I had never heard of those people, and they definitely weren't my parents. But before I could say anything, the man shook his head slightly so only I could see. I got the message loud and clear.

The others gathered back around me, looking at me with new eyes. I had been right about this man being in charge; when he spoke, they listened. And more important, they believed.

"Poor lass," remarked the man who had dragged me off the wagon, shaking his head with sorrow. "I'm so sorry about your parents." His face twisted. "I promise you, those Northuldra sorcerers will pay for their crimes! If it takes me till my dying day!" He squeezed his right hand into a fist, so tight his knuckles turned white. Then he waved his fist in the air as if he was ready to take on the entire Northuldra people right that very second. Frightened, I edged backward to get out of his punching range.

The man in charge groaned, grabbing the angry man's fist and lowering it back to his side with some force. Then he turned back to me. "It is indeed *very tragic* what happened to your parents in the forest," he agreed in a steely voice. "But do not worry, young Iduna," he added, saying my name very carefully, as if to help himself remember it. "We in Arendelle take care of our own. Since you are one of us," he said, again emphasizing each word, as if giving me a secret message, "you will never want for anything. We will care for you, feed you, keep you safe from harm."

I forced a nod, even though the lump in my throat had grown so large I felt like I would choke on it. I wanted to protest, to declare I would never be one of them. These strange people in their strange town were as unlike me as the sun was unlike the moon.

But I kept silent.

Instead I nodded, pulling the Arendellian cloak tighter over my body. "Thank you," I forced myself to say. "You are too kind, sir."

The man's shoulders relaxed. He knew I had gotten his message. He turned to the others. "I will escort her to the orphanage personally," he told them. "In the meantime, I assume you all have something better to do than stand around?"

The other men grunted but didn't argue, scattering from the wagon to go back to their homes. The man watched them go, then turned to me.

"I am Lord Peterssen," he said in a soft voice. "And you needn't be afraid. I meant what I said. No harm will come to you."

I nodded meekly. What else could I do? He held out a hand, helping me out of the wagon.

"Come," he said. "I will take you home."

CHAPTER FOUR

Agnarr

"AH, YOUNG PRINCE, YOU ARE AWAKE AT LAST."

I opened my eyes blearily, my vision still spotted as I looked around the room. Even so, I recognized it immediately. The rich greens and browns. The rosemaling scrollwork trailing down walls, embedded in doorways. The thick beige curtains of the canopy bed. The roaring fire in the hearth.

I was home. In Arendelle. In my bedroom.

Had it all been a dream? The forest? The battle? But no, my body felt as if it had been run over by a herd of reindeer. And when I attempted to sit up, my head spun and I quickly collapsed back onto my feather pillow.

The castle overseer, Kai, hovered over me, clucking his tongue. "Take it easy," he scolded. "You've had a rough go of it. It's going to take a while for you to be on the mend."

I nodded slightly. Even the small movement of my head against the pillow seemed to take a herculean effort.

I closed my eyes, trying to pull together memories of what had happened. How I'd ended up here, like this.

A day of celebration, twisted into violence. Northuldra and Arendellians, fighting one another. Then fire. Wind. Smoke.

Papa . . .

My eyes flew open. "Is Papa dead?" I asked, my voice raw. But even as I asked the question, I realized I already knew. I had seen it. My father, battling the Northuldra at the side of the dam. His foot slipping. His arms flailing.

Oh, no. No, no, no!

Kai gave me an anguished look, turning away. His gaze shot to the back of the room as if it held all of life's answers. A figure stepped from the doorway.

It was Lord Peterssen, one of my father's trusted advisors.

To my surprise, he dropped to one knee beside my bed. "Your Highness," he said, lowering his head in a bow. "I am sorry to be the bearer of such terrible news." He straightened, then looked me right in the eyes. His own were solemn as the grave. "Your father is lost. Perished in the battle between us and the Northuldra."

My heart wrenched. It was true then. My father. Gone. The strongest, most powerful man I'd ever met. The noble leader the Arendellians sang of in the taverns. The man who had devoted his entire life to keeping Arendelle safe and helping it prosper.

Gone. Just like that.

Guilt assailed me as my mind flashed back to our last

hours together. He'd been furious at me for wandering off. And why had I wandered off, anyway? I could have spent the day with him, helping him organize any loose ends with the Northuldra regarding the dam, serving as his squire. Maybe if I'd been there, I would have noticed something was wrong. I was good at that—seeing things that no one else did. Maybe I could have warned him before it was too late. But I'd failed again. I'd always been such a disappointment to my father.

Maybe it was my fault he was dead.

Lord Peterssen rose to his feet, putting a fatherly hand on my shoulder. "I am so sorry," he said again. "Arendelle has lost a good man. A good king. We will all miss him."

A sudden horrifying thought came to me. "And . . ." I struggled to sit up again, ignoring my aching head. "What of Lieutenant Mattias? Is he . . . ?" I trailed off, not able to form the words. I tried to think back again to the battle. Mattias had shoved me out of the way, trying to protect me as the forest erupted into violence.

The thought of losing my father and my friend on the same day was almost too much to bear.

Lord Peterssen shook his head slowly. "We don't know what happened to him," he admitted. "Some say he was still fighting when the mist rolled in."

I squinted at him in confusion. "The mist?"

He nodded. "They say it fell from the sky. Dropping down over the forest, heavy and thick. So thick no one could penetrate it. Many of our people were trapped—are still trapped—on the other side."

"But that's crazy!" I cried. "A mist can't trap people. It's not solid."

"This one is," Peterssen said solemnly. "I rode out yesterday to see it for myself. It's as solid as this wall right here." He rapped his knuckles lightly against my bedroom wall. "And from what we can tell, there's no way in and no way out."

Fear thrummed through me. My father had instilled in me from a young age awareness of the dangers of magic and sorcery. It was powerful. Wicked. A man who wielded magic did not fight fair. Sorcery corrupted the very soul, turning it black as night.

"Was it the Northuldra who did it? Are they magical?" I whispered, suddenly remembering the girl I'd watched in the forest. The one dancing in the wind. She'd been like a fairy from a storybook. Lithe, ethereal. In that moment, I couldn't have looked away. I closed my eyes for a moment, trying to recall more details, but it was mostly a blur apart from that stirring sense I had been witnessing something—and someone—incredible. I frowned, frustrated.

"Your father believed they were," Peterssen said. "But from what I saw in my time with the Northuldra as the dam was being constructed, they were simply friends of the elements. They used these gifts of nature to help them in their everyday lives. But I never saw them use magic of their own."

"But they could have made the mist," I pushed. "Or asked the elements to do it, right?"

"Perhaps. Though for what gain I am not sure. As far as we can tell, they were trapped inside as well." Peterssen sighed. "I promise, Your Highness, we will put our best men on this. To try to answer these questions and find a way through the mist. But for now, there's a more pressing issue at hand."

"What's that?"

He gave me a solemn look. "The king is dead. And you, Your Highness, are his only son . . . and therefore heir to the throne of Arendelle."

Horror shot through me. Of course, on some level I knew this, deep down. But to hear it spoken aloud . . .

"I'm too young to be king!" I blurted out before I could stop myself. I took a deep breath, trying to focus, or at least appear focused on the outside. This time when I spoke, I hoped I came off as calm. "I'm fourteen. I'm not prepared to rule a kingdom."

Peterssen laid a gentle but firm hand on my arm. "Perhaps not yet," he agreed. "Your father knew his death would come someday and stated that if you were not yet of age when it came to pass, I would serve as regent to the kingdom in your stead. Of course, I would not act without your approval," he added quickly. "But if you trust me, I will do my best to keep Arendelle in peace and prosperity until you come of age."

Relief flooded through me. This was exactly what I needed to hear. Someone besides me was still in charge.

"Thank goodness," I murmured under my breath. The ache in my head had returned with a vengeance, now accompanied by the bone-deep thrum of loss, and all I wanted was to close my eyes.

"We can talk more when you're fully healed," Peterssen declared, looking at me with sympathy. "For now, do not worry about a thing."

I began to sink back into my pillow, more than willing to let sleep overtake my aching bones and heart, when a sudden thought came to me. "How did I get out of the forest?" I asked. "I don't remember." I squeezed my eyes shut, trying to recall the events of that day. I remembered the fighting. Being knocked over by the wind. Hitting my head against a rock. The darkness . . .

To my surprise, Peterssen didn't answer at first. Then he shrugged. "We don't actually know," he admitted. "The soldiers lost track of you during the fighting. But you were found lying in one of their wagons just before the mist rolled in. You were hurt. Bleeding. Unconscious. Perhaps you crawled in there yourself and then passed out?" But his voice sounded doubtful, as if he didn't really believe it.

Neither did I.

A voice rose from the deep recesses of my mind. The most beautiful voice I'd ever heard, singing a pure, haunting, desperate song that still rang in my ears. I remembered hearing it back in the forest as I struggled to gain consciousness. Then the feeling of being lifted, but not by human hands. And suddenly I was floating. . . .

More magic? But no. There was a face. *Someone* had helped me get to that wagon. But who? Try as I might, I couldn't pull the face from the darkness of my mind. It was another blur, lost in the chaos of that day.

There was a knock at the door. Peterssen gestured for Kai to answer it. Gerda, the family steward, stood on the other side, wringing her hands nervously. "Is the prince ready?" she asked. "The people are waiting outside."

I frowned. "Waiting for what?"

"For you to address them, of course, Your Highness," Gerda sputtered. She turned accusingly to Kai. "Didn't you tell him? They're all out there. They're worried. They need to see he's all right."

Peterssen sighed. He turned to Kai and Gerda. "Leave us," he commanded. "I will see to it myself that His Highness is ready to address his subjects."

Gerda responded with an unhappy snort, as if this wasn't how things were supposed to be done, but thankfully exited the room, followed by Kai. Peterssen walked over and closed the door behind them, then turned back to me.

"What do I have to do?" I asked. My head was still pounding. I felt as if I was going to be sick.

"The people must see you," Peterssen said. "They are scared. They lost loved ones. They lost their king. They must gaze upon their prince now. See their country's future with their own eyes."

I stared at him in horror. "No! I can't do that. Not now. Make them wait!"

"They've waited three days already. It is time."

"Please," I said, trying my best not to beg. "It's too soon."

Peterssen's face softened. He knelt down before me, taking my hand in his own. "Sometimes a king doesn't have the luxury of grief," he explained slowly. "He must put his people's feelings before his own. When you go out there, you must stand taller than you are. Act braver than you feel. Show them, through every move you make, every word you say, that they have nothing to fear." He gave me a sympathetic look. "You must show them you are not afraid."

"Even when I am," I said, looking at the ground.

"You would be a fool not to be," Peterssen agreed. "But you must not show that fear to your people. Pull it deep inside you. Conceal it in your heart. Don't feel it. Don't let it show." He rose to his feet. "That is what your father did. And his father before him. That is what kings do to protect their people. And this is what you must do now."

"What if I don't want to be king?" I blurted out, knowing I sounded like a petulant child, knowing how angry my father would be if he were there to hear me. But I wasn't ready. I hadn't asked for this. A week ago, the only thing worrying me was failing my weekly spelling lesson. Now I had the responsibility of an entire kingdom? Real people, with real problems—depending on me.

The panic spiraled; I felt the walls closing in on me. Peterssen gave me a sharp look, understanding but maybe growing a little impatient. If only Lieutenant Mattias were here.

What would he say? What would he tell me to do?

The next right thing.

I swallowed hard, Mattias's words seeming to echo in my head, as if they'd been spoken aloud. The advice his father had once given him. The advice he'd then passed down to me.

Life will sometimes throw you onto a new path, he would say. *And when it does, don't give up. Take it one step at a time.*

I took several deep breaths, pushing the panic down. Then I turned to the lord regent and nodded. "All right," I said. "I will get dressed, and I will stand before my people. I owe them that much at least."

Peterssen's shoulders relaxed. "Very good, Your Highness. It will mean a lot to them. Shall I send the servants in to help you dress?"

"No. I will do it myself. Thank you."

The regent nodded and headed out of my bedroom, leaving me alone. For a moment I just sat there, my thoughts whirring in my head. Then I walked over to the mirror, staring into it. My eyes were hollow, shadowed by black circles. My skin was pale as milk. My hair had been shorn close to my head, probably so they could sew up my wound.

I don't look anything like a king, I thought with a grim smirk aimed at my reflection. More like a frightened boy.

I closed my eyes. "Conceal, don't feel," I murmured to myself, repeating Peterssen's words. "Don't let it show."

I opened my eyes. Squared my jaw. I could do this. I *had* to do this.

It was the next right thing.

CHAPTER FIVE

Iduna
One Month Later

"ROAR! I AM EVIL NORTHULDRA AND I WILL kill you deader than dead!"

I startled awake from my nap as two orphan children, a boy and a girl around six years old, raced into the dormitory, one chasing the other, a wicked grin on the chaser's face. The boy squealed, diving onto my bed and trying to hide behind me to escape the "evil Northuldra" while she jumped on top of him, grabbing the pillow from under my head and smashing it into his face.

"I will cast a horrible spell on you!" she jeered. "You will burst into flames!"

I stumbled out of bed, out of their line of destruction, still disoriented from being awoken from a deep sleep. The boy grabbed my pillow from the girl, tossing it away. They began wrestling madly until the boy fell off the bed, slamming his head against the wooden floor.

He burst into tears. "Ow!" he cried, rubbing his head. "You don't play fair!"

"Yeah, well, neither do the Northuldra!" the girl declared mischievously, not looking the least bit sorry for her part in the accident.

Suddenly, there were footsteps on the stairs. The housemother stepped into the doorway. "Aryn, Peter!" she scolded. "What did I tell you about roughhousing in the bedroom?" She clapped her hands. "Come now! I have plenty of chores to work off that energy!"

"Aw!" they moaned in unison, but did as they were told, slinking out of the bedroom to head downstairs.

I was alone again.

I drew in a breath, trying to still my racing heart. I reached down to collect my mother's shawl from under the bed and press it to my cheek, relieved that the children's antics hadn't unearthed this lone vestige of my previous life.

A lump rose in my throat as I walked across the room to the tiny window at the far side. It had been a month, and I still couldn't get used to sleeping in here—inside this closed-in, claustrophobic space with its rows of cots and scores of children, so far removed from nature and the elements.

Back home, the wind rustling the leaves and water tumbling over the stones in the river used to sing me to sleep. Now all I could hear were the whispers of the other children, telling each other scary stories after the lights went out, usually about the "wicked Northuldra," as if my family were some kind of magical monsters lurking under the beds, ready to strike.

Some of the children in the orphanage had been there at the dam celebration. Their parents had been killed, supposedly at Northuldra hands. All they wanted to talk about was how Arendelle would get its revenge, how they would repay these traitors who were given a great gift and returned the favor with murder.

Yes, their own king had been murdered that day. They believed one of my elders had killed him, shoving him off a cliff by the side of the dam. Which was ridiculous, of course. There was no way any of our gentle elders would have committed such a violent act against a fellow human.

Of course, I spoke none of this out loud. Instead, I stayed silent, minding Lord Peterssen's warning: if I spoke up and gave a clue as to who I really was and where I came from, he would no longer be able to protect me.

Because it wasn't just the children telling the tales. Everyone in Arendelle was talking about the Northuldra "traitors" and what they'd do if they ever came across one. If I didn't keep this secret, I might not live long enough to find my family again.

And find them I would. My ankle had recently healed. It just needed a little more time before it could bear the brunt of the long walk to the mist, and then I would go from this place. I would travel back to the forest. Find my family again.

I stared out the tiny bedroom window, onto the cold

afternoon streets. Light flakes of snow were falling from the sky, dusting the cobblestones below. Was winter here already? It was easier to lose track of the days shut up inside a wooden box. But I knew soon it would come, blanketing the world in white, the chill creeping into our bones. Back home, we'd all huddle by the fire on cold winter days, cozy under mountains of reindeer hides, cuddling close to keep each other warm. There would be stories. Songs.

I missed the songs most of all.

I opened my mouth to sing. My mother's song. A song of Ahtohallan, a magical river of memories. *Only Ahtohallan knows,* she would always say in answer to my endless questions.

A fierce longing rose inside me. Did Ahtohallan know what had happened the day of the dam celebration? I wished I knew how to find her, to ask her. But she was very far away. *Too far for a young girl like you to go,* the elders would always say when I'd ask if they would take me to the river. My throat constricted as I thought of them, thought of Yelana calling me to come knit on the day of the celebration. Why couldn't I have listened to her, just that once?

A sob rose to my throat. I missed them all so much. Would I ever see them again?

"Are you all right?"

I whirled at the sound of the voice and, to my shock, stood face to face with none other than the boy I had saved in the woods.

Agnarr.

I stared at him, disbelieving. He was dressed in a sharp red suit with a matching tie, and his blond hair was cropped close to his head. They must have shaved it to work on his wound. It made him look older and his leaf-green eyes even bigger.

I felt my face turn as red as his suit. What was he doing here? He couldn't be one of the orphans, not in that outfit. Had he come here from the village to thank me for my rescue? Did he even remember? I scanned his face for recognition but saw none. I thought back to that moment in the wagon, when he'd slipped his hand in mine. But he'd been so out of it. He probably didn't remember.

I could never forget.

He backed away, catching the look on my face. "S-sorry," he stammered. "I didn't mean to intrude. I just heard you singing, and . . . What was that song?"

I wasn't sure what to say. "Just something my mother used to sing to me," I confessed at last, though I wasn't certain this was wise to admit. It was a Northuldra song, after all.

Still, something in his face told me I could trust him. At least a little.

"That's nice," Agnarr said, sounding suddenly wistful. "I barely knew my mother. She left when I was a small child. And let's just say Father wasn't exactly the lullaby type." He gave a bitter laugh. "You know how kings are."

My pulse jumped. His father, a king? But that would make him . . .

"There you are, Prince Agnarr. I was wondering where you'd wandered off to."

A deep baritone rang out as Lord Peterssen stepped into the room. His eyes settled on me and he gave me a friendly smile. "Oh, good. You've already become acquainted. I hope Agnarr has been minding his manners," he added, poking Agnarr in the ribs. Agnarr playfully shoved him back.

"I am nothing if not the picture of decorum and grace!" he declared haughtily, but with a tease in his tone. Lord Peterssen snorted in disbelief.

Meanwhile, I was staring at the two of them, my mind racing so fast I could barely put a thought together. Agnarr, the boy I rescued. He was a prince? The heir to the throne of Arendelle?

I'd rescued the prince of Arendelle.

"Your—Your Majesty," I stammered, dropping to my knees as I desperately tried to recall from the Arendellian fairy tales I'd read how the common people greeted royals, hoping I was doing it right.

Only, it seemed I had gotten it wrong.

Agnarr shook his head, his cheeks coloring. "Oh, stop," he mumbled. "You don't need to do that."

"Sorry." I scrambled to my feet, my face burning with shame. "I don't . . . I mean . . . I didn't . . ."

The prince stepped forward, holding out his hand. I reached for it hesitantly, trying to pretend it was the first time we'd touched. "Name's Agnarr," he said. "It's very nice to meet you."

"I'm . . . Iduna," I said. Then I squared my shoulders and lifted my chin, acting as if I met princes all the time and it was really no big deal. "It's . . . nice to meet you, too."

He gave a perfunctory nod, all business now. He was no longer an injured boy but the heir apparent. "I hope they are treating you well here at the orphanage," he continued. "I know it's a little crowded right now. Many lost parents during the battle of the Enchanted Forest—myself included. But we're doing our best to care for everyone. Peterssen and I have asked the council to allocate additional funds for an expansion to the building. Along with extra food. And chocolate," he added with a grin. "That was my idea."

I thought back to the tiny square of chocolate he'd slipped me in the wagon. "A very good idea," I agreed. "Chocolate makes everything better."

He looked surprised as I parroted his words back to him. His brows creased as if he was trying to remember. Then he grinned. "I think you and I are going to get along very well."

Peterssen clapped his hands. "Great. Now that introductions have been made, it's time to head back to the castle. If you're ready, Iduna?"

I stared at Lord Peterssen in shock, unable to fully comprehend what he was saying. "You want me to come to the castle?"

"Yes, of course," he said in a voice that left no room for argument. "I said I'd take care of you, didn't I? Well, I apologize it's taken some time to get organized. Things have been—tumultuous the past few weeks, as you can imagine. Transitions of power, all that sort of thing." He waved a hand. "But now that the dust is settled, I have returned to keep my promise. You'll still live here, of course. But you will also start daily educational lessons at the castle. Agnarr's own tutor, Miss Larsen, will teach you. It's the very least that we could do for the sacrifices your parents made."

I stared at him, fear rising inside me. The castle? They wanted me to go to the castle? On a daily basis? Were they joking? If anyone learned who I was . . .

"I—I don't think I can . . ." I stammered.

"You *can*," Lord Peterssen said firmly. "And you will." He sighed. "Iduna," he continued, giving me a sympathetic look, "I know there have been a lot of changes lately. And I know it's been strange and difficult for you here. But I promise things will be easier from here on out. Now come. We'll take you there now and give you a little tour. Your first lesson will be on Monday morning."

I started to open my mouth, probably to argue again. But at that moment, the orphan children from earlier stormed back into the bedroom. Now it was the boy playing the part of the "evil Northuldra," coming after the squealing girl with a mad look in his eyes.

"I'm going to kill you!" he cried. "Like I killed the king!"

Agnarr's face turned stark white. My heart panged as I caught the anguish swimming in his green eyes.

He might have been the prince, but he was also a boy who had lost his father. Perhaps Peterssen would have stepped in and said something, but I beat him to it.

The children dove back on my bed, wrestling one another, still shouting about magic and treachery. I marched over to them.

"Magic?" I broke in with an exaggeratedly jovial tone. "Please. Who needs magic when you have super tickle powers?"

Without warning, I pounced, grabbing them and tickling them under their arms. They squealed in protest, trying to wiggle away as they begged for mercy, not unlike the Northuldra children back home. Tickle torture, it seemed, was universal.

"Let us go!" cried the boy. "Please!"

"We have chores to do!" the girl giggled, swatting my hands away.

"Chores?" I repeated in as innocent a voice as I could muster. I released them, rising back to my feet. "Why didn't you say so? I'd certainly never want to keep you from *chores!*"

"Yes, chores!" the girl agreed, a look of relief on her face. "Come on, Peter. Let's go do our chores!"

They leapt from the bed, nearly knocking Agnarr over as they fled for the stairs. He watched them go, his face still pale. But then he turned to me.

And he smiled.

It was a smile so bright it seemed to light up the entire room. Peterssen stood behind Agnarr, nodding his approval at how I'd handled the situation.

I smiled back shyly at the prince. "Let me get my coat."

CHAPTER SIX

Agnarr

"AND THIS IS MY GREAT-GREAT-GREAT-grandfather Eric. Will you look at that mustache? Talk about hair goals! And over here—that's Great-Grandmother Else. I always thought she looked like a nice lady. The kind who sneaks her grandchildren cookies when their parents aren't looking."

I glanced over at Iduna, who was staring up at the paintings in my family's portrait room, a polite but otherwise unreadable expression on her face. Was I boring her? Was I talking too much? I was probably talking too much. But who could blame me? After the dam tragedy, they'd all but shut the castle gates, with only essential staff remaining inside. And Lord Peterssen hadn't been so keen on letting me run around the village unescorted, declaring it was way too dangerous under our current political climate.

When a king died, a kingdom could go through a

period of unrest. Neighboring countries could start sniffing around, looking for weakness. Even within the kingdom, some ambitious great-nephew or -niece of the former king might start getting delusions of grandeur and decide they had some kind of claim to the throne. *If only that pesky son of the king weren't in the way. . . .*

And that didn't even count the Northuldra, who had become public enemy number one in Arendelle. What if they were, even now, people whispered, gathering their forces and preparing to lead an attack on our kingdom— to finish what was started back on their land?

It all sounded completely far-fetched to me, but as Peterssen always said, better to be safe than dead. Until all potential threats had been uncovered, I was to remain inside the castle gates and only be allowed to leave when escorted by a full company of guards.

Which meant I had been climbing the walls the past few weeks. Utterly bored and alone. Now, for the first time in forever, I had someone to talk to.

Of course, it didn't hurt that this someone had the shiniest pile of hair I had ever seen and eyes like the sky on a cloudless winter's day. Not that that mattered or anything. It was just a fact.

I shook off that last thought and grinned at Iduna, hoping it came off as a nice grin and not slightly deranged. She hadn't said much since she got here, her face unreadable but definitely tensed, with eyes darting around each room we entered as if assessing it for potential danger. It made sense: after all, it had only been a month since she'd lost her parents in an unexpected battle. It was hard to feel safe after going through something like that.

I knew from experience.

Ooh! I should show her the library. I wondered if she liked to read. There were so many good books in our library. Books with all sorts of adventures lying between their pages, like windows into other worlds. Worlds I, as a crown prince and heir to the throne, would probably never get a chance to see in real life since the castle gates were currently locked.

But no one could stop me from reading about them.

People always assumed being prince was such a glamorous thing. But in a way, it was like being a prisoner. My responsibility to my kingdom always had to come first over my own desires. And adventures? They were too dangerous to even consider. For if I were to die, the whole kingdom would suffer.

Like now, after my father's death. It would be years before Arendelle fully recovered. At least that's what the council said, during our latest meeting. Peterssen was a competent leader, but he wasn't a king. And our armies had been depleted from the battle in the Enchanted Forest, leaving us vulnerable. The council believed we should reach out to other kingdoms for assistance; the kingdom of Vassar, for example, had a great army. Perhaps they could be convinced to lend us aid if we ever needed it.

At least that's what members of the council argued for over an hour and a half at the meeting. Which had been so mind-numbingly dull I had almost fallen asleep three times. Who would have thought being a great leader would be so boring?

But now—now I had Iduna.

I grabbed her hand. "Come on!" I said. "I've got something amazing to show you."

Her eyes widened at the grip of my hand on hers, but after a moment she let me lead her.

"Ta-da!" I cried as I threw open the library doors.

For a moment, Iduna said nothing, her mouth just sort of dropping open.

"Do you like it?" I asked.

She walked into the room, sinking down onto a nearby padded stool. "These are all . . . your books?" she asked, her blue eyes wide as they took in the towering shelves. "All of them?" When I nodded in response, her eyes inexplicably filled with tears.

It wasn't quite the reaction I had been hoping for. "Iduna, what is it?" I asked.

Her eyes darted in all directions, looking everywhere but at me. "My . . . mother, she would have loved this room," she whispered at last. "She had a book. She used it to teach me to read." Her voice sounded soft and far away and sad.

Of course. What a dunce I could be! I dropped to my knees in front of her. "I'm sorry," I said, trying to make her meet my gaze. "I wasn't trying to upset you. Or remind you of your parents."

I groaned inwardly at my attempt at an apology. *Seriously, Agnarr? You are the worst. You're supposed to be trying to cheer her up. Instead you've made her cry.*

"We don't have to look at these," I added quickly, jumping back to my feet. "They're kind of musty anyway. Want to see the kitchen? I bet Olina has finished up the desserts for tonight's banquet. And I'm really good at distracting her for an advanced taste test."

She gave me a wan smile. "Maybe later," she said. "I'm not that hungry right now."

Argh. I was getting nowhere. I rubbed my head, frustrated, the cropped hair like stubbly grass between my fingers. "Do you want me to leave you alone?" I blurted. It was the last thing I wanted to do. But I didn't want her to think I couldn't take a hint. Peterssen had told me to be patient—that it might take some time for her to come out of her shell. I was probably coming off way too strong.

She rose to her feet, walking over to the large, circular wooden table in the center of the room, stopping in front of it and looking down. Too late I realized there were full-on blueprints of the dam my father had built, spread across its surface. The plans that had started this whole thing, drawn up long before I was born, when my father and his people had first arrived in Arendelle.

She traced a hand over the paper. "What do you think happened that day?" she asked, in a voice so soft I could barely hear her.

I stepped closer, staring down at the plans. "I don't

know," I said after a minute. "It started out as such a perfect day. The Enchanted Forest was so beautiful. Everyone was having fun. Laughing, joking. And then . . . they weren't." I swallowed hard as memories of the day came raging back at me. The stench of smoke. Swords clashing. People screaming. Wind blowing.

My father tumbling to his death.

"Do you think the Northuldra betrayed us?" she asked suddenly, turning to look at me. Her big blue eyes seemed to drill right through me, as if trying to peer into my soul. "Do you think they attacked first?"

It was, of course, the same question everyone had been asking since that fateful day. But somehow it sounded different coming from her mouth. Mostly because she was the first one who sounded like she really wanted an answer, instead of using the question as a preamble to rant on about the Northuldra and their vile magic.

"I don't know," I said at last, keeping my voice low so no one could accidentally hear us if they walked past. I was the crown prince of Arendelle, after all. Which meant I needed to side with my people, no matter what. And I did believe in them. Arendelle was a good kingdom. People were kind to their neighbors. They helped others in need. But still, it didn't make sense to me. Why would the Northuldra attack us after we gave them such a gift?

But then, why would we attack them?

Iduna looked up at me and I realized her eyes were

brimming with tears again. "Has anyone gone back?" she asked, her voice wobbly. "To see what's left? Who survived? Are the Northuldra destroyed?"

Oh! My eyes widened. She didn't know! Of course she didn't. No one outside the castle had any idea. They were already too riled up, even without knowing about the magical mist; Lord Peterssen hadn't wanted to cause a panic.

I gestured for her to follow me. We couldn't talk about something this important here, in the center of the castle. There were too many eyes and ears, lurking around every corner. It would be safer to talk in the courtyard garden, despite the cold. Hardly anyone ever went out there these days, especially since Peterssen had put the gardeners on leave when closing up the castle.

We stepped outside, into the courtyard. Everything was gnarled and barren in the throes of winter. But I ignored it all, leading Iduna straight to my favorite tree. My reading tree, I'd dubbed it, since I'd spent so much time from a young age sitting on the little bench underneath it, paging through books.

"Do you want to sit—?" I started to ask. But to my surprise, she had already swung herself into the tree itself, easily pulling herself up by her hands to reach the higher branches. I watched, mesmerized for a moment by her graceful, catlike movements, then decided to join her, hoisting myself up—albeit far more clumsily—onto one of the lower branches. A moment later, she crawled back down to my level, settling herself gracefully on a nearby branch. It was as if she were a bird that had lived in trees all her life.

She leaned toward me expectantly. "So, what is it?" she prompted.

I bit my lower lip. "Look, you have to keep this quiet, okay? They aren't telling everyone the truth. They're too afraid it'll cause a panic."

"What will?"

"The Enchanted Forest. It's . . . covered in mist."

Her eyes widened. But strangely she didn't look surprised.

"They say it's magical," I added. "Like, it totally looks as if you could walk through it, but you can't. And if you try, it bounces you back. No one can get in. And . . . well, I'm guessing no one can get out, either."

She plucked a twig from a branch, folding it in her hand. Her face had gone pale. "So you think people are still in there? Alive?" she asked.

Suddenly I realized why she was so interested. Lord Peterssen said her parents had been killed in the battle. But what if they hadn't been? What if they were trapped in the mist? Like I hoped Lieutenant Mattias was.

"I don't know," I admitted. "But I think there's a chance. Not that it matters. Unless the mist lifts some-day, we'll never know what's within it. All we can do is hope that—"

"I want to see."

I blinked at her, not understanding what she meant.

"The mist," she clarified at my bemused expression. "Do you know where it is? Can you take me there?" Her blue eyes flashed with inner fire.

I shook my head. "It's not that easy. For one thing, it's really far away. Like over a day's journey. And Lord Peterssen and the soldiers would never let us go. We're only kids. It's far too dangerous."

The expression on her face was so fierce that a shiver ran through me that had nothing to do with the biting cold. "I must see it," she declared. "We can leave tonight."

I stared at her, incredulous. Who *was* this girl? On the one hand she seemed completely crazy, but I also couldn't help admiring her courage. I would have never even thought to suggest something so bold.

And, unfortunately, I couldn't join her.

"I'm sorry. I can't. Not that I don't want to," I added quickly, after catching a flash of frustration on her face. "It's just that they watch me all the time; they even guard my bedroom while I sleep. I can barely go to Blodget's Bakery for cookies without a full-on army in tow."

She nodded slowly, then dropped fluidly out of the tree. I stared down at her through the branches, feeling my heart ache unexpectedly as I caught her slumped shoulders and bowed head.

I'd disappointed her, this girl who had already lost everything. But something about being the one to cause her any further pain made me feel a weight that was almost too much to bear.

"I'm sorry," I said again, slipping down from the tree

myself. "Maybe once things lighten up a little, I can make something happen. We could form a convoy. Journey out there together."

"Sure," she said absently as we turned to walk back inside the castle. But I could tell she had already dismissed me in her mind. Which hurt more than I wanted to admit. And suddenly all I wanted to do was find some way to help her with her quest.

But at the moment, that seemed even more impossible than getting the mist itself to part.

CHAPTER SEVEN

Iduna

I SNUCK OUT OF ARENDELLE LATE THAT night, over the bridge and into the hills, armed only with a satchel filled with bread and cheese, the horse I'd "borrowed" from the stables just outside the orphanage while everyone was sleeping, and an old map I'd found in the Arendelle library, which I'd used to plot out my trek. I was nervous, a little excited, but mostly freezing cold as we climbed the hills and the temperature continued to drop.

I didn't love the idea of journeying alone. I knew it was dangerous. The elders had always lectured us about going off by ourselves. They were great believers in strength in numbers. If only Agnarr had agreed to go with me. I could tell he wanted to, even though he couldn't. Which was ridiculous, right? A prince should be able to do whatever he wanted. And yet he seemed as trapped in the castle as my family was in the mist.

The mist... Would I have been trapped in it, too, had I not run back to the Arendellian camp for my mother's shawl?

Had I not stopped to save Agnarr...?

I didn't know whether to consider myself lucky or not. Which side of the mist did I want to be on? Trapped in the Enchanted Forest, but with my family? Or free in this strange new world where I had to hide who I was?

I shook my head. What I wanted didn't change a thing. The fact was I was on the outside, and I needed to see the mist for myself. Maybe if I went to it, I could call for Gale and the other spirits. Maybe they could give me some answers about what had happened. And how long this apparent curse would last.

As my horse crossed a long barren plain, snow began to fall from the sky. Big, fat flakes that landed in clumps on my hair and clothes. The Arendellian clothes I had on were a poor defense against extreme cold weather, and I longed for the old reindeer hides I'd used back home to keep warm.

But still I pressed on. I was Northuldra, after all. I knew how to live among the elements. This was nothing I hadn't faced before. Though... never *alone* before.

A wolf howled in the distance and I inhaled sharply.

It was almost dawn when I finally reached the map's end—a large empty clearing just outside the forest, devoid of trees. I knew the spot well—my mother used to take me here when I was little to see the four stone monoliths rising high into the sky. I remembered her explaining the symbols carved into the stones. The four spirits: earth, fire, water, and wind—each with the powers to help the Northuldra with their daily lives, so long as we respected them and their mother, the mighty river Ahtohallan.

But that day the stones were gone. They'd completely disappeared behind smoky grayish-blue clouds that were as thick as soup and completely opaque, swirling around in a perfect storm and rising high into the sky.

This was it. The mist.

I slid off my horse, my heart pounding as I approached it. By the time I reached it, my whole body was shaking with trepidation. I reached out, brushing the clouds with my fingertips. The mist pushed me away, as if it couldn't bear my touch. And when I attempted to step through, I bounced right back.

I stared at the mist, my mind racing with horror. So it *was* real. But how? Had the spirits somehow conjured up the mist to keep people out of their forest? Or to keep people in? Was it to protect the Northuldra? The Arendellians? The forest itself?

Or was it to punish them? Us. Everyone.

More importantly, how long would it last? Was this a temporary thing? Or would it go on forever?

I scrambled to my feet, determination rising inside me. Maybe all it would take was a little more force. I backed up, then ran forward, hard as I could toward the mist.

BAM!

I hit the cold ground hard as the mist shook me off

and threw me backward like a rag doll. Determined, I leapt back to my feet, charging at it again, this time holding out my arms, ready to shove it away with both hands.

But the mist repelled my advance once again. I flew through the air, then dropped unceremoniously, landing hard on my recently healed ankle. It crumpled beneath me and I cried out as daggers of pain shot up my leg.

I collapsed, clutching my leg in agony. Tears welled in my eyes and I angrily wiped them away. I tried to stand, but my ankle barked in pain and I realized I couldn't put any weight on it again. It was swelling, too, already double its normal size with skin that had taken on a purplish hue. I curled my hand into a fist and slammed it against the ground in frustration.

"Why?" I demanded, looking up at the mist. "You tell me why, right now!"

But there was no answer. The mist just swirled its endless gray clouds. Blocking me from my only home. My family, my friends, completely walled off from reach.

Despair settled like a heavy weight in my stomach. What came next? Should I head back to Arendelle, keep living the lie? Leave everything I ever knew and loved behind? Become someone else entirely?

Daughter of Greta and Torra. Whoever they were.

I sat up, rubbing my sore ankle. I stared bitterly at the mist. "You couldn't have given me one more person?" I growled. "Even one?" *Why did I have to be the only Northuldra to escape?*

Because you chose another path, I imagined it saying back to me. *You chose to save your enemy.*

I scowled at the fog. "What was I supposed to do?" I demanded. "Just leave him there to die?"

If the mist had an answer, it chose not to share it with me.

I wrapped my arms around my chest, shivering. The sun had risen, but its early morning rays were barely visible behind thick storm clouds. It would snow again soon; I could smell it in the air. The temperature had dropped further and the wind had picked up, icy blasts stinging my cheeks and nose. I needed to get back to the orphanage before my absence was noticed.

Gritting my teeth against the sure pain, I tried again to rise to my feet. But my ankle wasn't having it, forcing me to collapse back onto the cold, hard ground.

In the distance, a wolf howled, followed by another.

Desperate, I lifted my voice to the sky, attempting to call for Gale. *"Ah ah ah ah!"*

The Wind Spirit had always been there for me in the past. Swooping in to save me anytime I found myself in a mess.

But that day my repeated calls went unanswered. And only an angry, unfriendly wind howled through the trees, chilling me to the bone. Was Gale also trapped behind the mist? Or was the Wind Spirit simply angry at me?

The thought made me sad. In so many ways, the

Wind Spirit had been my best friend. My *only* true friend. Had it really abandoned me? Would it ever return?

Would I be alive when it did?

Only Ahtohallan knows. . . .

My mother's voice rose once again in my heart as I stared out at the impenetrable mist. A crushing despair began to weigh on my chest. Everyone I ever loved was there behind that wall. And I was stuck on the outside, utterly alone.

But I was not dead yet.

Grimacing, I forced myself to my hands and knees, ignoring the pain shooting up my leg. I began a halting crawl around the unforgiving surroundings, scooping up piles of leaves and tiny sticks and gathering them into a small pile. I reached into my satchel, thankful I'd at least remembered to bring my flint. Back home, I'd simply have called for Bruni, the Fire Spirit, to help me light my flame. But the elders insisted we also learn to make a spark the human way, just in case Bruni—whose temper could be as hot as its fire—wasn't in the mood to give aid. Or, you know, trapped behind a magical mist in this case. Thankfully I'd paid attention.

Huddling by the tiny pile, I struck the flint together as I had been taught to do. At first nothing happened. Then there was a spark of light that died quickly on leaves damp with the first breath of snow. Finally, I managed to create a small flame with a single dry leaf. The flame spread to the next leaf and then a twig. The crackling sound was a merry contrast to the desolate setting.

I had a fire. A tiny one—Bruni would have smiled at its feeble flame—but it was better than nothing. I held my freezing hands over it, warming them as best I could. As the heat from it spread through my fingertips, a small shred of hope rose in my heart. The wolves in the distance howled again, but I ignored them this time, instead drowning out their voices with a song of my own.

Until I heard a noise behind me.

CHAPTER EIGHT

Iduna

I CLAMPED MY MOUTH SHUT, WHIRLING around, my heart in my throat at the sudden sound. A heavily cloaked figure rode into view astride a tall white horse. At first I thought it must be an illusion–the kind of hallucination one might see before freezing to death. But when I blinked, the figure was still there.

It was Agnarr.

"Sorry I'm late," he said with a bashful grin.

Emotion flooded me before I could stop it. He'd come! He'd actually come. Not that I'd needed him, of course, I scolded myself. Obviously. I wasn't some damsel in distress from one of those Arendellian books, in need of rescue from a handsome prince.

Still, I couldn't stop the fountain of joy from bubbling up inside me as I watched him approach on his horse. I wasn't alone anymore.

I gasped as he climbed down from the horse and strode toward me.

"Are you all right?" he asked, his smile fading as he got closer to me and observed my swollen ankle. My pathetic little fire.

"I'm fine," I shot back quickly, though it was obvious I wasn't. "I thought you weren't coming," I added. "I thought they wouldn't let you leave the castle."

"Eh." He shrugged. "I figured in this case it might be better to ask forgiveness than permission." His mouth quirked. "Besides, everyone probably thinks I'm holed up in my room with a good book, as usual. They won't start looking for me for ages."

I watched as he walked over to the mist, dragging a hand across its surface, his eyes as wide as saucers. "So, this is it," he marveled. "The magical mist everyone's been talking about."

"Don't try to walk through it," I warned him ruefully. "It may look like mist, but it's solid as rock."

"Did you walk around it? See if there were any openings?"

I shook my head. "But if there were, people would have come out by now, right? They would have made their way back to Arendelle."

"Yeah." His smile faded. "I guess you're right."

Another gust of wind blew through the clearing and I shivered violently, the cold seeping into my bones despite the warmth of the fire. Agnarr noticed immediately and abandoned the mist, walking over to me and pulling off his thick woolen cloak, then draping it over my shoulders.

"You'll be cold," I protested.

He waved a hand. "The cold never bothers me."

"Liar," I accused as his body betrayed him with a fierce, all-consuming shiver. He grinned sheepishly.

"Okay fine. I hate the cold. But I'm not taking back my cloak."

"Then come share it with me," I said, beckoning him over. "This thing is huge. Surely it can warm us both."

Something flashed across Agnarr's face that I didn't quite recognize, but after a moment's pause, he relented and dropped down to join me by the fire, crawling under the thick fabric I held open and wrapping it around his body. I could feel his shoulder press up against mine, and a strange sensation wormed through my stomach. Back home, my family had always huddled together on cold nights, using our shared body heat to keep warm. This was no different, right?

Except somehow it was. It felt a lot different.

"Scooch in," I said jokingly, trying to ease the sudden tension. It was what we used to say back home. "There's plenty of room for two."

"I'm not surprised," he replied, inching us closer to the fire. "It was my father's cloak. He was a large man."

He trailed off, his gaze going back to the mist. A look of longing came over his face. And suddenly I was struck by the fact that I was not the only one who had lost people that day. Agnarr had lost his father. And likely others, too.

"Do you miss him?" I asked. "Your father."

He didn't answer at first, still staring into the swirling gray fog. Then he gave a long sigh. "My father and I had a . . . complicated . . . relationship. We fought that day at the dam. He was angry at me for wandering off to explore. He said I was acting like a child, not a prince." He scowled. "He scolded me in front of everyone—all the soldiers and shield-maidens. I was embarrassed. Angry, too. I've been angry with him for a long time. It was like nothing I ever did was good enough for him. That he wished he had a better son." He gulped a breath, like he was about to say something he wasn't certain should be said out loud. "The truth is, as much as I miss him, I think I'm still pretty angry with him now."

He dropped his gaze to his hands. My heart panged at the conflicting emotions I saw on his face. When he looked up at me again, his eyes were rimmed with unshed tears. "But I feel guilty, too. If we hadn't fought that day, I would have been by his side when it all happened. Maybe I could have helped. Maybe I could have saved him." His voice broke. "Maybe he wouldn't be dead."

I nodded slowly, not trusting my voice to speak. I thought about my own last day in the forest. Yelana calling me to my lessons. Had I listened to her, I would never have discovered Agnarr. I would not be here, now, wrapped in his father's cloak, his warm shoulder pressed against mine.

I sighed resignedly. As much as I wanted to, I couldn't regret what I had done. And I knew, in my heart, I would have done it anyway, even knowing the cost. I did not deserve to be locked away from everyone I loved. But Agnarr did not deserve to die alone on the forest floor because he'd had a fight with his father. Whatever happened that day to anger the spirits and cause all of this, it was not his fault. Nor was it mine. And while we might be on different sides of this fight, we had both lost so much. Our friends. Our family. Our place in the world. In an odd way we were more alike than different.

"Let's make a pact," he declared. "We'll come back here twice a year. Every spring and autumn," he added. "We'll travel out here and we'll check the mist. Maybe it'll start to fade gradually. Maybe we'll start finding weak spots. Maybe we'll eventually find a place we can push through." His eyes shone as he spoke, and I found myself getting swept up in his hope, however naive. The mist parting. Us stepping through.

Our families, our friends, greeting us on the other side.

Instinctively, I reached out, clasping his hand in my own and squeezing it tight. He turned to look at me, his eyes sparkling.

"So, is that a yes?" he asked. "We'll return in six months?"

I nodded solemnly. "Six months," I agreed, before shivering again. I laughed. "Though next time I'm bringing a much warmer coat."

"And I'm bringing chocolate," Agnarr added with a mischievous grin. "A lot of chocolate."

And just like that, I found my very first friend on the other side of the mist.

CHAPTER NINE

Iduna

Four Years Later

"AND SO, IT BEGINS! OUR EIGHTH BIANNUAL trek to the glorious, yet still stubbornly mist-bound Enchanted Forest!" I said as I jumped into the wagon beside Agnarr.

He flicked the reins from the driver's seat and the two horses dutifully sprang into action, the wagon lurching in their wake before I was properly seated. I squealed in protest, grabbing the prince's arm to prevent myself from tumbling off altogether.

"Someone's in a hurry," I teased after regaining my balance. I shoved him playfully in the other direction, to give him a taste of his own medicine.

"I'm just relieved to finally be on our way!" he declared. "We're three weeks late this spring, you know!"

"Oh, I'm *so* sorry, Your Majesty," I retorted, rolling my eyes. "Some of us have to work, you know. We can't just drop everything to traipse off to enchanted forests willy-nilly."

About a year ago, I'd started apprenticing under an inventor named Johan, who was working to find a way to harness wind power in order to create a natural fuel source for grain mills and water pumps. It was fascinating work, and it turned out I was good at it, too. After all, I did know something about the power of wind.

The past few weeks we'd had terrific weather conditions brought about by an unexpected late spring storm that blew gales of glorious wind into our fjord, so when I wasn't continuing my studies under the close and demanding eye of Miss Larsen at the castle, I'd been working every spare moment. It hadn't been easy to find time to get away.

Agnarr gave me a mock offended look. "I work hard, too, you know," he reminded me. "Arendelle does not just rule itself."

"I know, I know," I assured him, giving him a comforting pat. "Heavy is the head that wears the crown."

Even though Lord Peterssen was still acting as regent for the next three years—until Agnarr would assume the throne—the young prince had a ton of responsibilities to his kingdom. And they seemingly grew more and more each day. Agnarr sat in on all the council meetings where they discussed state affairs, and listened to petitions from the people of Arendelle every week. He was always patient, listening carefully, trying to come up with reasonable solutions. And the people loved him for that. I'd constantly hear them singing the praises of the fair-minded, rational, and intelligent soon-to-be king as I walked through town. It warmed my heart to know he was such a beloved ruler even before officially taking the throne. From what I'd gathered, his father had been respected—feared, even—but the people had never truly warmed to him the way they seemed to have already warmed to Agnarr.

Agnarr reached into his satchel, pulling out a chunk of chocolate and snapping it in two. He kept one, handing the larger half to me. I smiled as I bit into the sweetness, savoring the rich taste on my tongue. One of my favorite things about Arendelle—the chocolate.

That, and all the books at my disposal, thanks to the castle library. Even four years into our shared lessons, I never tired of exploring the dusty shelves and seeing what new adventures I could find.

As the wagon rolled across the bridge and out of the village, then started up into the hills, I reached into my own satchel, pulling out the book I'd been reading. Agnarr rolled his eyes.

"I'm boring you already, huh? And here we've barely left town."

My eyes sparkled as I cracked open the book. "Nothing personal. I'm just at a really good part."

"Oh, fine," he said, turning back to the horses. "Guess I'll have to entertain myself." He cleared his throat and broke out into a loud, bellowing, and really terrible rendition of a popular Arendellian song:

"I smell that reindeer pee, blowing through the fjord.
Iduna's ignoring me, so I'm really bored. . . ."

Urgh. I shook my head, dropping my book to plug my fingers in my ears. "Seriously?"

"What?" he asked, shooting me an all-too-innocent look. "You don't like my singing?"

"No one likes your singing, Agnarr. Not even the horses."

"Is that true?" he asked the horses in question, flicking the reins again. The two mares snorted loudly—a definitive answer, if I ever heard one. I started giggling. Agnarr sighed.

"Everyone's a critic." He flashed me a silly grin, telling me he didn't really mind. I smiled back at him, setting the book on my lap.

"You're in a good mood," I noted.

"And why wouldn't I be?" he shot back, stretching his arm out to the landscape in front of us. "The sun is shining. The sky is blue. I've got my best friend by my side and we're leaving the dreary castle for a few days of freedom."

"With all twenty-two of our very best friends," I added, glancing back at the Arendelle mounted guard at our backs. Agnarr had insisted they stay at least twenty yards behind us, but it was difficult to ignore their presence altogether.

"Ugh. Don't look at them," he groaned. "Pretend it's just me and you, like the old days."

I smiled at this. Back in the "old days" as he called them, we'd made this journey on the sly, sneaking out of Arendelle every six months to fulfill our promise to each other to check on the mist twice a year. We'd managed to get away with it three times before Peterssen finally realized what was going on. After that, he insisted we take protection with us if we wanted to keep going at all.

At this point, it had become such a time-honored tradition that it was hard to remember that first year, when I'd headed out alone, scared and sad and reckless, desperate to learn the fate of my family. When Agnarr had come after me—to make sure I was safe—even at the risk of getting in serious trouble once he returned home.

Back then he had been a stranger. My enemy. And yet somehow it hadn't felt like that as I watched him step up to the mist. As I saw the grief washing over his boyish face. As he spoke of his dead father and all the things he'd never gotten a chance to say to him. It was the first time I realized we were more alike than different.

That we should be friends, not enemies.

The next few trips had been a lot more fun. We'd sneak out of Arendelle in the dead of night with only the provisions we could carry on our backs. Which had led to some difficulties that second trip when we'd run out of snacks halfway there. Luckily for my indoorsy prince, I knew how to live off the land and showed him which berries were safe to eat and which streams were safe to drink from. Unfortunately, he'd still gotten quite the stomachache after drinking some supposedly clean river water, which I felt bad about. Though not bad enough to stop me from teasing him about his "delicate princely stomach" . . . which made him want to push me into the river.

"What are you reading, anyways?" Agnarr asked now, throwing me a glance. I held the cover up to him. "'*Creatures of Mists and Legends*'?" he read. "Sounds . . . interesting."

"Oh, it is." I nodded, warming to the topic of my latest literary conquest. "Right now, I'm reading about the Huldréfolk."

"Hold-a-fork-of-what?"

"*Huldréfolk*," I corrected with a laugh. "They're mysterious creatures who live amongst us, but we can't see them because they're so good at hiding. They also might, possibly have tails, but they never let you see their backsides to be sure."

"That's creepy."

"It's *fascinating*," I corrected. "And they have this special power, too. To find lost things."

"What do they do with them once they find them?"

"They keep them."

"Okay. *Not* useful. Also, not fair. They should return them to their rightful owners!" Agnarr protested.

I snorted. "Sure. I'll let you tell them that. Or maybe you can make it a law, once you're king."

"Absolutely. In fact, it'll be my very first act as rightful ruler of Arendelle!" he declared. "Who knows, maybe I'll get all those lost socks back."

"Ah, yes. King Agnarr, first of his name. Returner of Stinky Socks. You're sure to be a legend," I teased as I turned back to my book.

A comfortable silence fell over us as the wagon continued to roll down the path. It was a beautiful day, the world springing back to life after sleeping all winter. Tiny green buds poked their heads out from the earth. Emerald leaves unfurled from tree branches. It was as if there was a promise in the air. A rebirth. It made my heart swell with joy.

It also reminded me of home.

Although by now, my concept of "home" had become somewhat complicated. Arendelle no longer seemed a scary place, with shadows lurking in every corner. Instead, it was familiar, expected, comforting. It *was* my home, in a sense. The village people were kind and cheery and always had a friendly word to say when I passed.

Though I did wonder, deep down, if they would still be so welcoming if they knew the truth of who I was. Where my real home lay.

Because that was the dark cloud that still hung over an otherwise upbeat kingdom. The resentment and suspicion of the Northuldra and their supposed sorcery were still on the tips of every tongue and had become the convenient explanation for anything going wrong in town. The wine had gone sour? Northuldra magic! Leaky roof?

A Northuldra had snuck up at night and ripped off your shingles. The Northuldra people would have had to make Arendelle a full-time job to possibly accomplish all the harm they were supposedly responsible for. They were spies lurking among us, learning our secrets so they could use them against us. They were monsters hiding under the beds of children who refused to go to sleep. All of this, even though no Northuldra had been spotted in all the years since the battle had raged.

But instead of souring their wine, this Northuldra was helping their farmers become self-sufficient. Instead of tearing shingles from roofs, I was poring over books, studying the science of wind. Instead of lurking under children's beds, I had started teaching orphans to read. Living a normal life, with no magic flowing through my perfectly average, human veins.

In fact, I hadn't even been able to ask the spirits for help since the mist had fallen. I still tried to call for Gale every once in a while, but the Wind Spirit never answered. It was as if they'd all fallen fast—and firmly—asleep.

But that didn't make for a good story, did it?

CHAPTER TEN

Iduna

WE SETTLED DOWN TO CAMP FOR THE NIGHT, still a few miles away from the mist. We did this each time, though we probably could have made it in a single day if we really pushed ourselves. But Agnarr loved the excuse to be away from the castle, his studies, and the endless meetings, even if it meant having an entourage in tow.

"How do I start this fire again?" Agnarr asked, frustrated, struggling with the flint. I rolled my eyes good-naturedly. No matter how many times we went through this ritual, the prince could not seem to grasp the simple tasks of outdoor living. The product of growing up in a bespoke castle, I supposed.

I came over to help him, flicking the stones together in one swift motion to create a spark. Then I leaned over the pile of twigs he'd gathered and blew gently, coaxing them to light. Once they were aflame, I added more leaves, then a few sticks of wood. Soon we had a cheery little fire.

"I don't know how you do it," he said, shaking his head. "First time, every time! It's like magic."

I frowned. "Not magic," I said firmly. "Only practice. And patience."

He grinned at me, leaning back against a nearby boulder and placing his hands behind his head. He glanced at the company of guards, setting up camp a short distance away. We would join them later in the evening, when it was time to go to sleep. Agnarr and I each had our own tent, circled by guards. But for now, they allowed us a tiny bit of time alone with one another.

"Practice," he scoffed. "As if I have time for that. I swear Lord Peterssen has been setting up more meetings on purpose these days, just to keep me busy." He shook his head. "First thing I do when I become king? Outlaw meetings throughout the land." He winked at me. "I can do that, right?"

"Oh, yes," I agreed. "I'm sure *everyone* will be totally fine with that. In fact, they'll probably mark a day of celebration in your honor. You will henceforth be known as Agnarr: Annihilator of Meetings."

"Annihilator of Meetings. Returner of Stinky Socks. I've got quite a legacy going, don't I?" he said jokingly. Then he sighed. "You don't know how lucky you are to not have to think about this ruling-the-kingdom stuff. I wouldn't wish it on my worst enemy."

I gave him a sympathetic look. While we liked to tease each other, I knew how hard Agnarr worked each day, trying to make Arendelle a better place. It wasn't easy.

"But enough about me," he declared, sitting up straighter, changing the subject. "*You're* much more interesting." He grinned. "Tell me, did the new windmill work when you tested it?"

I smiled, happy that he remembered my latest project, though not surprised. Agnarr was always asking about my work and genuinely wanting to know about my progress and failures, celebrating alongside me when I had a breakthrough and consoling me when a new idea flopped. He treated my apprenticeship as if it were just as important as ruling a kingdom. But that was Agnarr. He always took an interest in the little things happening around the kingdom: how the crops were growing, how the people were getting along, the new babies who were born, the elders who died. All that on top of the big-picture kingdom stuff he had to deal with, with all its alliances and trade partners and enemies.

"We're getting there," I said. "We're still working out some kinks. But I had a new brainstorm the other day and Johan's going to try it out while we're gone. Hopefully he'll finally get it to work."

It was funny; when I'd first seen the "apprentice wanted" posting a year ago, I'd immediately applied, thinking maybe it might help me find Gale. But while the Wind Spirit remained in hiding, I began to fall in love with the work itself. It gave me something to do and it made me feel like I was an important part of the town.

Something more than just being the prince's best friend.

"That's great!" Agnarr exclaimed. "And then maybe Johan will invite you to join him permanently!"

He knew this was my greatest dream. My apprentice-ship would end in a few months, along with my formal lessons with Miss Larsen. That meant I would be able to take on a full-time role with Johan, if he agreed. No longer simply working *for* him, but rather alongside him.

"I hope so," I said. "If not now, then maybe someday."

"You know, I could always put out a royal decree," Agnarr teased. "I could even make it a law."

I laughed. "Nah. I'd rather earn it on my own," I told him. "It will mean more that way."

"And you will," he said fervently. "I know it. If anyone can do it, you can."

His warm words sent a shiver rippling through me, and I put my hands out to warm them by the fire. Night had begun to fall and with it a chill had crept into the air. Agnarr hopped to his feet and walked over to the wagon, pulling out his father's old cloak. The same one he'd draped over my shoulders the very first time we'd encountered the mist together. He didn't wear it much anymore, but he liked to bring it along on these journeys for sentimental reasons.

He walked over to me now, draping it over my shoulders. "That better?" he asked.

"Much," I agreed, smiling up at him. Way up. While Agnarr used to be not that much taller than me, he'd shot up in the past couple of years, sprouting broad shoulders and long, lean muscles, seemingly overnight. His hair had darkened, too, though it was still blondish red, and it was longer than the cropped-close-to-his-head style he'd had for a while after the dam tragedy. And he had a bit of stubble on his upper lip, as if he wanted to grow a mustache but wasn't quite ready to commit.

But for all these changes, his eyes remained the same: as emerald green as the forest itself in the richest months of summer, flecked with blues and yellows that seemed to dance when he smiled.

When he smiled at me.

Now this big, strong man-boy shivered noticeably, evidently cold himself. I opened up the cloak to invite him under it, like I'd done that first time by the mist and every trip since. He grinned.

"Scooch in?" he asked, quoting me.

"If you can manage it," I teased as he attempted to fit inside. "Seriously, if you keep growing we're going to have to bring two cloaks next time."

"Nah," he said, pulling one end of the cloak over his shoulder, his warm body pressing against mine. His thigh to my thigh. His arm tucking around my waist. My head sinking down onto his shoulder.

"See?" he said, his voice dropping lower. "Plenty of room."

"Oh, yes," I agreed, my tone light even as I ignored my

racing pulse. "Plenty. Perhaps we should invite the horses in, too. And the guards . . ."

He snorted, sighing contentedly as he looked up at the sky. "I love these trips," he declared. "I wish we could do them every night of the year. Sit by a warm fire. Sleep under the stars." He nudged me with one arm. "Why did people invent roofs anyway?"

"Um, to keep out the rain perhaps?"

"Oh. Right." He grinned. "You're such a know-it-all."

He closed his eyes. I tried not to notice how warm and solid he felt pressed up against me. Something I was trying and failing at quite a bit these past few months. Which was ridiculous.

This is just Agnarr, I scolded myself. *The goofy boy who can barely manage not to fall out of a tree.*

Yet still, when this goofy boy dragged his thumb across my palm, I couldn't resist a small tremble, my whole body seeming to alight with fire at his simple touch.

He noticed, looking down at me with sleepy eyes. "Are you all right?" he asked.

"Yep, perfectly fine," I responded quickly, hoping he couldn't see my blushing face in the dim light cast by the fire. We'd been holding each other's hands since that very first day in the castle when he dragged me along from room to room while giving me a tour. Since that first night out by the mist, when I'd been so lost in my despair. His touch had always been comforting, friendly. A promise that everything would be okay.

But now? It felt different. A promise, still. But maybe of another sort.

I let out a small sigh.

Agnarr suddenly scrambled to his feet, breaking the warm connection between us. "Are you hungry?" he asked. "Thirsty? Cold? Hot?"

"I'm fine," I assured him. "Just . . . a little nervous for tomorrow. As always."

He gave me a sympathetic look, sitting back down, this time across from me, not under the cloak. He was still close though. Close enough that I could reach out and touch him if I wanted to.

Instead, I buried my hands under the cloak, clasping them together to give them something to do.

"I get it," Agnarr said. "As fun as these trips are, the conclusion is always hard."

I nodded slowly. Every trip was always the same. The buildup, the anticipation. Only to end in familiar disappointment. The mist was still there, thick and impenetrable as always. I was beginning to think it would remain that way forever.

"What would you do if the mist was gone?" I asked him. "The very first thing?"

It was an old game—one we indulged in every trip to the mist—and I knew his answer before he spoke it. But something about the familiarity of it was soothing, quelling the rising uneasiness inside.

He hugged his knees to his chest, staring into the fire. "First, I'd look for Mattias," he said. "I know he's still alive in there. Somewhere. After all, he was the best soldier in the land. No way was he taken down in battle."

"And when you found him?" I prompted, as I always did.

"First I'd give him the biggest hug. Which he'd hate, of course. He's always saying real soldiers don't hug." He grinned. "But he'd like it, deep down. Also, I'd promote him to general of the Arendelle guard."

"Anything else?"

Agnarr's eyes sparkled. "I'd give him all the gossip about Halima down at the village. He's crazy about her. He'd want to know everything."

"She's pretty crazy about him, too, from what I've gathered," I said with a giggle, thinking back to the woman who worked at Hudson's Hearth, a local eatery where everyone gathered to chat or for one of their famous buttered biscuits. Men were always trying to flirt with her, but she turned them down every time. There was only one man for her, she'd declare, even if he was gone forever.

It was impossibly romantic.

"Oh, and one other thing," Agnarr suddenly added, his eyes shining.

I looked up. This wasn't part of our script. "What's that?"

"I'd like to find my rescuer."

Something thudded in my heart. "Your . . . rescuer?"

"You know, the person who saved me. The one who got me to the wagon. I bet he or she is still stuck in the mist, too."

"Why do you think that?"

"Well, they'd have to be. Or they would have come forward by now. I'm a prince, after all. People who save princes get rewarded. But no one has ever come forward asking for one."

"Maybe they believe saving your life was reward enough?" I suggested casually, my heart fluttering at this unfamiliar territory. In all the years Agnarr and I had been close, he'd never once mentioned wanting to find his rescuer. I had begun to wonder if he remembered the rescue at all.

"Well, of course it is," Agnarr agreed with a laugh. "But still, I feel like we'd have met by now if they were on the outside." He shrugged. "I think they're still locked in the mist somewhere. Probably wondering if I survived. So if the mist parted, first thing, I'd find them and thank them."

I smiled uneasily, closing my eyes in mock weariness to avoid having to meet his gaze. Agnarr had no idea all that had transpired behind the scenes to make his rescue possible. If I hadn't abandoned my lessons. If I hadn't followed him to camp. If I hadn't left my shawl in that tree. If I hadn't stumbled upon him, lying there. If I hadn't . . .

I would be in the mist.

And he would be dead.

"I think it was one of the Northuldra," Agnarr announced suddenly.

My eyes flew open. "What? Why do you say that?"

He poked the fire with a stick. "No real reason. Just . . . a feeling. After all, they were the ones who connected with the spirits of the forest. And I remember the feeling of floating at one point."

I opened my mouth to speak. My heart was pounding so hard at this point I felt like I might crack a rib. Should I tell him? What would he say if I did? He couldn't be mad, right? I mean, saving his life? That was a good thing.

"Though it doesn't make much sense now that I think about it," he added before I could say anything. "I mean, they were trying to slaughter us. Why would they want to kill my dad and save me?"

My heart sank. I closed my mouth. What had I been thinking? I could never tell him the truth. It was too dangerous. Too risky. I thought back to my first day in Arendelle, Peterssen whispering to me urgently. He could protect me, but only if I stayed quiet. No one could know.

Especially not the crown prince of Arendelle.

I awkwardly stretched my hands over my head, faking a yawn. "I'm exhausted," I claimed, though it wasn't exactly true. "I'm going to get some sleep." I stood up and walked over to the wagon, busying myself with the blankets.

Agnarr bounded over. "Hang on," he said, rummaging through the wagon. He pulled out a thick reindeer hide from somewhere inside. "This will help cushion the ground."

"Isn't that yours?"

He shrugged. "I'm fine. Besides, I think I'm going to stay up for a while. Keep watch."

"Um, isn't that what your regiment of guards is for?" I

asked, glancing over at the company of men with swords not twenty yards away.

"Hey, they might need my help, fending off wolves or something."

I raised an eyebrow. "What would *you* do if you saw a wolf? Try to scare him off with your terrible singing voice?"

"Please. I'd wake *you* up and make you sing," he declared. "You'd charm the mighty beasts with your sweet, clear notes and they would all lay down in your lap like puppies, to listen."

I smiled, stepping away from the wagon. "Is this your roundabout way of asking me for a song, Your Majesty?" I teased. We were back in familiar territory. Agnarr always wanted a song on outdoor, fire-filled nights like these. I would protest at first, but in the end, I always gave in.

He grinned sheepishly. "Not if you're tired."

"I suppose I can stay awake for one song," I allowed, hiding my pleasure at being asked. I walked back over to the fire and sat down in front of it, placing the reindeer hide on my lap, then smoothing it with my hands. Agnarr lay down beside me, stretching out his long legs and putting his head in my lap with a contented sigh.

It shouldn't have felt as right as it did.

I lifted my voice to sing. I was wobbly at first, but soon the notes poured from my throat like water from a stream as I sang an Arendellian song I'd learned in the village.

"Your voice is like an angel's," he murmured, closing

his eyes and breathing in deeply. It didn't take long before he was fast asleep. So much for keeping watch. I stroked his hair, feeling the strands slip through my fingers.

Like sand slipping through an hourglass.

This could very well be our last pilgrimage, I realized suddenly. Agnarr was now eighteen, after all. Soon he would take a bride. And no way would his new wife allow him to trek into the wilderness with some random village girl. If I wanted to keep going to the mist, I would be going alone.

The thought made me sadder than I wanted it to. And before I even realized I was doing it, I had switched songs. To the song of my people, my real family. I hummed the tune softly, the words coursing through my mind like water. Like Ahtohallan, the river of memories. Tears welled in my eyes as I gazed down at my sleeping prince.

Because soon, I knew, memories of these nights would be all I had left.

CHAPTER ELEVEN

Agnarr

"FIND ANYTHING?"

I called out to Iduna, who was standing a few yards away, checking the wall of mist, careful not to miss a spot. She didn't answer at first, clearly too wrapped up in her work to hear me. Typical. She always got like this when we came here. As if she'd crawled down into a deep memory of the past, and the present barely registered.

But who could blame her, really? To be here. To see the mist. To touch it. To know what—who—might be waiting on the other side. Trapped. Maybe forever.

It made me feel pretty strange, too.

I crept over toward Iduna, who was still running her hands along the outer shell. She was concentrating so hard she didn't hear me approach. When I touched her shoulder, she jumped in surprise, letting out a startled yelp.

"Sorry," I said, giving her an apologetic grin. "I didn't mean to sneak up on you."

"It's fine." Her eyes did not leave the mist. "Did you finish your section?"

"Yup."

"And . . . ?"

"Oh. There's a big gaping hole. Crazy huge. Sorry, was I supposed to tell you?"

She didn't laugh.

"Sorry. Bad joke." I felt dumb. I should know better than to mess with her at the mist.

"And yet somehow you manage to repeat it every year," she grumbled, testing out another section of mist. I watched as she pressed against it, holding her hands there for a moment, then released it, moving on to the next spot. She was as thorough as ever.

"You want a snack?" I asked, walking over to my satchel, which I'd left on a big rock. "I've got more chocolate."

"I want to finish first," she answered, distracted.

"Do you want me to help?"

"I'm fine. Eat your snack."

I sighed, sitting down on the rock, pulling out a section of chocolate, and crunching down on it as I watched her continue. I wanted to tell her to stop. That she'd checked it plenty—that the guards had, too. There were no weak spots. No holes. No changes at all since we'd first come here four years before. What made her think it would suddenly change now?

And yet she always seemed to hold out hope.

For me, our pilgrimages had become more tradition than anything else. I was thoroughly convinced the mist would remain forever. But that didn't mean I didn't enjoy the journey. Being away from the castle, out in nature, with no worries or responsibilities . . .

Getting to spend time alone with Iduna next to a fire and under the stars.

"Maybe you need a magic spell or something," I called out to her, still munching on chocolate. "I mean, it was magic that brought the mist to begin with. Maybe magic could make it disappear."

She froze in her tracks, her hands still on the mist. "I don't know any magic," she snapped, her voice sharper than I usually heard it.

I cringed. *You're such a moron.* Iduna had always been sensitive about the topic of magic. Probably since magic had led to her parents being killed or at least trapped in the mist. It had been four years since the mist came down and most of the people of Arendelle were still terrified of any hint of magic—especially coming from the Northuldra on the other side of the gray fog. In fact, they assumed the reason we made these trips was to make sure that the mist was still solid and strong . . . that they remained safe from the Enchanted Forest and the people within.

In reality, I was more conflicted. Like Iduna, I was driven by wondering what might be on the other side. How many Arendellians remained alive and trapped, just waiting for the mist to part so they could rejoin their loved ones. Mattias, perhaps Iduna's parents—how wonderful would it be to reunite after all these years?

But I also worried. For if the mist were to part, it would free more than just our loved ones. What if the spirits still raged? What if the Northuldra intended to seek revenge? As ruler of Arendelle, I had to keep my people safe. Which meant I couldn't be selfish and hope for the mist to part just so Iduna and I could be reunited with our loved ones.

I looked over at Iduna. I wanted nothing more than for her to have her greatest wish come true. To be reunited with those she loved.

But at what cost to Arendelle?

Iduna was still checking on the mist, but her movements had become quicker now, more erratic. Her hands swept over the mist in desperate motions and her face had become pale and frustrated. I watched as she scowled at the mist, then swung her fist against it, crying out in pain as the mist pushed it back.

I leapt to my feet and ran over to her, taking her injured hand in mine. She tried to yank it away, but I held on tight, rubbing my fingers over her swollen knuckles. With my other hand, I reached out, tipping up her chin till her eyes met my own. They were wild and angry, sad and desperate. Like every time before.

She never gave up. And she always got hurt.

"Stop," I said gently. "You have to stop."

She squeezed her eyes shut, tears leaking from the

corners. I dropped my hand to reach around the small of her back, pulling her close. She buried her face in my chest and I stroked her hair softly, breathing in her warm scent. Her hair still smelled like lavender and sunshine, even after spending the night by a smoky fire. In the meantime, I probably smelled like sweaty old socks. Luckily, she didn't seem to mind.

For a moment, we just stood there, wrapped in one another's arms. I could feel her heartbeat, fast and fierce against my chest, her ragged breaths at my throat. Her hands gripping my sides, tightly at first, then relaxing a little, giving into the warmth of our embrace. I kissed the top of her head, my hands stroking her back, trying to calm her with soft whispers.

"Breathe," I said. "Just breathe."

She pulled away then, tilting her face to look up at me. Her cheeks were stained with tears and her face was blotchy. Her eyes were rimmed in red. "Why do I do this to myself every time?" she asked in a small voice.

"Because you still hope," I told her, reaching out to swipe a fresh tear away. "That's not a bad thing, you know."

"Yeah, well, it's a stupid thing. Clearly the mist is going nowhere. This is all a big waste of time."

I frowned. "No. I don't believe that."

"What?"

"It's not a waste of time," I told her. "Not to me anyway." I paused, then added, "Because I get to spend it with you."

She jerked away, turning from me to stare at the vacant plain stretching out toward the horizon. Worry wormed through my stomach.

"What is it, Iduna?" I asked softly. She'd always been a little sad after coming to the mist. But I'd never seen her this distraught. "Whatever it is, you can tell me. You can tell me anything."

She turned back to me, her face pale and her blue eyes anguished. "How long can we keep doing this, Agnarr?" she demanded. "These silly trips of ours. Soon you'll be king of Arendelle. You think they'll let you keep traipsing off on this fool's errand each fall and spring with some random orphan girl from town?"

I stared at her, shocked. Of course she wasn't wrong. I knew, in the back of my mind, that once I became king, some things would have to change. But that was three years away. Did we have to think of that now? Couldn't we enjoy the time I had left?

I swallowed hard, trying to pull together my racing thoughts. "First," I said firmly, "you are not some random orphan girl. You are my best friend. And nothing will change that. I promise. Our friendship is as solid and strong as this stupid magical mist. And I think you'll agree this stuff is pretty resilient."

To prove my point, I charged at the mist, throwing myself full force against it. It was a move I'd jokingly done during past trips and it had always cheered her up some to watch me bounce off the side and land sprawling on my butt in the mud. But this time, she just watched me with tortured eyes. So I leapt up and charged again, once more getting thrown to the ground.

"Stop it, you crazy person!" she cried, her tone finally carrying a stirring of lightness. "You're going to hurt yourself! Don't you know it's a crime to purposely harm the future king?"

She jumped between me and the mist. But I had already lunged again. I tried to dig in my heels, to stop myself, but it was too late. I slammed into her, shoving her back against the wall of mist. Suddenly our bodies were pressed up against one another. Our faces inches apart.

My breath caught in my throat. I stared down at her, suddenly mesmerized by every detail of her face. Her wide blue eyes, her full pink lips, her small nose, slightly turned up at the tip. The light freckles dusting her cheeks. Her body flush with mine. My heart pounded, matching the beats of her own. And for a moment there was nothing else. No mist, no Enchanted Forest, no guards. Just her and me, not moving. Not able to move.

And then she reached out, pushing me gently away. I stumbled backward, almost losing my balance again. When I looked up at Iduna, I saw her face was bright red. Probably mirroring my own.

"You are a crazy man!" she declared, choking out a nervous laugh, clearly trying to lighten the moment. "I can't believe they're going to let you be king!"

I grinned impishly. "Well, they still have three years

to come to their senses," I reminded her. "Maybe I'll get lucky."

"Maybe," she agreed. "Or maybe by then the mist will have parted. You never know."

"You never know," I echoed, pleased to see her unflappable optimism returning. It was one of the things I adored about Iduna. She always saw the best in the world. She never stopped believing things could change for the better.

I lifted my hand to the mist, making a big show of waving goodbye. Just as I had done every time before. "Till next time," I called out to it. "You stubborn old thing."

And with that, I led Iduna over to the wagon, letting the soldiers know it was time to leave. She scrambled up onto the front seat and I joined her a moment later, after checking on the horses. Before setting off, I gave her a searching look.

"You okay?" I asked.

For a moment she said nothing, and I worried I'd lost her to the gloom of the mist once more. Then a small smile emerged. "I will be," she said. "If you share the rest of that chocolate with me."

I grinned, my shoulders slumping in relief. "I think I can manage that."

CHAPTER TWELVE

Iduna

"IDUNA! YOU'RE BACK!"

I lifted my eyes, squinting in the early morning sunshine. Johan, the man I was apprenticing for, was running down the hill toward me, a huge smile on his face. He was young—only six years older than I was. And with his sparkling brown eyes and mop of curly black hair, it seemed he always had a few village girls vying for his attention. But he was focused on only one thing—inventing.

And his invention of the moment was centered on wind.

"I'm so glad you're here," he declared. "You've got to see this."

I laughed at his enthusiasm as he dragged me to the top of the hill where we'd set up our test windmills. To my surprise, the blades were rotating steadily, even though I could barely feel a breeze.

"They're working!" I cried in excitement. "How did you get them to work?"

We'd been having trouble with this for months now and Johan had been getting very discouraged. When the weather was just right, his mills worked perfectly, the blades catching the wind and rotating, powering up the mill and allowing it to grind grain or pump water. But capturing that wind wasn't as easy as it sounded.

Johan's face was alight with excitement. "I used your idea," he said. "To make them moveable. So the post in the middle stays in place. But the blades can be rotated around the post, depending on the weather conditions. This way, whichever direction the wind is coming from, they can pick it up."

"And it worked?"

Johan pointed at the windmill.

I grinned, watching the blades spin around and around. A warm feeling of pride rolled over me with each rotation. We had made it happen. And now—who knew what the possibilities might be?

I couldn't wait to tell Agnarr.

"Can you believe how far we've come, Iduna?" Johan cried, coming over to me and putting a hand on my back. He'd grown up poor in the village, with big dreams of making something of himself, but the townspeople had never taken him too seriously. *Crazy Johan and his inventions,* they used to say, laughing.

But no one would be laughing now. Not when they saw this.

"I hope you'll put in a good word for me with your friends at the castle," Johan added, brushing his hands against his pants to wipe off the grease that had accumulated on them. "We need them to approve these windmills before we can offer them to the citizens of Arendelle. They might not like it," he added with a warning tone. "It could detract from their own profits."

"Agnarr will love it," I assured him, walking over to the windmill and looking at it with delight. I could feel the breeze on my face and it reminded me of Gale. I hoped my dear friend would be proud of how I had put the knowledge gathered from our time together to practical use.

To feed the hungry. To empower the people.

It felt good. So good.

"What will I love?"

I whirled around, delighted to see none other than Agnarr himself, climbing the hill, accompanied by a few of his personal guards. My face broke out into another huge smile.

"What are you doing here?" I asked. "And how are you up so early? Why, it's not even noon!"

"Ha ha. I can rise early!" he protested, looking a little offended. Not that he had any right to be—he was a notoriously late sleeper. Perks of being a prince, I guess.

I smirked. "Let me guess. Council meeting this morning."

"Yes. Which, so sadly, I couldn't attend," Agnarr agreed, with a great and regretful sigh. "Since I have already committed myself to attending to the people of Arendelle this fine morning. I cannot disappoint my loyal subjects."

"How . . . noble of you." There was nothing Agnarr hated more than council meetings. "And let me guess. You started your very important rounds at Blodget's Bakery?"

A smile crept to his lips. "Bakeries are a very important part of any kingdom, I'll have you know."

"Oh, I know. And a good prince must always avail himself to a cookie taste test, right?"

"Sacrifices must be made," Agnarr agreed solemnly. "For the good of the realm."

"Your Majesty," Johan broke in as he bowed from the waist. "I am truly honored to have you visit my humble mill. Please let me know if I can be of any assistance in any way possible."

I resisted the urge to roll my eyes. Johan wasn't exactly the biggest fan of the monarchy. And he definitely didn't like Agnarr, the spoiled prince, as he called him. Which was totally unfair, since Agnarr was not spoiled at all. But any time I tried to defend him, Johan would get angry and tell me I didn't understand.

But now, here he was, putting on a great show. Probably so Agnarr would sign off on his windmills. Which was totally unnecessary. Agnarr would always do the right thing if it helped his people. No sucking up required.

Agnarr smiled down at him, unaware of Johan's true feelings. "You don't have to do that," he assured him.

"Iduna has told me all about your work together. I'd love to see these mills for myself."

"Of course, Your Majesty!" Johan scrambled to his feet, his face red as a tomato. He turned to the post-mill, which was still rotating steadily. "It's an important invention. Sure to revolutionize farming from this moment forward. . . ."

He started explaining the rotating blade part of the mill. The part I had come up with. But to my surprise, he didn't mention my part in it. He took all the credit for himself—as if it had all been his idea. Not that I needed credit. I was just an apprentice after all. But still! At least a little acknowledgment might have been nice.

"This is all very interesting," Agnarr said when Johan had finished. "I can't wait to see it put to practical use. What will you charge for these post-mills?"

Johan waved a hand. "Very little," he said. "Just enough over cost for me to live a simple life. After all, I do this work for the people, not my own personal gain." He gave the prince a smug look.

Agnarr, to his credit, nodded sincerely. "That's wonderful to hear," he said. "Anything to help Arendelle and her people. Please do let me know if you need anything from me. Anything at all that might help."

"Your Majesty is too kind," Johan replied, bowing his head again. "But . . . how will I reach you? We commoners can't exactly just waltz into the castle and start demanding favors of our betters, now can we?"

I frowned at the tone in his voice, setting Agnarr up

in a trap. But the prince didn't acknowledge the barb—if he noticed it. Instead he just waved a hand.

"Oh, just ask Iduna. She'll deliver the message, won't you?" Agnarr smiled at me before turning back to my employer. "You know, you're very lucky to have someone so smart in your employ. She's really a good worker, isn't she?" He gave Johan a knowing look.

I groaned. I knew exactly what he was trying to do. And it wasn't helping.

"Well! It was *so* great to see you, Your Majesty," I broke in, giving him a warning look. "But I'm sure you are so busy right now, visiting *all* of your people. Please do not feel you have to linger a moment longer."

"I suppose you are right," Agnarr replied with a mischievous look. "And when I'm finished, I believe I have some important *reading* to do?" *Reading* was our code word to meet at our favorite tree in the castle courtyard. Though oftentimes there was no actual reading involved.

"Reading sounds great," I assured him. "Perhaps I will also read something once I have finished my important work."

Agnarr shook his head, as if in amazement. "She's such a hard worker, isn't she, Johan? So dedicated! So smart. So—"

"*Goodbye*, Your Majesty," I interjected, resisting the urge to roll my eyes. He was too much.

"Goodbye, Iduna." He winked at me. "Work hard! Like you always do!"

And with that, Agnarr and his guards rejoined the

road, heading farther up into the hills. Probably to pay a visit to the farmers and shepherds above. I watched him go for a moment, smiling to myself. Even if his methods were crude and completely obvious, I appreciated the sentiment. He knew how much I wanted this job. Why it was important to me.

"He thinks he's so great, doesn't he?" Johan shared once Agnarr had departed.

I turned, not surprised to see Johan was no longer smiling. He was watching Agnarr climb the hill with a scowl on his face.

"What are you talking about?" I asked with a sigh. *Here we go again.* "He said he loved your windmills. He offered to help."

"I don't need his help. Don't you get it?" Johan retorted "Once the monarchy gets involved, it will be all about them. They'll try to take over my project. Use my invention for their own personal gain."

"Agnarr would never do that!" I protested.

"You think you know him so well. But trust me, all monarchy is the same. They're selfish, entitled, and they only think of themselves. I know he's your friend now, Iduna," he added. "But beware. When push comes to shove, he will choose his crown over his friends. They always do."

I frowned. "You're one to talk," I said. "You didn't even mention that the rotating posts were my idea."

Johan's frown softened. "I'm sorry about that," he replied. "I was . . . caught off guard by his sudden appearance. I didn't explain anything well. I certainly didn't mean to discredit all your hard work." He stepped toward me, reaching out to take my hands in his. Hands so different from Agnarr's—rough and calloused, whereas the prince's were strong but smooth. "You are amazing," he told me. "I could never have done this without you. And the next time I see the prince, I will tell him that."

I felt my cheeks heat up. "You don't have to do that," I said. "It doesn't matter anyway. It wasn't just me. It was us. We did it together."

"We did. We're a great team, you and I," he declared, looking up at the post-mill. Then he dropped my hands. "Now. Come. Unlike certain spoiled princes, we have much work to do."

CHAPTER THIRTEEN

Iduna

"WHAT ARE YOU READING, YOUR MAJESTY?"

I hooked my knees around the tree branch, swinging backward until I was upside down and face to face with Agnarr, who had just sat under the tree and cracked his book open. He startled, clearly not having realized I was up there, lying in wait. Then he flashed me a grin.

"Some new Danish author," he said, holding up his book.

I swung my legs around, gracefully flipping out of the tree and landing on the ground in front of him with a flourish. He groaned.

"I seriously believe you are part cat," he declared. "How else do you always land on your feet?"

"The bigger question is, how do you *never* land on yours?" I teased back, dancing over to him. "I mean, it feels like the laws of nature should give you at least a fifty-fifty chance."

He rolled his eyes, giving me a pained look. I shrugged impishly and plopped down beside him on the bench. I plucked the book from his hand and skimmed the cover. "*'The Little Mermaid'*?" I read. "Sounds interesting."

He grabbed the book from me. "It is." He opened it back up, flipping through it until he found his page. I tapped my finger impatiently on my knee, refusing to be ignored.

"What's it about?"

He looked up. "A mermaid."

"Wow. Descriptive."

"Sorry." His mouth quirked. "A *little* mermaid."

I groaned. "You are the worst book describer ever."

"Hey! I just don't want to spoil it for you," he said with an all-too-innocent smirk. "You're welcome to read it yourself after I'm finished."

"You're also the *slowest* reader ever. I'll literally have died of old age by the time you hand over the book." I made an overly dramatic swooning motion, as if I were expiring, right then and there. "Tragically sent to my grave without ever knowing the story behind the mermaid who is also little for some random reason that my best friend won't reveal out of sheer cruelty and malice."

Agnarr closed the book. "You're impossible, you know."

I leaned in, then lowered my voice as though we were sharing our deepest secrets. "So you'll tell me?"

"Absolutely not. But let's try to find you a second copy in the library."

I grinned. "I suppose that would be all right, too."

Agnarr stuffed the book in his satchel, and together we headed back inside the castle, down the hall, and toward the library. It was still my favorite room in the whole gigantean place. I loved the smell of musty books and old leather. And the treasures it held—like mermaids, little or otherwise—were only the beginning.

I watched as Agnarr began to search the shelves, a familiar warmth rising in my chest. It'd been three months since we'd last traveled to the mist, and something about that journey had changed us forever. We were still best friends, of course. We still joked and bantered and teased one another with fluid ease. But there was something else there now, a gravity to our friendship, lingering beneath the surface.

Not to mention an unspoken desire to be near one another at all times.

When he wasn't in meetings, and I wasn't working, and we both didn't need to study, we'd always find some excuse to meet up. Under the name of friendship, nothing more.

Except there *was* something more; I could feel it growing each day.

And I didn't know whether to be delighted . . . or scared to death.

"Hmm. Now to find it . . ." Agnarr's voice snapped me back to attention. "I swear I saw another copy somewhere." He started digging into the stacks.

I tiptoed behind him, careful not to be seen. When

he wasn't looking, I plucked the book from his satchel, then made a great show of finding it in the stacks.

"Oh, look! Here it is!" I cried excitedly. "My very own copy. How lucky is that?"

His eyes narrowed suspiciously. "You just found that there now? Just like that? Amongst the thousands of books in here?"

"Just lucky I guess!" I beamed. "Now if you'll excuse me, I have some important reading to do."

I plopped down into a nearby leather armchair, opening the book. Agnarr watched me for a moment, then sighed, reaching into his satchel for his own copy, which, of course, was no longer there.

I tried my best to keep a straight face, staring very seriously into the book, as, from the corner of my eye, I saw his expression morph from confusion to understanding to annoyance. But then the giggles came.

I could never stop the giggles.

"You are so dead!" he declared, diving at me. But I was too quick, leaping over the back of the chair and dashing through the library. He gave quick pursuit and soon we were in a full-on game of chase, dodging furniture and maybe—but definitely accidentally—knocking over old things that were probably way too old and valuable to be knocked down.

We were well beyond the age of kids who should have been playing this kind of thing, of course. At least that was what Gerda and Kai would always say when they found us chasing each other or playing hide-and-seek through the castle. But we didn't care. It was fun. And weren't older people allowed to have fun, too?

Suddenly, Agnarr changed course, taking a sharp left to cut me off. I screeched as he lunged for the book, throwing myself to the side only to knock into a statue of a horse.

A very familiar-looking horse. Wait, was that a statue of the Water Nokk?

I dove to try to save it, but I was too late. It fell forward with a loud . . .

Grinding sound?

What on earth?

Agnarr and I both froze in our tracks. Dust billowed in the air. The bookcase behind the statue had swung open wide, revealing an arched passageway beyond.

I glanced over at Agnarr. His shocked expression confirmed he'd had no idea there was a secret door in the library. He'd shown me other secret passages. Useful ones that could be used to sneak out of the castle unseen. But this was new.

"What is this?" Agnarr asked, stepping forward to examine the bookcase. As if that was the most interesting part about all of this. I watched, impatiently, as he checked out the hinges, then turned to the Water Nokk, as if trying to piece the mechanics together.

I nearly screamed in frustration. All I cared about was the secret room.

Unwilling to wait any longer, I grabbed a candlestick off the wall and dashed through the passageway, which dead-ended into a dark, small, windowless room with a table in the center. On the table was an ornate candelabra, which I lit with my small candlestick. Soon the whole room began to sparkle and shine, the light catching tiny flecks of crystals embedded in stone shelves that rose floor to ceiling on all sides. I drew in an admiring breath, twirling around. What a magical place!

Magical and . . . messy. The shelves were covered in dusty old objects that clearly hadn't been used for years: glass beakers, silver scales meant to weigh small things, dusty vases filled with dried-up flowers.

And books. So many books.

Not ordinary books like the ones in the regular library either, which were old but not as old as these. These books looked like they'd been in here, gathering dust, for a thousand years.

My eyes were also drawn to a rickety old table in the center of the room. It was covered in scrolls of ancient paper that crumbled at the corners, all with writing in languages I couldn't decipher. Among the scrolls were piles of old maps with drawings of foreign lands and sea monsters scrawled across their pages.

"This is amazing!" I cried, twirling around the room. "How long has it been here? Does anyone know it exists?"

"My father did, evidently," Agnarr replied, stepping up beside me.

I whirled around, confused. He pointed to blueprints I hadn't noticed yet, lying at the edge of the table. "That's his handwriting," he said flatly. Then he turned and pointed to a dusty portrait in the corner of a woman wearing a crown. "And that's my mother."

I stared at the portrait, surprised. Agnarr never talked about his mother. I didn't even know her name. I stared at the portrait, immediately identifying the resemblance between the woman and her son. Same reddish-blond hair. Same green eyes. But unlike Agnarr's eyes, which always sparkled like the sun, this woman's eyes looked unbearably sad. As if she held a terrible secret.

"You never talk about your mother," I said softly, for the first time wondering why.

"She . . . disappeared when I was young," he said slowly. "They searched and searched for her, but never found her." He shrugged impatiently, as if he didn't care. "At least that's what they told me. I have no idea if it's true."

"Why wouldn't it be true?" I asked, though I wondered if I should press him. He looked so upset, his face dark and brooding. As if he was on the verge of crying. Or maybe punching someone in the mouth. Which wasn't like the Agnarr I knew.

I guess we all had our secrets.

"You know what, who cares?" I announced resolutely, trying to lighten his mood. "It's just a dumb old room anyway. Smelly, too. Let's close it up and forget we ever saw it. There's nothing interesting in here anyway."

It was the last thing I wanted to do, of course. I mean, who knew what kind of ancient wisdom might be buried in a room like this? Perhaps it even held some sort of clue to breaking through the mist. Some historical record of when something like the mist had happened before—and how the people of the past had dispersed it.

But Agnarr looked so distraught. Like simply standing in the room was causing him physical pain. I had to get him out of there. And fast.

I held up *The Little Mermaid*, waving it in his face. "Oh, look what I found!" I tried.

But he only pushed it away, walking to the other side of the room. He stared up at the old books, his face twisted with anger. "All these secrets!" he burst out. "My whole life! No one told me anything. It was all secrets, secrets, secrets! And now my father's dead. And my mother's gone. And all the answers are gone with them."

He slammed his fist against the wall. Then he turned to me, his brilliant green eyes practically gleaming with misery.

"Please, Iduna. Promise me now. No secrets between us. Ever."

My heart suddenly gave a jolt. I dropped the book, which landed on the table with a heavy thud. But I couldn't bring myself to reach down to pick it up, too afraid I'd topple over if I tried.

No secrets? How could he ask for that? But then, of course, he didn't know. To him, I was an open book. He had no idea the depths of my deception. How I'd lied to him every day since we'd met. Lies stacked upon lies on top of lies, like some crazy house of cards that could come crashing down at the slightest breeze.

The lump in my throat threatened to choke me. But I forced myself to suck in a breath, trying desperately to channel some inner calm. What was it Agnarr always said before he went to address the people?

Conceal, don't feel.

"I've got to go!" I blurted out, doing a particularly terrible job at the whole "concealing" thing. My best friend—the boy I loved more than anyone else in the world—was standing before me, asking me to tell the truth.

And I couldn't do it. Even for him. *Especially* for him.

"Iduna, what's wrong?" Agnarr asked, looking alarmed at my reaction. He reached out, taking my hands in his own and squeezing them tight. My heart fluttered as he met my eyes with his own. Eyes so deep and green and bright, but filled with such confusion.

He didn't understand.

He'd *never* understand. Because I could never tell him.

"What's wrong, Iduna?" he repeated, softer this time, reaching up to trace my cheek with feathery fingers, leaving a trail of fire in their wake. I should go. I should leave. I should run from this room and never come back.

But, of course, I couldn't. I could no more walk out of the room than I could break through the mist itself.

Instead, I closed my eyes. Tried to still my racing heart. "Nothing," I whispered. "I just . . ."

I trailed off, unsure what to say. Not sure if I'd ever know what to say again. Every word that came from my mouth tasted like a lie, even the ones that were true. What was I going to do?

"I think I know."

My eyes flew open. "What?"

"I know what you're hiding."

A cold knot formed in my stomach. "What I'm hiding?" I repeated. "You . . . do?" I could barely get out the words. My whole world felt as if it were teetering on the edge of a cliff, ready to fall into the abyss.

He nodded slowly, his eyes never leaving mine. The confusion was gone, I realized. And in its place a striking look of clarity. And . . . something else entirely.

"Don't worry," he whispered. "I feel it, too. I've been feeling it for a while now. Since our last journey out to the dam." His face turned bright red. "Though I wasn't sure at first if you did, too. But now . . . I think . . ." He choked out a laugh. "Wow. I'm really bad at this, huh?"

And suddenly I realized exactly what he was trying to say. What secret of mine he'd uncovered. A secret that had been bursting inside of me for months now, even though it had gone unacknowledged until that very moment.

Relief crashed over me like a tidal wave and I found myself starting to laugh. It was a totally wrong reaction, but I couldn't help it. I couldn't stop laughing.

His face fell. His eyes clouded again. "Oh," he said. "Maybe I was wrong—"

And then my lips met his.

For a moment he stood there as if frozen in place. Then, slowly, his hands reached out and cupped my cheeks, pulling me close to him.

And he kissed me back.

This was wrong. I knew it was wrong. And yet—perhaps it was that very wrongness that made it feel so right. So good and perfect and sweet. We were all alone, in a secret room. No one could see. No one would know.

And we were kissing.

Our lips joined felt clumsy at first, but somehow that made it all the better, a new adventure we'd embarked upon together. His mouth moved hungrily against mine, and his hands tangled in my hair. I clamped my hands on his hips, pulling him closer. Our bodies seemed to melt into one another until I was unsure where I ended and he began.

Thud!

We broke apart, startled by the noise. It took us a moment to realize it was just the *Little Mermaid* book, knocked from the table. I gave a brittle laugh, suddenly bashful, quickly dropping to my knees to grab the book, mostly as an excuse to duck out of sight for a moment and try to get myself under control.

"Uh . . ." Agnarr stammered when I rose to my feet again, as if he'd lost all power of speech. "Wow. That was . . . wow."

"Wow," I agreed, daring to look at him again. His eyes were glazed over. But he looked happy.

Almost as happy as I felt.

Feeling brave, I leaned forward again, planting a kiss on his cheek. Then, before he could react, I danced over to the exit, waving the *Little Mermaid* book gleefully as I went.

"I'm going to read this first," I told him.

Agnarr stared at me. His face was adorably flushed, redder than I'd ever seen it before. I gave a small wave before heading down the passageway, the book clutched to my chest. I'd almost made it out before he finally spoke.

"Iduna . . ."

I stopped. Turned. "Yes, Your Majesty?"

He grinned at me. "Don't tell me how it ends."

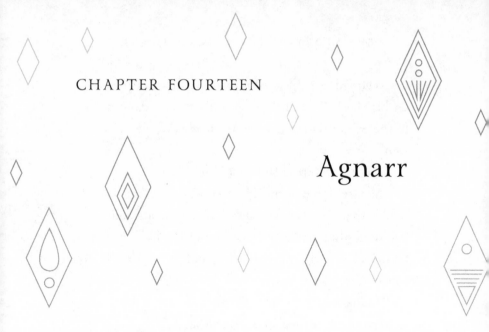

CHAPTER FOURTEEN

Agnarr

SHE'D KISSED ME. SHE'D KISSED *ME*! OUT OF the blue—I hadn't even been expecting it. I mean, I'd wanted it. I'd been wanting it. I'd been dreaming of it, too. How many nights had I laid awake in bed, imagining what Iduna's lips would feel like on mine? But I had no idea that she would just—

"Agnarr! Could you at least pretend to be paying attention?"

I looked up, realizing everyone in the council meeting room was staring at me. We'd been having another one of those endlessly boring diplomacy meetings all afternoon, but I hadn't been able to pay attention to anything being said. And who could blame me? How could one focus on politics and foreign relations when one had a memory of a perfect kiss from a perfect girl running through one's head?

"Agnarr, please. We need your input here." Lord

Peterssen was beginning to sound cross. I sighed and straightened in my chair, doing my best to push thoughts of Iduna out of my brain. Which was impossible, of course, but at least they could dance in the back part for a while, instead of taking up my entire attention.

"What are we talking about again?" I asked, trying to look like a good prince.

"The kingdom of Vassar. It's got a nice port. Great trade opportunities. It would be a boon for us to join our two kingdoms together in an alliance," Peterssen said.

"Uh, sure. That sounds great." Why did I care about any of this again?

"Really? Then you agree? You don't want to think about it first?" Peterssen was peering at me curiously. "Or at least meet the girl?"

I almost fell out of my chair. "Wait, what?"

"The king of Vassar's daughter? Runa? He's offered you her hand in marriage." Peterssen gave me a pointed look, silently scolding me for not listening earlier.

"A fine lady," piped in Frederick, one of the council members. He was short and burly, and had the biggest, reddest mustache I'd ever seen on a man. "Quite beautiful, too, from what I understand. Would make for a regal queen and a good mother."

Queen? Mother? I stood up, succeeding mainly in knocking over my chair. It fell to the floor with a loud crash. "What are you talking about?"

Peterssen sighed deeply. "Agnarr, you're eighteen. In a few years, you'll be taking the throne of Arendelle. Which means you need to sire an heir to the throne. Maybe two. And to do that, you need a wife. Sooner rather than later."

My mind immediately flashed to Iduna. Which was ridiculous, of course. They'd never let me marry her. She was, by all rights, a commoner. I was supposed to marry a princess from a different kingdom to strengthen Arendelle's position. Especially after my father's death. Peterssen had done his best as regent, but the wolves were always sniffing at the doors of a kingdom with a young ruler.

I knew all this in my head. I had always known it, deep down.

But in my heart . . .

Without thinking, I rubbed my thumb across my lower lip. I could still feel the phantom bliss of her soft mouth moving against mine.

Iduna.

I faked a cough. Ridiculous, certainly, but all I could come up with on short notice. "I'm not feeling well," I announced. "I need a break. We can talk about this another day." I started toward the door.

"But, sire!" protested Peterssen.

I stopped in my tracks. "I've gone eighteen years without a wife," I said slowly. "Surely you gentlemen can wait a few more days to foist one on me."

"We're not asking you to decide right now," Frederick responded. "Just for you to keep an open mind. And allow the young lady to come visit us in Arendelle. So she can experience the beauty and charm of our kingdom for herself."

"Sure. That's fine. Whatever you want to do." I was already halfway to the door, desperate to escape those gazes, the looks of men who expected me to lead but doubted my ability to do so. I could feel Peterssen's eyes on me, but I refused to look in his direction. *This is your fault!* I wanted to cry. *You brought her here. The most beautiful, kind, funny girl in the world. What did you expect would happen?*

But I couldn't say any of that. They'd never understand. And so, with as much dignity as I could muster, I lifted my head high and strode out of the council chambers like the king I was.

Conceal, don't feel.

Don't let it show. . . .

CHAPTER FIFTEEN

Iduna

"YOUR USUAL, MISS IDUNA?" ASKED MRS. Blodget as I practically skipped into her bakery later that day. I peered into the glass cabinet where she kept all her special treats. Flaky pastries, gigantic cookies, and, of course, chocolate.

So much chocolate.

"Yes," I said. "Two dozen cookies. And, that right there, whatever that is," I added impulsively, pointing to what looked like a miniature Arendelle Castle made entirely of chocolate. The cookies would be for the younger children in the orphanage. Now that I was working and had an income, I liked to bring them treats. While the orphanage did well at stretching their budget to make sure everyone was fed, there was never much left over for desserts.

The chocolate however, was for me.

As Mrs. Blodget bustled to package up the cookies, I

wandered around the store, looking in all the cases. But even as I peered through the glass, my mind was completely elsewhere.

Namely, on Agnarr's kiss.

"You look happy today," Mrs. Blodget remarked as she came over with the box of cookies, tied with a red ribbon. "Of course, you always do." She handed them to me, along with the bag containing the tiny chocolate castle. She gave me a wink. "I added an extra half dozen cookies," she said in a conspiratorial tone. "For the children."

"Thank you," I said, beaming. "You didn't have to do that."

"I know. I wanted to. Such a sweet thing you do for them. Those poor little dears."

I shrugged. "It's the least I can do."

"Well, not all would bother to do the same, trust me," she said, clucking her tongue. "They are lucky to have you. *We* are lucky to have you," she added. "My husband told me what you and Johan are working on up in the hills with the wind. He said it will revolutionize our town."

"I hope so." I smiled.

Mrs. Blodget's eyes misted over. "Your parents would have been so proud."

"Thank you," I said, a little uneasy about the parents part. It was so tough, always lying to people. Especially people as nice as Mrs. Blodget. How long would I have to do this? My mind flashed back to Agnarr's words in the library.

Please, Iduna. Promise me now. No secrets between us. Ever.

A promise I could never make. Even to the boy I loved.

"Good morning, sunshine," Johan greeted me as I entered his barn early the next morning. "You're looking bright and cheery this morning."

I gave him a wan smile, exhaustion settling on my shoulders like a wet blanket. I hadn't been able to sleep much the night before, tossing and turning and thinking of Agnarr. Some of it was nice—reliving our secret kisses in the library room. Other parts were not, though. I tried and tried to come up with a way to tell him the truth about my past without ruining everything between us.

Maybe he wouldn't care, I told myself. Maybe he would be totally fine finding out where I came from. Especially if he knew I was his rescuer. How could you hate someone who saved your life?

But then I remembered his words in the library. How his whole life had been ensconced in secrets. If he found out I'd been lying to him this whole time, he would think me no better than anyone else. He'd be so hurt. All the trust we'd built up between us would be lost. He'd probably end up hating me.

I couldn't bear to have Agnarr hate me. He was all I had in the world.

Well, that and my job. I realized Johan was staring at me worriedly.

"What's wrong?" he asked, putting an arm around me. I allowed him to lead me over to a nearby bench. "You look like someone ate your pet reindeer."

I gave him a rueful smile, sinking down onto the bench. "I'm fine," I assured him. "Just tired."

He sat down next to me. "And why wouldn't you be? You've been working so hard," he said, patting my knee. "Don't think I haven't noticed. I couldn't have asked for a better apprentice, Iduna. I'm proud of all we've accomplished together." He squeezed my knee.

I swallowed hard, suddenly feeling slightly uncomfortable about his proximity. Which was strange, of course. After all, Johan and I had been working closely together for over a year at this point. We'd always been close. But something seemed different about him that day. Though I couldn't quite put my finger on it.

"I love this job," I declared, rising to my feet, mostly to put distance between us. I walked to the window, staring out at our mill. The blades were rotating steadily and I couldn't help a swell of pride rising inside of me. I had done this. Something magnificent that would change Arendelle's future. "I wouldn't want to work anywhere else."

"I'm glad to hear it." Johan joined me at the window, pulling me around until I faced him. His expression was serious. "Iduna, I know your apprenticeship ends in a few months," he said. "But I'm hoping you'll agree to keep on with me after it's over." He paused, then added with a sly smile, "Though not just as my apprentice this time."

Whoa. My heart started to beat faster in my chest.

Was this finally it? Was this finally the moment I'd been waiting for? The moment he asked me to stay on with him full time?

"You . . . want to hire me?" I asked, my voice trembling so hard I could barely get the words out. Was this really happening? Was I really getting my dream job?

To my surprise, Johan started to laugh. As if I'd said the funniest thing in the world.

"Iduna." To my shock, he dropped down to one knee in front of me. "I want to *marry* you."

What?

I stared down at him, too shocked to speak. He smiled up at me, reaching out to clasp my hands in his own. Horrified, I leapt backward, instinctively putting distance between us.

His earnest expression crumbled. He scrambled back to his feet.

"I . . ." I began, my mind racing to take back control. "I didn't . . . I'm sorry."

What was I apologizing for? I hadn't done anything wrong. I was just surprised—shocked. I thought he was offering me a job.

Not marriage!

He sucked in a deep breath and the disappointment emptied from his face, replaced by a blank mask. "I thought . . ."

"You thought . . . what?" I could barely breathe.

"I thought we worked well together," he sputtered. "I thought we were a good team."

"We do. We . . . are."

"Then why not be more?" he asked, his eyes now pleading. "Iduna, we could be happy together. You and I."

My thoughts and mind were racing so fast it was almost impossible for anything to make sense. How long had he been harboring these feelings for me? Had I been blind to his true intentions all this time? I liked Johan. He was smart. Creative. A good boss. But that was where my feelings ended.

But not his, evidently.

"I'm sorry," I stammered, wringing my hands together in front of me. "You're a good friend. And I love working with you. It's just . . ." I trailed off, not knowing what else to say. This was not good. Not good at all.

Sure enough, his face turned beet red, anger rising to the surface.

"What, do you think you're too good for me?" he demanded. "You, with your fancy education at the castle? Your fancy friendship with the prince?"

I felt the blood drain from my face. My mind flashed to Agnarr in the secret room. His lips brushing over mine. Kisses so tender. So sweet. Had that only been days before?

Johan caught my expression. His eyebrows rose. "Oh." He started to laugh. "I see.

"You're in love with the prince."

I staggered backward. "I am not!"

He nodded slowly, realization dawning in his eyes. "Yes, that's it, isn't it? That's why you'd never lower yourself to marry a commoner like me! You have delusions of grandeur. You think he's going to make you queen? You are such a fool!"

"I don't think that!" I protested.

"I hope not," he shot back. "Because it will never happen. People like him, they don't care about people like us. Self-made people who don't need their benevolence to survive." He gave me a patronizing look. "And, trust me, while they may flirt with you and see fit to sully your honor, in the end they only marry their own kind."

Johan's cruel words shot through me like a lightning bolt to the heart. I knew this, of course. I'd known it from the very first day I'd started having feelings for Agnarr. But a part of me had still held out hope, especially after our kiss.

Johan must have seen the effect his words had wrought in my shell-shocked expression, because his voice softened, relenting. "Look, I'm sorry," he said. "I'm not trying to hurt your feelings. And I'm sorry if I came on too strong. But I care about you, Iduna. I don't want your girlish crush to get you hurt."

"I don't have a crush!" I tried to say, but knew it was useless. Everything he was saying was right. Agnarr and I could never be together. And it would be so much smarter to turn my back on him now, before it was too late. To pair up with a man like Johan instead. Someone who was my equal. And, hey—maybe I could learn to love him someday. Or at least grow old in mutual respect. Many marriages survived on less.

But no. It was already too late for me. I was desperately in love with my prince. The way he made me laugh, the way he made me think. The way he made chills run down my spine when he reached out and caressed my cheek with his soft fingers. Agnarr made me feel things I'd never felt before. And if I couldn't have him, I wanted no one at all.

I realized Johan was still waiting for me to respond. I finally found my voice.

"Look, this doesn't have to change anything," I tried, hoping to defuse the situation as gently as I could. "We're still friends, right? We can still work together?"

Johan's face twisted. "That's all you care about, isn't it?" he said in an accusing voice. "The stupid windmills."

"What do you mean?"

"Go home, Iduna. You've made your choice. I hope it gets you what you want."

I froze. "Wait, are you . . . firing me?" I asked, eyes wide with horror.

"What do you want me to do?" he spit out. "I've laid out my heart to you and you've trampled on it. How does one go back to talking about wind after something like that?"

Of course. I had rejected him, and he was going to make me pay. With the one thing he knew mattered to me most of all. My job.

I felt tears well in my eyes, but I refused to let them fall. "You know, you talk a good game about helping people become independent," I said, trying not to let him see how upset I was. "But when it all comes down to it? You're as selfish as the rest."

"Iduna—"

"Goodbye, Johan. Good luck with your windmills."

And with that, I pivoted on my heel, storming down the hill. I could hear him calling after me, but I refused to turn around. I wouldn't give him the satisfaction.

At the bottom of the hill, I turned right by force of habit. Headed to the castle.

I needed to see Agnarr.

Now.

CHAPTER SIXTEEN

Iduna

HE WAS ALREADY IN THE TREE WHEN I GOT there. As if he'd been waiting, right where I needed him to be. I wanted to tackle him with relief when I saw him there, curled up on a low-hanging branch, his nose buried in a thick tome.

But I held back, Johan's voice seeming to echo in my ears.

You have delusions of grandeur. You think he's going to make you queen?

What if Johan was right and Agnarr had already decided the whole thing between us had been nothing more than a big mistake?

I couldn't bear to lose both my job and my best friend in one day.

Agnarr looked up from his book, hearing me approach. His face brightened with a huge smile that made me want to break out into tears of relief. Johan had no idea what he was talking about. Agnarr cared about me. What we had together—it was special. It mattered.

I climbed into the tree. Agnarr's smile faded as he caught my face.

"What's wrong?" he asked, setting aside his book immediately.

I hung my head, at first not wanting to talk about it. I felt so ashamed—had I missed the signs? Had I given off signals that had led Johan to the wrong conclusions?

But no. I had given him an honest day's work.

"Iduna. Talk to me." Agnarr's face was inches from mine. "Are you all right? Are you . . ." His face turned pale. "Are you upset about what happened in the library? 'Cause we can talk about it. If you thought it was a mistake—"

I choked out a laugh. And here I had been worrying he was thinking the same thing about me.

"No," I assured him, giving him a sad smile as I laid my hand on his shoulder. It was all I could do not to crawl into his arms, let him hold me. Tell me everything would be all right. But I had to get this out first. "In fact, the library thing was the good part about this week."

His brows furrowed. "What happened?"

"Well, for starters, Johan proposed."

Agnarr's face turned as white as a ghost's. "He d-did?" he stammered. "Um, that's . . . wow." He swallowed hard. "What did you say?"

"I told him no. Obviously," I snapped, feeling annoyed

I even had to answer that question. That on some level Agnarr wouldn't already know. But how could he? We'd never talked about these kinds of things. We'd never even expressed feelings for one another until recently.

"Phew." Agnarr's face shone with relief. "I mean, he's totally wrong for you," he added hastily when I gave him a look.

I swallowed down a bitter laugh. *Wrong for me.* On the contrary, Johan was exactly the type that was right for me. A self-made man who had come from nothing. He was someone who had worked hard and persevered against all odds. Not unlike me.

It was Agnarr who was wrong for me. The one unattached man in Arendelle I could never have.

The only one I wanted.

In the end they only marry their own kind.

I closed my eyes, trying to reset my sanity. "Anyway, when I said no to his proposal, he basically fired me. Which means I'm not going to get to work on windmills anymore."

"What?" Agnarr looked horrified. "He can't do that!"

"He already has." Suddenly I felt a million years old.

"Well, he has to rehire you then. That's illegal. Or it should be, if it's not. I can make it illegal. I could send over some guards to talk to him. I could ... put him in jail even. I mean, unjust firing of perfectly qualified apprentices who simply aren't into marriage ... or something? That has to be a crime of some sort."

I couldn't help a small smile at this. His outrage on my behalf made me feel better. Even if I didn't want him to follow through with any of it.

"Thank you," I said. "I appreciate the support. But I'd prefer to deal with this myself. It's my problem, not yours."

"I know, but . . ." His shoulders slumped in defeat. "I want to help you."

"And I love that you do. But I'm not some damsel in distress from one of your books. I have always taken care of myself. And I will take care of this, too."

"I understand," he said. And my heart swelled at the acceptance on his face. He wanted to help. But he was also willing to step back and let me do it my way. He wouldn't force me or guilt me into something I didn't want. All he wanted was for me to be happy. And he would do anything, I knew, to make it so—even if that meant doing nothing at all.

"Isn't there anything I can do for you?" he asked softly. He reached out, brushing a lock of hair from my face. His eyes were tender, kind. "What do you need, Iduna?"

My emotions flooded my heart at his simple words. And suddenly I realized there was only one thing I needed. The one thing I should not ask for. The one thing I wasn't sure I could live without.

"I need you," I whispered. "Just you."

His breath caught in his throat. For a moment, he

just looked at me. Just looked and looked and looked until time itself seemed to freeze in his gaze.

And then he kissed me.

It didn't begin gently this time, like the kiss we'd shared in the secret room. Instead, it felt desperate in its intensity. And as he dug his hands deep into my hair, heat rose inside me, until I felt as if I would literally burst into flames.

"Agnarr," I whispered, my mouth against his.

"Iduna . . ."

I don't know how long we kissed in that tree. It could have been hours, years, minutes, or only a few blissful seconds. But when we finally pulled apart, flushed and breathless, we looked each other in the eyes, no longer bashful. As if nothing in the world mattered outside that tree. No past, no potential future. Nothing could steal this moment away from the two of us.

"I love you," he whispered. So softly at first that I was half convinced I was making it up in my head. But then his voice rose. More confident. The voice of a boy who would soon be king. "I've *always* loved you," he added. "Since that first day in the orphanage when I walked in on you singing."

"I love you, too," I replied, my voice so croaky that I wondered if he could even understand me. My admission wasn't perfect, but there it was, all the same: vulnerable and true. My heart was his for the taking whether I liked it or not. I reached out and slipped my hand in his and squeezed it hard. His hands were soft, not rough and cal-loused. But that didn't mean they weren't strong and fully capable. "Since . . . the day we first climbed this tree."

It wasn't what I wanted to say, of course. I wanted to tell him I'd loved him far longer. Since that very first day he arrived in the Enchanted Forest. When I'd seen the wonder in his eyes as he stroked the baby reindeer. When his father yelled at him and I watched his narrow shoulders slump and his head bow in shame.

When he lay bleeding on the ground and I made the choice to save him—instead of myself.

But I couldn't say any of that. Not now at least. Not while everything was so fragile, so new. I knew in my heart this perfect moment would not last forever. Our circumstances were far too different for any of this to end happily in the long run. But while we might not have tomorrow, we had this precious now. And now was all that mattered.

I smiled at the prince. He smiled back at me, looking pretty pleased with himself.

Agnarr.

"If only we could do this forever," I said with a happy sigh.

"We can!" he declared. "In fact, I'll make a royal proc-lamation. Kissing no longer has to have any time limits whatsoever!"

I giggled. "There are no time limits now!"

His eyes met mine. They were soft and dreamy, a

likely reflection of my own. "Then why can't we do this forever?" he whispered.

I could have offered up a million practical reasons. Instead, I kissed him again.

CHAPTER SEVENTEEN

Iduna

"'AND SO THE ARENDELLIANS SETTLED DOWN on the grassy, green banks of what would henceforth be known as Arenfjord.'"

A giggle escaped me, and Miss Larsen looked up from her history text, eyeing us with a suspicious expression. Agnarr's face grew wide and innocent as I bit my lower lip to stop from laughing, giving the prince a scolding look. How was I supposed to pay attention to our history lessons if he kept reaching under the table, grazing my knee with his hand and sending shivers straight up my spine? Good shivers, but still!

"Is something amusing, Miss Iduna?" Miss Larsen asked pointedly.

"No, ma'am," I assured her. "I was just . . . thinking of something."

"Next class, let's try to keep your concentration on learning, shall we?" Miss Larsen asked.

I nodded as I gathered my things and headed for the secret library, knowing Agnarr was not far behind.

In fact, over the past few months I had found it almost impossible to concentrate on anything but Agnarr and our secret romance. (Well, that and keeping it secret.) We still spent almost all our free time together now, when not in lessons or in council meetings, evading his guards and slipping out of the village. We'd wander the hills, hand in hand, talking for hours about nothing and everything. Then we'd find a tree or bush to hide behind and kiss until it felt like I couldn't breathe.

The secret room in the library had become our most frequented spot, both because it was so tucked away and because it was the place where we'd first given in to the rushes of feeling flooding through us. We'd turned the room into our own special hideaway, with Agnarr reading aloud from various books or scrolls he'd uncovered while I painted stars on the ceiling with paint that seemed to glow in the dark. When I had finished, we lay on the floor, staring up at the vast sky, hands linked, as if we were on one of our mist trips.

But as magical as these moments were, I still had to deal with real life. Like what was I going to do to earn a living now that I was no longer an apprentice.

Agnarr tapped his finger to his chin, considering the options. "What if you started your own windmill business? Give Johan a little competition."

"That would great," I said with a chuckle. "But how

would I start a business? No one's going to invest in a sixteen-year-old girl."

"*I* would. If she were you."

I groaned. "For the last time, I'm not taking your money, Agnarr."

"I don't see why not. I have more than enough to spare. Also, you're a good investment. I know you'd pay me back."

I kissed him in the space between his ear and collarbone, the place I knew always made him shiver. "Agnarr. I appreciate your faith in me. But this is something I have to do on my own."

"Oh, fine." He sat up and ran his hand through his hair. "So you don't have money. What *do* you have?"

I scrunched up my nose. "Knowledge? I mean, I know how to build a windmill. I just don't have the money to buy the supplies to do it."

"That's it!" Agnarr cried, pointing at me. "I got it!"

"What?"

"You can be a teacher."

"A teacher? Like Miss Larsen?"

He shook his head. "What I'm thinking is something a little more specialized."

"What do you mean?"

"You told me Johan actually constructs these windmills on farmers' lands, right? Well, what if they want to save money by just paying for the knowledge of how to build them and actually doing the construction themselves?"

My eyes widened. "Oh!"

"You could teach them, right? You'd provide the expertise and the building plans, for a reasonable fee. And they'd gather all the materials and labor."

"That's . . . not a bad idea," I said, trying to organize the thoughts whirling through my head. "This way people wouldn't have to sacrifice half their life savings to get a windmill."

"And you're such a good teacher," Agnarr said. "You're so patient with everyone. Even me!"

"*Especially* you," I teased, poking him in the arm.

"So, what do you think?" he asked.

"I think you're brilliant," I declared. "But don't let it go to your head."

He smiled. "There's only one thing in my head right now, Iduna." He lowered his mouth so his lips were right against mine. "And she's going to make a terrific teacher."

CHAPTER EIGHTEEN

Iduna

Six Weeks Later

"ALL RIGHT, SO YOU HAVE SOME CHOICES here. You can just build your basic windmill–which will require fewer materials and is less labor intensive. Or you can add a roundhouse to the design. This will cost more up front as it requires a lot more lumber. However, you'll gain a covered storage area for your grain or farm tools."

"Hm. What do you suggest?" asked Mr. Hansen, studying the plans that I'd sketched and laid out before him. "I don't want to waste any money, but . . ."

"A roundhouse will also protect your trestle—that's basically the legs of the windmill—from bad weather," I told him. "Which, we tend to have a lot of around here. If you can afford it, I would definitely recommend it."

Mr. Hansen looked up. "Well then, let's go with that!"

I smiled, rolling up the plans and putting out my hand. He shook it with a firm grip. "Great," I said. "I'll revise these to include the roundhouse and get them back to you first thing tomorrow. Sound good?"

"Fantastic. This is going to save me a fortune from what I was going to pay Johan. And I don't mind doing the work myself. I prefer it, actually. This way I get exactly what I want." He grinned at me. "Thank you, Iduna."

"Thank *you*," I corrected with a smile. "And please tell all your friends. I'd love to design windmills for them as well."

"Oh, you better believe I will," he declared. "I'll sing your praises in the pub tonight. By morning, you'll have more business than you can handle."

"Don't worry. I can handle quite a bit," I assured him. "Thank you again. I'll see you tomorrow."

And with that, I headed back down the hill, whistling cheerfully. It was a beautiful day. I was once again gainfully employed. *Self*-employed—which was even better. After all, I had the best boss in the world. Even if she was a bit of a tyrant.

I still couldn't believe how much fun I'd been having over the past few weeks. It was hard work—yes. And at the end of the day, I was exhausted. But I was earning money every day, and I'd already raised almost enough to rent my own place. My own little home in the village—it sounded like a dream come true.

And Agnarr had been so encouraging. Sure, he was busy, too—with all the council meetings and his royal duties. But he never missed a chance to meet me at the end of the day in our secret room in the library. We would curl up in one another's arms, utterly spent from our very different days, and he'd make me tell him everything—even the boring stuff. And he'd act interested in all of it.

I reached the bridge that led into Arendelle, waving at a few people as I crossed. My mind wandered to the first day I'd come to the town, still but a girl, frightened and alone. The walls had seemed so tall and imposing then. The streets so narrow and tight. I couldn't imagine, at the time, living in a place like this.

But now, it felt like home.

It would never replace the forest I grew up in. I still mourned my old life and family and all I had lost that day. But it had been so long now, that life had begun to feel almost like a dream. A beautiful dream of an enchanted forest, with magical spirits and a family that loved me.

There was a time when I truly believed I would die if I could never enter the forest again. If the mist was never to part. But that time, I realized, was long gone. And I had so much more to live for now. My life in Arendelle wasn't what I planned for, but I had made it mine all the same, and I was proud of what I'd accomplished so far—and of the things I still planned to do. And now my dreams were less about returning to the past and more about striking out into the future—whatever it might bring.

I just hoped, somehow, Agnarr could be a part of that future, too.

CHAPTER NINETEEN

Agnarr

"I WAS MINDING MY OWN BUSINESS!" declared Mrs. Olsen, a local fishing boater sporting a ropy silver braid that trailed down her back. "Sitting in my boat, sewing up my nets for the next day's haul. When all of a sudden, I felt like I couldn't breathe! It was as if I had a noose tied around my neck. But when I reached up to try to remove it, there was nothing there!" She shook her head. "I've been too afraid to get on my boat ever since."

I nodded along, careful to keep my expression neutral from my seat on the dais in the Great Hall, as she continued with her tirade. The Tuesday petitioner session—where the people of Arendelle would come to air their grievances to the crown and ask for help or advice—often proved to be a difficult balancing act for me. As their would-be ruler, I needed to act concerned and sympathetic, but at the same time impartial. Sometimes it was hard to keep a straight face, while at other times it was hard not to rush over to them with a hug and comforting words.

Some of their complaints were petty, like the neighbor's goat had eaten their prize tulips. Others, though, were truly heartbreaking: like the one from a woman whose husband had died in a freak accident; she, sadly, had no job (and no income) and was left with five children to feed and support. But more and more frequently, these sessions had started centering on the strange reports we were receiving of incidents occurring down by the docks and outside the village. Some swore they were about the misuse of magical powers—and how those affected couldn't protect themselves.

A shepherd named Aksel stood to echo Mrs. Olsen. "I've always kept a herd of sheep grazing in the hills," he began. "Never had a single problem keeping them there. But yesterday I went up to check on them? And they had all turned purple!"

"Purple?" I frowned. "What do you mean, purple?"

"I mean, purple! Day before their wool was as white as the driven snow. Now it's bright purple! They're acting spooked, too. I'm sure they're under some kind of evil spell."

"It's the spirits," declared Gunnar, our town's new blacksmith, who had been standing near the back of the room. He'd only arrived a month ago and had been a troublemaker ever since, stirring up the crowds with his constant talk of evil spirits. "The same ones from the day at the dam. They're toying with us now. But mark my words, soon they'll come down from the hills. They will attack Arendelle with their black magic. We must be ready for them."

I groaned under my breath. Not again. "Has anyone actually seen a spirit?" I cut in, my tone brusque. "In Arendelle, I mean, or anywhere nearby?" I turned to Aksel. "Did you see any by your sheep? Or, Mrs. Olsen, by your boat? Has anyone seen a single spirit in real life, ever?"

Everyone shrugged noncommittally, looking down at their feet.

"Could it be possible that something else is causing the problems then? Something non-magical in nature?" I asked. "Mrs. Olsen, have you been checked by a doctor lately? The pollen is fierce this spring. Maybe you had an allergy attack. And, Aksel, could one of the shepherds from a neighboring town be jealous of your prizewinning wool—and hoped to gain advantage by dyeing your sheep when you weren't looking?"

"So, you're saying you don't believe us?" Gunnar asked. "That the crown won't even investigate these extremely valid concerns, as odd as they may seem to you?" The room erupted in angry chatter.

Frustration flared through me. "No, what I'm saying is—"

Lord Peterssen rose to his feet, placing a stilling hand on my shoulder. "Of course Prince Agnarr believes you," he said. "And no matter who or what is behind these acts, they must stop immediately. We will double our patrols, both in town and in the hills. If we find any suspicious individuals, or, uh, spirits skulking around, we will track them down and bring them in to face the law."

There were a few grunts from the crowd, but most did not seem appeased. What did they want us to do? This supposed enemy had never been seen. How were we to guard against magical spirits?

"I think that's enough for today," Peterssen added, his voice rising above the din. "We will reconvene next week to hear any new grievances. For now, please join us for refreshments in the Second Great Hall."

The mood of the crowd lightened immediately at this, all evil spirits forgotten, and they quickly evacuated the throne room to get themselves some treats. Peterssen watched them file out, not saying a word. When at last they were all gone, I turned to him.

"What is it with everyone and the spirits?" I asked, my tone unusually short with my closest advisor. "We haven't seen any evidence of them since the mist rolled in. Why does everything get blamed on them still?"

Peterssen patted my shoulder. "People will always need something to blame for their troubles," he explained. "And magical spirits are an easy target—since they can't exactly defend themselves. Also, to be frank, Agnarr, the people are just following the precedent set by your father. Whenever something bad happened in Arendelle, he'd blame it on magic or evil spirits. I don't know if he truly believed it, or felt it was easier than taking responsibility. But I'm sure the people remember." His face clouded over.

"And it only seems to have gotten worse since the battle all those years ago."

A distant memory floated into my consciousness. "He blamed them for my mother," I said. I hadn't thought of that moment in ages. But now it seemed clear as day. Me, age five, playing with a wooden horse in my bedroom. My father's hulking shape, standing silhouetted in the doorway. I looked up, startled. He'd cleared his throat before speaking.

Agnarr, your mother is gone. She was taken by evil spirits. And she's likely not coming back.

I hadn't been able to sleep for a week after that. I kept looking for her during the day, praying the spirits would see fit to bring her back. At night, I lay awake, trembling with fear, imagining every shadow was an evil presence, lurking and waiting to take me away, too.

But no spirits came. And my mother never returned.

"Yes." Peterssen nodded thoughtfully. "That was likely an easier story for him to accept than the alternative."

"Which was . . . ?" My heart pounded. Was I finally going to be told some truth about my mother? If she hadn't been taken by spirits, that meant she could still be out there, somewhere.

She could still be alive.

But Peterssen only waved a hand. "I don't know, Agnarr," he said. But I could tell by his eyes that he did. Or at least he knew something, if not the full extent of the story.

More secrets. Would I die buried in secrets?

I shook my head, forcing myself back on task. My mother could wait for another day. "So, what do we do?" I asked. "We can't very well fight against an imaginary force!"

"No. But we *can* make the people feel safe. That's our primary job."

I sighed. Ruling a kingdom was turning out to be a lot more difficult than I had imagined. No wonder my father had always been in such a grumpy mood. I wanted to do the right thing for Arendelle. But what that was, I wasn't sure.

I rose from my seat and started toward the exit. I was meant to meet Iduna in the village and I was already late. It was a big day for her—she'd finally saved up enough money from her windmill business to rent her own place—and she was getting the keys this afternoon. I was so proud of her and all she'd accomplished over the past few months. She'd been working tirelessly, putting in long hours, but it had paid off. I couldn't wait to celebrate with her.

Before I could get very far, however, Peterssen called to me.

"Agnarr?" He shifted from foot to foot, suddenly looking nervous "There is . . . one thing you could do to satisfy the people."

"Really?" Hope stirred in my chest. "What is it?"

"Next week," he began, "we will have some visitors at the castle."

"Visitors?"

"The king of Vassar." Peterssen cleared his throat. "And his daughter, Runa."

My heart plummeted. I had hoped that my telling them to do what they wanted had been enough of a non-reaction that it had dissuaded the council from the idea of marriage. But evidently, it'd been in the works all this time.

I'd just been too busy with Iduna to notice.

"Do you really think now is a good time?" I asked, trying to keep my voice neutral. "I mean, there's so much unrest. People choking, purple sheep . . ." My voice trailed off as I realized how ridiculous and desperate I sounded.

"Oh, so you're concerned about those sheep now, are you?" Peterssen's mouth quirked. Then he gave me a fatherly smile. "It's okay, Agnarr," he assured me. "There's nothing to be nervous about."

"Who said I was nervous?" I blurted out. "I just don't need to meet anyone right now! I'm only nineteen."

"And soon you will be twenty, then twenty-one. You'll be taking the throne, and it's always better if there is already an heir lined up when that happens."

So not only was I expected to marry this stranger, but I was meant to procreate with her without delay. My stomach swam with nausea.

"I don't get any say in this at all?" I demanded. I knew I was not acting like the heir apparent, but I couldn't help it. I didn't want to meet anyone.

Not when I already had Iduna.

I knew from the start that Iduna and I could never

marry. Royalty married royalty—that was how it was always done. And with the kingdom of Arendelle still fragile in the wake of my father's death and Peterssen as regent, this was not the time to buck the trends. We needed trade partners. We needed allies. We needed an army.

But I needed Iduna.

I hadn't meant to fall in love with her. But who could blame me? She was smart, kind, funny, and good. She was everything I ever wanted in a partner. A best friend, a true love. She made me laugh. She made my heart race.

Life without Iduna?

I couldn't bear the thought.

Peterssen sighed. "Agnarr, you asked how you could help your people feel safe. Well, Vassar is well known for its considerable army. An alliance with them would help us secure our harbors and farmlands. Make Arendelle safe."

"I'm fine with an alliance!" I protested. "But can't we just make it into a trade deal or something? Why does it have to involve marriage?"

"Because that's how it's done, Agnarr. That's how they can ensure the deal between the two nations sticks. No one betrays their own family." Peterssen walked over and put a hand on my shoulder. "Look, I know this is all scary and new. But when King Nicholas and his daughter arrive next week, I cannot have you standing there looking like a scared rabbit. It will suggest weakness. And we cannot afford to look weak right now."

"I know." I groaned. "Conceal, don't feel. Blah, blah, blah."

"Yes." Peterssen's gaze drilled into me. "If not for your own sake, then for the sake of your people. You don't *have* to marry Princess Runa. But you must treat her with the respect due to a noble of a neighboring nation. If you do not—"

"Of course I will," I broke in, mostly to get the conversation over with. I felt like I was going to be sick. "Don't worry about me."

"I always worry about you, Agnarr," Peterssen said, patting me on the arm. "That is my job. But I also trust you. I know you care about Arendelle. And I know you will do the right thing."

CHAPTER TWENTY

Iduna

"AND THESE WILL BE YOUR KEYS, DEAR."

I smiled distractedly as Mrs. Christiansen, a local woman who had offered up a cottage for rent, handed me a set of keys strung on a small metal loop. As I closed my hand around them, my eyes rose in the direction of the castle on the far side of town, then dropped to the empty street in front of us. A stirring of disappointment wound through my stomach.

Where was Agnarr? He was supposed to be here for this. I knew he had a meeting earlier, but he'd promised to be here on time. He knew how important this was to me.

"Iduna?" Mrs. Christiansen frowned. "Aren't you going to go in?"

"Oh. Sorry. Yes." I shook my head, turning to the door of my new place, a cottage just up the hill from Blodget's Bakery. It was only two rooms, but it had a kitchen with a cooking top and an actual ice box for keeping food fresh. Just off the kitchen was a seating area, with a door that led to a cozy bedroom. There was even a patio in the back, big enough to put a chair out on—making it a perfect reading spot.

It was simple. Humble. But it was mine. All mine. After sleeping twelve to a room in an orphanage for years, it was a private slice of heaven.

My hand trembled as I slid the key in the lock. I knew I was moving slowly, but hoped Mrs. Christiansen didn't notice. I just kept hoping Agnarr would appear. We had planned to do this together. Step into my new home for the first time, side by side, entering this new life together.

Where was he?

The door creaked open. I gave one last glance backward, but the street remained empty. Sighing, I stepped over the threshold, alone.

"So, what do you think?" Mrs. Christiansen asked, coming in behind me. "It's a darling place, right? Perfect for a single girl like you."

I flinched at the unintended jab.

"It's wonderful," I assured her. "Just perfect."

And it was. Perfect.

But also very empty.

"Well, rent is due on the fifth of the month. You're already paid up this month, so I'll come around in thirty days. If you have any problems, please don't hesitate to knock on my door. I'm only three houses down." She grinned, putting out her hand. "Congratulations, Iduna. This is a big step for you. You should be very proud."

"I am. Thank you." I shook her hand, trying to give her a smile.

We said our goodbyes, and Mrs. Christiansen headed out, pulling the door shut behind her. Now alone, I looked around the place, poking my head into various cabinets and the closet in the back room. I tested the bed, bouncing on it a little. Seemed comfy enough.

But still, I felt restless. Unsettled.

Where was Agnarr? Was he all right? What if something had happened to him?

I rose from the bed. I needed to go find out.

I found him in the secret room. He was sitting in a chair, head in his hands. Hair mussed, eyes wild. I frowned, concern welling inside me. I'd never seen him look so ill at ease.

"Is everything all right?" I asked, worried. "I thought you were going to meet me at the house."

He looked up, his face turning even more pale. "Oh," he said, rising to his feet. "I'm so sorry. I totally forgot."

He forgot? This was like the biggest thing to happen to me all year! Something was definitely wrong. Agnarr wasn't the type to just forget.

"What's wrong, Agnarr?" I asked gently. "Whatever it is, you can tell me."

He moaned and began to pace the room, back and forth like a caged wolf, his steps eating up the distance between the walls. His eyes darted to the stone shelves, the table, the floor—anywhere other than my face.

"You're going to hate me," he said.

Wow. He was really upset. I walked over to him, slipping my hand in his. It was clammy and cold. "You know I could never hate you, Agnarr," I said quietly. "Now tell me."

He hung his head. "There will be visitors to the castle in two weeks. The king of Vassar."

I was puzzled. "So?"

"And his . . . daughter. Runa."

Oh. Ice trickled down my spine. I dropped his hand. "I see."

Agnarr turned to me, his gaze wild. "I tried to tell Peterssen I wasn't ready. That this wasn't the right time! But he insisted I at least meet her." He dragged his fingertips through his hair. "I mean, I guess it's not a big deal, right? I meet people every day."

I felt dizzy, a pit forming in my stomach. But Agnarr was staring at me with such desperation that I found myself nodding along. "Yes," I said. "You meet people every day."

But we both knew that this wasn't just any person. This was a royal suitor. A woman the people of Arendelle might desire as a match for their king. She would be noble, genteel, well groomed.

Unlike me. An orphan. A nobody.

They may flirt with you and sully your honor, Johan mocked in my head. *In the end, they only marry their own kind.*

I squeezed my eyes shut. *This is your own fault,* I scolded myself. *You knew from the start this was wrong. That this could never be anything but a flight of fancy. There was never any future for you and Agnarr. You knew that—and yet you chose to indulge in yet another lie. A lie that you knew would end in heartbreak.*

This story was never going to have a happy ending for me. Agnarr would marry a princess. Father children. Raise a family inside these walls while ruling the kingdom outside.

And I would be forced to watch it all from afar, my heart ripped from my chest.

Despite my best efforts, a strangled sob escaped my throat. Agnarr grabbed me, pulling me into his arms in a hold so tight I was half convinced he'd crush me. But at the same time, I didn't want him to let me go.

I never wanted him to let me go.

"Iduna, I love you," he whispered, his mouth brushing against my ear, sending all-too-familiar tingles all the way to my toes. "I love you more than the stars in the sky. I love you more than the breath in my body."

"I love you, too," I replied. But my voice sounded older than my years. Tired.

He pulled away, cupping my face in his hands. His

eyes were so green. I could never get enough of them. And yet soon—too soon—I might never see them up close again.

"I will figure this out," he declared. "I am to be king, right? That has to mean something. If I say I won't marry her, then that should be the end of it."

I nodded slowly. I knew he was just trying to make me feel better. And besides, I had no strength left to argue. "If you say so."

"I do," he declared in a fierce voice. "Now come on. Let's go check out your new place! I've been dying to see it."

I sighed, his enthusiasm causing an ache to well in my stomach. Just an hour before, I'd been so excited to show him. So proud of the little place I'd gotten all by myself. I'd imagined inviting Agnarr over for dinner, cooking on the little stove. Probably burning the fårikål, but he wouldn't mind. He would tell me it was delicious. The best he'd ever tasted.

But now . . .

"It's really not that interesting," I protested weakly. "Just a silly cottage."

"*Your* silly cottage," he corrected, reaching out to take my hands in his own. They were so warm, while mine were now cold as ice and trembling. "Which makes it *very* interesting to me," he added, meeting my eyes. He gave me a goofy half smile, as if begging me to trust him. To believe everything would turn out okay.

And I wanted to. Oh, god, I wanted to.

"All right," I said at last. "We can stop at Blodget's on the way. Grab some chocolate."

Agnarr's grin widened. "You know the way to my heart, Iduna."

If only that were enough. . . .

CHAPTER TWENTY-ONE

Iduna

AFTER THAT, WE HARDLY PARTED EACH other's company. Even without saying the words, we both knew that these days together might be our last. We'd meet first thing in the morning in our favorite tree. We'd say goodbye to one another late at night outside my cottage door. We'd spend hours in the library secret room—our only truly safe haven—wrapped in one another's arms.

It was as if we both felt the time slipping through our fingers. As if our relationship was like a vacation, with an end date looming, and we were desperate to make the most of the time we had left. We didn't talk about it, of course. Our conversations stayed light and easy. Both of us danced around the subject of the upcoming royal visit from a certain foreign princess, which, it seemed, the rest of Arendelle was spending all their time preparing for. Cakes were being made. Ice sculptures designed.

Both great halls scrubbed down within an inch of their lives and colorfully decorated for a royal ball. I was pretty sure Olina hadn't left the kitchen in a week and certainly hadn't gotten any sleep. She almost bit our heads off when Agnarr stole a krumkake from a towering pile.

It was wonderful. It was also terrible. And so, so wrong. Every day, I told myself that this would be the last. That I would cut this all off while I was still able to be the one to do so. Before the choice was no longer mine to make.

But then I'd see Agnarr's hopeful smile. Feel his fingers stroking my skin. And I would once again be powerless to stop any of it. I was already too far gone. Drowning in love, with no desire to come up for air, even if it meant my doom.

And my doom it would be. The princess would be here in a week. We were running out of time.

"Let's go on an adventure!"

I looked up from my book, across the table at Agnarr, who had been engrossed in a pile of maps he'd found on one of the shelves in the secret room. He looked back at me, a mischievous smile on his face.

"It's been way too long," he added. "I mean, we didn't even get a chance to travel to the mist this year. How unfair is that?"

I nodded. Peterssen had nixed any trips to the mist due to the unusual occurrences in Arendelle. He said the village was in a state of too much unrest right now for Agnarr to wander far from town.

Which meant adventures, in general, were out.

"You know Peterssen is never going to let you go," I reminded him.

He scowled. "What he doesn't know won't hurt him." His eyes sparkled. "We can sneak out of town through that secret passageway off of the kitchen. No one will ever have to know."

"And when they notice we're gone?"

"We'll be back before they do. We'll just make it a day trip. Not far." He reached across the table, his eyes pleading. "Come on, Iduna. You know you want to."

His enthusiasm was catching. And I did want to. I loved our adventures. And I knew this one might very well be our last. How could I say no?

"Where are you thinking of going?" I asked.

Agnarr grinned, knowing he'd gotten his way. He swept his hand over the stack of maps. "Your choice! Pick a map, Iduna. Any map. We'll follow it to the end. See what we'll find."

"All right," I teased, making a big show of closing my eyes and waving my hands over the pile. "But if I randomly pick the map to the World's Largest Ball of Yarn, we're still going."

"I couldn't think of a better destination," Agnarr declared. "Now pick already!"

"All right, all right." I reached down to the table and grabbed a map at random, digging deep into the pile.

Then I opened my eyes and looked at it. The map was of the mountains just outside of Arendelle. And someone had drawn a pathway through, leading to a small valley nestled between two large mountains.

"'The Valley of the Living Rock,'" I read. Then I looked up at Agnarr. "Well, it beats the World's Largest Ball of Yarn. Though I'm not sure by how much—"

To my surprise, Agnarr suddenly grabbed the map, turning it over in his hands. His mouth dipped to a frown, his eyebrows furrowed.

"What's wrong?" I asked. "Were you holding out for the ball of yarn? 'Cause truthfully, I'm not exactly sure if that really—"

Agnarr planted his finger on the map, pointing to some writing in the corner I hadn't noticed before. It was in a language I couldn't read.

I cocked my head. "Can you read it?" I asked.

"No." He shook his head. "But I recognize the handwriting." His voice had a tremble to it that made me suddenly uneasy.

"You do?"

"It's my mother's," he said softly. "I've seen it on other papers in this room. My father must have brought all her things here, after she disappeared."

I could hear the bitterness in his voice as he spoke. Especially on the word *disappeared.*"

Suddenly I really wished I had found the ball of yarn map instead.

"We can pick another one. It's no big deal," I tried.

"No." He shook his head fiercely. "This is the one."

He rose from his seat, rolling the map in his hands. I could see the pain on his face, but also a sudden spark of what looked like hope. And suddenly I knew what he was thinking. What if we followed this map and found something at the end of it? What if we found out about his mother and the reason she had vanished so many years ago . . . ?

CHAPTER TWENTY-TWO

Iduna

BEFORE DAWN THE NEXT MORNING, WHILE everyone was still asleep, we slipped out of Arendelle miraculously unseen. The air was crisp and cool as we crossed the bridge in a shroud of darkness, excitement prickling our skin. Even the horses seemed ready for an adventure, their steps light and prancing as we headed for the hills.

Once we reached the hills, Agnarr and I were playful, almost giddy, as we put the real world aside and set off on our journey, buoyed by the sense of carelessness that accompanies doing something reckless. We knew what we were doing was wrong, dangerous, and completely irresponsible. Especially for a prince. But Agnarr insisted he didn't care. He was sick of playing by other people's rules. Living up to other people's expectations.

He wanted this—he *needed* this.

And, in a way, I did, too.

We followed the map north, deep into the mountains—on a different path from the one that led to the Enchanted Forest and the mist. On the way there, we stopped for a late lunch at a picturesque trading post and sauna, where we warmed up and attempted to haggle over some *way*-too-overpriced supplies. In fact, I almost got myself thrown out of the place after expressing my honest opinion on the obvious price gouging going on in the remote establishment, angering the burly redheaded teen behind the counter. But Agnarr just plunked down the money with his usual magnanimousness and gently moved me along.

As we began to climb higher into the mountains, the journey became more treacherous, with icy roads winding around steep cliffs with sheer drops. The last stretch of the journey was up a footpath, too narrow for horses. We tied them to the trees and headed for it. When we came to the top, the the sun had disappeared over the horizon, bathing the landscape in dusk, but all we encountered was an empty valley of rocks.

"Well, this is certainly less exciting than I had pictured it," Agnarr joked as he looked around the valley. He glanced down at the map, pursing his lips. I could see the disappointment in his eyes as he looked up again. I knew how badly he was hoping for some answer about his mother. But what had he expected? For her to be at the end of the map? Like a treasure, just waiting to be found?

"Maybe there was something here once," I said gently.

"Things don't always stay as they are, you know." I had been familiar with movement, fluctuation, from a young age. My family had always been wanderers. Constantly on the move, following the paths of the reindeer. No map could lead you to the nomadic Northuldra.

No map could lead Agnarr to his mother.

Suddenly my ears caught a noise. I grabbed Agnarr, yanking him back behind a nearby tree, shoving my hand over his mouth to muffle his sound of surprise. We watched as a young woman came over the horizon, walking slowly down into the valley from the other side. Her hair was brown and unbraided. And she was dressed like a Northuldra in a simple undyed robe, cinched at the waist with a colorful belt.

My heart beat fast. Could it really be one of my family, escaped from the mist? I didn't recognize her, but the Northuldra had expanded quite a bit before the day of the dam celebration. Also, it had been almost five years. People changed.

Agnarr moved my hand so he could speak. "I recognize her," he whispered. "I think she's one of the ice harvesters."

My heart sank a little. That made sense. The ice harvesters were nomadic, like the Northuldra. They followed the ice throughout the winter season and came to Arendelle every summer with huge blocks that could be used to keep food fresh or could be carved into decorative sculptures for the town squares.

The woman stepped into the center of the valley. She raised her chin and started to sing. My heart leapt as my ears caught the clear song rising into the air.

I closed my eyes as the woman continued to sing. Memories flooded through me with each soulful note. While I'd never heard this particular song, I'd heard similar ones growing up with the Northuldra. My mother used to tell me they were gifts to our people from the fairies and elves of the arctic lands. She would sing them to me to help me sleep—her lilting voice, melodic and sweet, lulling me into dreamland, offering a soothing sound in my head. A deep longing rose inside of me.

"It's beautiful," Agnarr said softly, also seeming caught up in the song. "I've never heard anything like—"

His words were cut off by a sudden thundering sound. Like rocks rolling downhill. The woman's singing stopped. Curious, I peeked out from behind the tree again.

And I realized the rocks were *moving*.

Like actually moving.

"Whoa!" I whispered in awe as big and small boulders rolled down the hill, coming to rest at the woman's feet. "Are you seeing this?" I asked Agnarr.

He nodded. "Is it magic?" he whispered.

I glanced over at him, wondering if it would be a problem if it was. But I saw only fascination in his eyes, not fear.

Before I could answer, the rocks suddenly popped open, revealing themselves not to be rocks at all, but rather trolls. Short, roly-poly gray rock trolls with huge ears and noses and hair made out of grass. Some even had moss growing out of their ears. They were wearing green tunics, and each one had little necklaces made of glowing crystals.

"I read about these!" I whispered in excitement. "They were in the book that had the Huldréfolk in it."

"What are they?" Agnarr asked, his eyes not leaving the scene.

"I think they're called trolls," I replied. "From what I understand they're the oldest creatures alive. They can live hundreds of years. And . . . this may sound weird, but evidently they're experts in love."

Agnarr raised an eyebrow. "Okay, that I would not have guessed."

"Shhh," I said, hushing him. "Something's happening."

My eyes locked on to the ice harvester, who was now standing in the center of what had become a troll circle and wringing her hands together.

"Grand Pabbie," she said in a trembling voice, "you helped my mother once before. Now I need your help as well."

"What is it, my child?" asked the oldest and largest of the trolls.

"My Elias died in an ice accident last week," she replied. A tear slipped down her cheek. "It was sudden. Tragic . . ."

She dropped to her knees, her shoulders racked with

sobs. A few of the female trolls rolled up to her to give her comforting hugs and rub her back.

"He was my world. My sun and my stars," she cried. "I cannot go on without him."

"I am truly sorry to hear this," the older troll—Grand Pabbie—replied solemnly. "Elias was a good man. He did not deserve his fate."

The woman swallowed hard. "A good man. And a good husband." She brought a hand to her stomach. "He would have made a good father, too. Alas, he died before he knew I carried his child inside me."

The female trolls now broke into excited chatter, reaching out to place their hands on the woman's stomach. She smiled uncertainly through her tears, as though wondering if she should shoo them away or welcome this enthusiastic response.

"It's a boy!" the eldest female troll crowed. "A big, bouncing baby boy!"

The woman's eyes widened. "You can tell?"

"Of course!" said the troll who had made the announcement. She had what looked like dandelions growing out of her head. "Bulda knows all when it comes to babies!"

"Ooh! You should name the baby Bulda!" declared another female troll. "It's such a pretty name."

"Or Pebble! I've *always* been fond of the name Pebble!" added a young girl troll with crooked teeth and a big smile. "It's just the cutest!"

The woman did not look like *she* thought the name Pebble was the cutest. But she kept silent, likely afraid of offending.

"Don't listen to them," Bulda broke in. "Those are all troll names. You need a people name." She tapped her finger to her stony chin. "What about simply naming him after his father? That would be a wonderful tribute and a way to remember him."

The woman struggled to her feet. "Don't you understand?" Her voice took on a near-hysterical pitch. "That's why I'm here! I don't *want* to remember him!"

Grand Pabbie stepped forward with a solemn look on his stony face. "You want to forget," he said. It wasn't a question. She nodded, tears coursing silently down her cheeks.

"I can't sleep at night. I can't work during the day. All I can see is him. I can't bear it anymore! Please, take the memories from me. I beg you!"

Grand Pabbie motioned for her to kneel before him. "I can do what you ask," he said. "But it will come at a price. I can make your mind forget. But the heart is not so easily changed. You may not remember Elias. But you will always feel him in your heart. Like a phantom pain that will never completely go away. And you will not know why."

"That's what I want," she choked out. "*Anything* to take the memories away."

"Very well," Grand Pabbie replied solemnly. He lay a hand on her forehead and closed his eyes. Agnarr and I watched, mesmerized, as the Northern Lights in the sky above her head seemed to change. For a split second I saw an image of a man, tall, strong, carrying an ax, hacking away at a block of ice. Then, just as quickly as it had appeared, it burst away in a cloud of stardust. As if it had never been there at all.

A moment later, the woman rose unsteadily to her feet. She looked dazed.

But the tears, I noticed, had stopped.

"What am I doing here?" she asked, sounding perplexed.

"You came for a blessing for your baby!" Bulda told her gently. "Remember?"

"My . . . baby?" She stared at Bulda for a moment, then nodded, reaching for her stomach again. She remembered that.

"Yes. You told us his name was Pebble," added the young troll, winking at her friend.

Grand Pabbie steered her away from the women. "You must get back to the ice now," he instructed. "Your family is waiting for you there."

"My family." A small smile crossed her face. "Yes. I must get back to my family." She waved at the trolls. "Thank you for the blessing!"

And with that, she disappeared into the night. The trolls remained, however, hanging out and munching on some nearby mushrooms, chatting among themselves.

I turned back to Agnarr. "That was crazy," I whispered. "I've never seen anything like it."

"Magic," he said slowly. "True magic." He shook his head. "Good thing the people of Arendelle don't know about these guys."

I rolled my eyes. "Aksel would probably blame them for his purple sheep."

Agnarr snorted. "Hey, maybe if they meet the trolls, they can stop blaming the Northuldra for everything that goes wrong in town."

I tried not to flinch at his causal joke. At least he didn't believe that the Northuldra were to blame for everything. But I hated the reminder that many people still did.

"I can't believe the trolls just wiped her memory like that," I said, mostly to change the subject. "Or that she wanted them to! Who would want their memories wiped?"

Agnarr opened his mouth, then clamped it shut again, his face going stark white.

I frowned. "What's wrong?"

"You don't think . . ." His voice trailed off.

But I realized exactly what he was thinking. The map we'd followed had belonged to his mother. That meant she probably knew about the trolls. Maybe she had come here, too, before she vanished. Maybe she'd had a similar request.

To forget her life in Arendelle.

To forget her husband and son.

"Come on!" I urged Agnarr, grabbing his hand. "Let's go talk to them."

"What? No!" he cried, alarmed. "We can't!"

"Why not?"

"They could be dangerous."

I glanced over at the trolls. Two of them were playing a game by rolling round stones. Another was rocking a little troll baby. I looked back at Agnarr with one eyebrow raised.

Agnarr let out a frustrated breath. "Fine," he said. "Let's go meet some trolls."

We emerged from behind the tree and made our way down into the valley. It was starting to get darker, and the crystals around the trolls' necks had begun to glow. Hearing us, they looked up. For a moment they just stared as we stared back, an uncomfortable silence growing between us.

But then Grand Pabbie stepped forward.

"Your Majesties," he said with a reverential bow. "I didn't expect to see you here so soon."

CHAPTER TWENTY-THREE

Iduna

I STARED AT THE ELDER TROLL, CONFUSION swirling through me. How could he possibly have been expecting us? Was this more magic?

"I—I think there must be some mistake," Agnarr stammered.

Grand Pabbie pressed his stone lips together. "Are you not King Agnarr?"

"Well, I'm Agnarr. Technically I'm not king yet. Not till my twenty-first birthday."

"I see." Grand Pabbie turned to me. "And you, my dear. Does that make you Princess Iduna? I am not always clear how titles work in your land."

"Just plain Iduna," I said, drumming my fingers on my thigh. "I'm not royalty at all."

Grand Pabbie nodded solemnly. "You two are not married yet?"

I felt my cheeks heat up, and I was able only to shake my head in answer. This was getting embarrassing.

Grand Pabbie shook his head as though trying to rid himself of a pesky thought. "I am sorry," he said. "The Northern Lights show me many things. But sometimes they come out of order. You are not here, then, I take it, to ask me to save your daughter's life."

"We don't have a daughter," I answered, feeling a little annoyed now. This troll was dangling everything I had ever wanted right in front of me as though it were fact.

Agnarr and I married.

With a little girl.

The vision was so powerful it hurt my stomach. Because I knew it could never come true.

I swallowed hard, but when I spoke, my voice was resolute. "We're not married. We're just friends."

The trolls burst out laughing. I glanced at Agnarr. "What's so funny?" he demanded, also sounding annoyed.

"You two are not just friends," Bulda proclaimed with a wide, toothy grin. "And if you're not married yet, well, we can easily fix that, can't we, ladies?"

The female trolls cheered.

"We should go," Agnarr said, grabbing my hand and trying to pull me away. This whole thing was clearly freaking him out. "Come on, Iduna."

But I stood firm, planting my feet. We'd come this far. And the trolls were strange, maybe, but they didn't seem evil or malicious. And if they could help . . .

I looked down at Grand Pabbie. "We're here to find information about Agnarr's mother," I told him. "Do you know if she came here once? Maybe to seek help of some kind?"

The trolls all started whispering furiously among themselves. Agnarr was beginning to look really nervous. I knew he wanted to know but at the same time was petrified of finding out.

"This is ridiculous," he whispered to me. "They clearly don't know anything. We should—"

"Yes," Grand Pabbie interrupted.

Agnarr's face turned pale. "You knew her?"

"She came to us many years ago," he said. "I remember her well. She was very sad, your mother."

I could see Agnarr's hard swallow. The slight tremble in his legs. I reached out and slipped my hand into his, trying to give him strength.

"I do not wish to speak ill of any man," Grand Pabbie continued. "But suffice to say your mother married out of duty to her kingdom, not for love. And the marriage was not a happy one. And though she loved her baby boy, she could not see the sun through the clouds. She told us she would lie in bed all day crying. Mourning the life and kingdom she left behind. Your father grew impatient at her behavior. He couldn't understand why she was so sad when he had given her everything she could possibly desire. But there was one thing he could never give her."

"Love," Bulda whispered to me, cuddling up against

my leg. A tear slipped down her stony cheek. "Poor dear was starving for love."

"She struggled with her sadness for years," Grand Pabbie continued. "But at last she could take it no more. She fled the castle with only the clothes on her back—"

"And left her son behind," Agnarr interrupted, his voice now layered with contempt. "How could a mother do that? To her own child!"

Grand Pabbie gave him a look. "You must understand. It was the hardest thing she ever had to do. Also, the bravest. She knew she could not make a life for you outside the castle. If she took you, they would come after you. It would likely start a war between her home country and Arendelle. Many would die. And your life would hang in the balance." His eyes met Agnarr's. "Leaving you behind wasn't selfish. In fact, it was the most selfless act she could have chosen."

I felt a lump in my throat, imagining what Agnarr's mother must have gone through. How much she must have been hurting to take such drastic measures, and how anguished she must have been at having to leave her only child behind to keep him safe. I risked a glance at Agnarr. His face was still pale. He'd wanted answers. But perhaps not these answers.

"So she came here?" I prompted.

Grand Pabbie nodded. "She did. She knew we had the ability to help her forget. And forgetting was the only way she could live with what she'd done. She wanted to forget who she was. Who she'd left behind."

He paused, then added, "But before we performed the spell, she had one other request. To see her son, not as he was then, but as he would be." Grand Pabbie's eyes zeroed in on Agnarr. "So we searched the Northern Lights for visions of your future. It is how I knew you would come to us someday."

"But you thought we'd be married," I reminded him. "With a daughter."

"Two daughters, actually," Bulda piped up. "Two beautiful little girls." She closed her eyes and sighed happily.

Two daughters? I looked at Agnarr with incredulity, but he had turned and walked a few feet away, his head bowed and his hands clasped in front of him. I went to him and wrapped my arms around his waist.

"Are you all right?" I whispered. "I know that's a lot to hear."

"It's just so awful," he said, his voice cracking on the words. "To think she was so unhappy. And I couldn't do anything to help her."

Tears welled in my eyes at the pain in his voice. "No. You couldn't. You were only a child, Agnarr. And also, you can't make people happy. They have to find it inside themselves."

He nodded stiffly, going quiet. I didn't want to press him, so I just stood there, holding him close. But deep down, I couldn't help wondering if he had realized the parallel of his mother's story to his own. She had been forced to marry someone she didn't love. And now her son was being asked to do the same. For the good of the realm.

But what would it do to Agnarr?

The trolls might claim to see the future, but I saw ours clear in front of me.

And it did not end with a happily ever after.

CHAPTER TWENTY-FOUR

Agnarr

"DO YOU KNOW WHAT A PANIC YOU CAUSED, Agnarr?" Lord Peterssen demanded when we returned, exhausted and drained from our adventure, late that night. One of the soldiers had spotted us coming over the bridge and had dragged us both back to the castle, under strict orders from the regent. "Do you know how many men wasted their day searching for your body, thinking we'd find you dead in a ditch somewhere? You can't just wander off like that without telling anyone!"

I slumped in my chair in the council room, wishing the floor would open up and swallow me whole as Iduna bore witness to the biggest dressing down I'd received in my life.

One I totally deserved.

"Look, I—"

"I warn you, do not interrupt me right now, Agnarr."

Peterssen's voice had never sounded as threatening—and disappointed—as it did in this moment.

My mouth snapped shut. He had every right to be livid. It was bad enough I had left the castle without my guards. But also, there had been several violent attacks carried out in the nearby hills while we were gone, all targeting the additional soldiers Peterssen had deployed to look for us . . . for me. While no one had been killed, several men and women were being treated for various injuries. And when interviewed, they all told the same tale: strange men coming out of nowhere, all wearing masks depicting the sun.

All making threats against the prince of Arendelle.

When I couldn't be found, the castle assumed the worst. The council had even started working on a new plan for succession, just in case.

All the while I had been off gallivanting with Iduna.

"We didn't go far," I protested, guiltily trying to justify my actions. But there was no justification. No matter how unhappy I'd been, no matter how much I needed escape, I had broken protocol. I had put people in danger and had created an emergency that wasted castle resources. I had been stupid and reckless.

Imagine what my father would say if he were still here.

"It doesn't matter," Peterssen snapped back. "The attacks all happened in the nearby hills. What if these masked men had found you, all alone, unprotected?"

"Um . . . Iduna would have protected me?" I said, lamely attempting a joke to defuse the situation.

Bad idea.

Peterssen raked a hand through his hair, frustrated with me. "This is not a joke, Agnarr!" he shouted. "This is not purple sheep or imaginary spirits. Our own soldiers were attacked by enemies of the crown. People were hurt. Our citizens are terrified. There are even rumors swirling around the village that the Northuldra have returned for revenge."

"That's ridiculous!" Iduna, who had been silent up to this point, burst out. But Peterssen was not to be dissuaded.

"Is it? The masks they wore depicted the sun. Northuldra are the people of the sun. It doesn't take too much to make the connection."

"The Northuldra don't wear masks like that!" Iduna protested. She looked panicked. "Also, they're peaceful people. They'd never attack someone unprovoked!"

Peterssen's face grew stormy. "Enough, Iduna. I mean it."

She glared at him, looking as if she wanted to tear him limb from limb. I reached out and squeezed her hand, trying to comfort her. But she only yanked it away. Her whole body started trembling; she was clearly alarmed at the idea of the Northuldra returning to seek revenge against the people of Arendelle—and the prince who should never have escaped that day.

"Calm down, Iduna!" I tried to reassure her. "It's all

right. We're safe. We won't allow them to get you, or me, or anyone."

She set her gaze on me, horror in her eyes. "Wait. *You* don't think it's them, do you?" she croaked. "You can't possibly . . ."

Peterssen cleared his throat. "We obviously don't know who is behind the attacks. We can only speculate. But that being said, the attacks *did* happen—and threats were made against the prince." He gave me a hard stare. "Until we figure out what's going on, I need you to stay in the castle. We'll close the gates, bar the windows. You will be under the protection and surveillance of a full guard at all times."

I wanted to protest. But I knew when Peterssen got that look in his eyes, there was no arguing with him, and I had caused enough trouble for a lifetime.

But I couldn't be cooped up in the castle like a prisoner.

At least, not alone.

"Fine," I said. "I'll stay put. As long as Iduna can join us here."

"What?" Iduna asked in surprise.

Peterssen shook his head. "Iduna has her own home."

"Yeah. Outside the castle walls. Where you literally just told me it was unsafe to be."

"Unsafe for *you*, Your Majesty. The attackers threatened you personally. There is no reason to assume Iduna would be a target."

"Agnarr," Iduna began. Her voice was stern. "It's all

right. I'll be fine. Besides, I have work to do. The wind-mills, remember? I have people depending on me. I can't hole up here and abandon them."

"Yeah, but what if—"

"I'll be *fine.*" This time she said it through gritted teeth, clearly annoyed. That usually would have made me back down immediately, but I ignored my better instincts and kept pushing.

"You don't know that," I said angrily. Why was she being so stubborn?

"Agnarr—"

I couldn't take it anymore. "Iduna, I *order* you to stay in the castle. For your own safety. Until the threat is gone."

"Excuse me?" Her face turned purple. "You can't do that!"

"I'm the crown prince of Arendelle, so actually, I can," I shot back.

The second the words left my mouth I regretted them. I was being stupid, ugly, cruel. To her, of all people.

She looked at me as if she wanted to punch me in the mouth.

Peterssen chose that moment to step in. "Prince Agnarr. A word alone, please?"

I let out a frustrated breath. "Fine." I turned back to Iduna. "But we're not done talking."

"Oh, yes we are," she said with a short laugh completely devoid of any mirth. "We definitely are."

And with that, she pushed back in her chair and

stormed off. I moved to go after her, but Peterssen grabbed my arm.

"Come on," he said. "Let her go. You can apologize for being a blockhead later. Right now, you and I need to have words. One on one."

Reluctantly, I followed him into the library. Peterssen motioned for me to sit in a nearby leather armchair. I slumped down, scrubbing my face with my hands. When I looked up again, he'd sat down across from me and was leaning forward, elbows on his knees.

"Agnarr. We need to talk about Iduna."

"So you agree, then. She should stay in the castle until the threat has passed," I said, surprised, but happy he was on my side.

But he only sighed and shook his head. Suddenly, he looked very old. "Look, I know I was the one who brought Iduna to the castle in the first place. I felt bad for her because of her situation—losing her parents and all. And I thought it would be nice for you to have someone your own age around the castle."

I nodded impatiently. "It was. It is. Iduna's the best, which is why we need her to stay here."

"Iduna is wonderful," Peterssen agreed. "And we all love her, Agnarr. We do. But . . ."

"But what?" I asked, beginning to get exasperated. What was he trying to say?

"But I'm becoming concerned that you love her in a . . . different sense than the rest of us."

I felt my face flush. Not because I was embarrassed

about my feelings for Iduna. If anything, it had become nearly impossible not to shout about them from the rooftops. But at the same time, I wasn't stupid. I knew what the council would think if they knew about our relationship. They liked her fine as my friend. But in their eyes, she was no princess. No future queen.

My expression told Peterssen everything he needed to know. He nodded but didn't speak. For several minutes the only sound in the library was the ticking of an old clock. Then he rose from his chair. He walked out onto the balcony and stared down at the town below.

"Maybe if it were a different time," he mused. "Maybe if things weren't so volatile. Maybe if your father hadn't been murdered. If soldiers weren't being assaulted by men in masks."

"That has nothing to do with Iduna!"

"And yet it has everything to do with you." Peterssen sounded sad now. "Arendelle lost her king overnight. I've tried to be the best regent I can, but things have been unstable. The citizens are uneasy again. They'll be more so now, after the attacks. And in these times, they look to the crown to ease their fears."

He turned from the balcony to meet my gaze. "Meaning you must be the king they need you to be. And a big part of that is marrying into another strong royal family. Forming an alliance that will help protect Arendelle in the years to come."

I hung my head, my heart plummeting to my knees. My stomach felt as if I'd swallowed lead.

But that didn't change how I felt about Iduna. My beautiful, smart, funny best friend.

How could I marry someone else? Someone who was bound to be inferior to Iduna in every possible way. And once I was married, what would happen to our friendship? It seemed unlikely we would spend time together once I had a wife, at least alone. It wouldn't be proper.

If only I had been born a peasant. A soldier's son, perhaps. If only Mattias had been my father instead of the one I actually had. He would have loved Iduna. Especially her amazing laugh. It reminded me of his. I closed my eyes for a moment, imagining the two of them together.

And suddenly I understood my mother's pain. Why she had left as she had. Trapped in a loveless marriage with my father. Maybe she, too, had loved someone out in the world once, someone her heart told her was right when everyone around her said he was wrong.

Maybe she had to leave him behind when she came to Arendelle to become our queen.

Peterssen was watching me, a sorrowful look on his face. Sorrowful and . . . if I didn't know better, I'd say guilty, too. What was he hiding? I groaned. Just what I needed—more secrets. "What aren't you telling me?" I demanded, finally feeling able to ask for the answers I had wanted for so long.

"Agnarr—" But at that moment the captain of the guard rushed in, her face pale.

"There's been another attack!" she reported. "A villager this time, inside of Arendelle. He was leaving his shop when it happened. A man in a sun mask jumped out and started beating him. He barely managed to fight him off, and the man ran away." She paused, then added, "He says he's pretty sure it was a Northuldra."

Peterssen let out a low growl. "And I suppose he's running around, telling everyone this tale?"

"He doesn't have to. Everyone's already gathered in the town square to hear him speak. They're frightened to death. They're talking about forming a militia. They say if the crown will not protect them, they will move to protect themselves."

"This must stop!" Peterssen exploded. He pushed off the balcony railing and strode across the library to the guard. For a moment, they conferred softly so I couldn't hear. Then Peterssen turned back to me.

"Agnarr, it's past time you go and address your people. You need to promise them that you will take action. That you will do everything within your power to keep them safe."

I nodded stiffly. "Just tell me where and when."

Peterssen's shoulders relaxed. He spoke again to the guard. "Tell everyone that the prince will address the people in ten minutes. Be sure they gather to listen."

The guard gave a salute, then disappeared out the door, trailed by Peterssen. I ventured to the library's windows and looked down onto the streets below. The citizens of Arendelle were milling about anxiously. They all looked afraid.

Peterssen wasn't wrong. They needed a leader. They needed a king.

I just wasn't certain anymore that I wanted it to be me.

"Conceal, don't feel," I whispered to myself. It was the only thing left to do.

CHAPTER TWENTY-FIVE

Iduna

"AND THEY ALL LIVED HAPPILY EVER AFTER!"

I closed the book, smiling at the children who sat on a colorful rug in the warm, cozy Arendelle library. There were only a handful today, though usually at least a dozen came to my weekly story time after school let out. I guessed the rest of their parents had kept them home, too afraid of going out onto the streets of Arendelle after all the recent violence.

It had been a week since the first attacks, but the seemingly random acts had continued with alarming frequency. The people of Arendelle were living in fear—never knowing what was around the corner. The castle had closed its gates. No one was allowed to enter or leave until they determined what was going on. Soldiers stepped up their patrols, but they seemed to do no good. The attacks continued. And no one knew who was behind them.

It was a scary time.

But I kept a brave face, continuing to meet with the farmers to help them with their windmills. They always commented on how brave I was, a woman traveling alone in times of such unrest. But fear wasn't going to power their mills, pump their water. It wouldn't feed their children.

I also kept up with story time. I knew it was something the children—especially the orphans—looked forward to each week. Their lives had been turned upside down. I wanted to give them something happy and safe to enjoy.

I smiled at my small group now. "Any questions?" I asked, setting the book on my lap.

A boy of about seven raised his hand. "Are the bad guys in masks going to kill us all?"

I sighed. I had meant questions about the story I had just finished. But I knew it was hard to concentrate on fairy tales right now, when real life had become so scary.

"Of course not," I assured him. "They won't even be able to get close. Not when we have such wonderful, brave soldiers patrolling the streets of Arendelle. They are smart and strong and they will keep us safe."

A little girl around four raised her hand. "I'm scared, Miss Iduna," she said; then she stuck her thumb in her mouth.

"It's okay to be scared," I assured her. "You know, I get scared sometimes, too."

The children stared at me, so wide-eyed that I almost

laughed. To them, I was a grown-up. And grown-ups weren't supposed to be scared.

If only they knew.

"You know what I do when I'm scared?" I asked, setting down my book by my side. "I sing." I smiled down at them. "Anyone want to sing with me now?"

They all did, of course, and so I taught them a silly song about reindeer and carrots and a really stubborn pig. By the end of it, they were laughing hysterically and no one looked afraid anymore.

"Okay," I said, rising to my feet. "I hope to see you next week!"

They filed out, talking among themselves. Some were even still singing. I watched them go, feeling a warmth in my heart.

"You're so good with them," Mrs. Reedy, the librarian, complimented me, coming over to stand beside me. "They're lucky to have you."

"I'm lucky to have them," I assured her. "They always make me smile."

"Our Iduna, what would we do without you?" Mrs. Reedy declared, drawing me in for a hug. "You are a true gift to Arendelle. A princess of the people!"

I laughed her off, even though her comment stung a little more than I wanted to admit. Not that she would realize it, of course. "Oh yes! A true princess," I joked, "in mud-stained boots."

After we exchanged goodbyes, I headed out of the library. My plan was to bake bread for some of the older ladies and men around town who were too sick or too worried to go to the market. I was still learning to bake, now that I had my kitchen. And some of my results had been... questionable. But still, there was something about it that always put my troubled mind at rest. The act of measuring each ingredient out so exactly and creating something entirely new somehow put me at ease.

Made me forget, for a moment, even about Agnarr.

I hadn't seen him since the night they'd closed the castle gates, the night of Peterssen's stern reminder and our fight. He'd been hustled to a makeshift stage in the town square, surrounded by a ridiculous number of guards and dressed in his official Arendelle military uniform. I'd fled the castle after our argument, enraged at how entitled and privileged he'd acted, and watched from far back in the crowd as he gave a grand speech about working to root out the enemy and keep Arendelle safe. It was his number one priority.

And I had to admit he looked and sounded like a true king.

I missed him more than I wanted to, but I was still upset about our last conversation, when he'd all but bought into the idea that the gentle, peaceful Northuldra could be responsible for these attacks. I'd thought he was different, the only one who believed, like I did, that there was more to the story about that day by the dam. But it turned out that when push came to shove, he was just like everyone else, letting fear and rumors lead him.

I sighed, reaching for my key to open the front door

to my small haven. It was for the best, I told myself. Agnarr and I never had a future anyway. Everything we'd shared was nothing more than a beautiful dream.

And it was high time I woke up and faced reality.

I had just pulled my final loaf of steaming hot fresh bread from the oven when I heard a knock on my door. I was surprised to see Lord Peterssen on the other side. From what I understood, he didn't leave the castle very often anymore, especially now, with the gates closed. But he stood alone, without even any guards, waiting at my front door.

I ushered him in quickly.

"Sorry to come unannounced," he said, taking off his hat and setting it down on the table. His hair had begun to thin, I noticed. And I could see shadows of strain on his face.

"Not a problem," I assured him. "Would you like some tea?"

It wasn't the question I was dying to ask, of course. I wanted to ask if they'd made any headway in figuring out who was behind the attacks. And I wanted to ask about Agnarr. How was he holding up?

Did he miss me?

Peterssen shook his head. "No thank you," he said. I caught him glancing toward the door. "Look, I need to tell you something important. May I speak frankly?"

Fear shot through me at his words, but I kept my tone level. "Yes. Of course," I said.

"In an attempt to root out the source of the recent attacks, the council has enlisted the help of a specialist. His name is Sorenson and he's a scientist of some regard. He claims he's created a foolproof test to uncover lies. The council plans to use it on every citizen of Arendelle to find out what they might know about the men with the sun masks." He looked regretful. "They're going to be asking questions. Lots of questions. Looking into everyone's histories."

I stared at him in horror. "*Everyone?*" I whispered, realizing what this could mean. "Even . . . you?"

"No. Not me. And likely Agnarr will also be spared. You, however . . ." He trailed off, giving me a knowing look.

He didn't have to go on for me to get his meaning. "I haven't done anything wrong," I protested, my heart pounding in my chest. "I was only a child when it all happened."

"I know that, of course. But the townspeople are on a rampage. Their fear flies through the streets. It's irrational, but real. And dangerous. If they learned that the crown has been harboring a Northuldra for the last five years . . . if they knew their future king was in love with one . . ."

I stared at him in surprise. We'd gone to such great lengths to be careful. "Lord Peterssen—I—"

He waved me off, looking tired. "I'm not blind, all right? I know about you and Agnarr. I may have known before you knew it yourselves. Your secret is written all over your faces. In the glances you give one another when you think no one's looking." He sighed deeply. "I should have never brought you to the castle. It was folly! I only wanted to help you. And to give the prince a chance at a true friend. If I had any inkling of what would happen . . ." He stared down at his hands. "I was oblivious, obviously. And now . . ."

My heart slammed against my rib cage. Every beat felt like a punch. "What do I do?" I asked, my voice hoarse. "Should I leave town?"

"No. The guards are asking so many questions of people going in and out of the village that if you leave now, you'll only arouse suspicion. But if you stay, I cannot guarantee you won't be called in for an interview. I'll do my best to shield you. You're the prince's best friend. Beyond suspicion. Whatever it takes. But if they start to dig, they may begin to realize the inconsistencies in your story." He rushed through his next sentence, as though it pained him to say the words out loud. "And if they discover who you truly are? Well, I'm afraid there's not much I can do."

I lifted my chin defiantly. "Well, maybe it's time the truth came out, anyway. I'm not ashamed of who I am. Where I came from. Maybe it's time I come clean. Let them judge me as they will."

"That's very noble," Peterssen replied with a wry

smile, almost as if he had expected that to be my answer. "And under other circumstances, I'd agree it would be the best plan. Unfortunately, in this case, you alone are not at risk of losing everything. It won't take them long to realize my involvement in the matter. They will strip me of my title. And possibly begin a challenge to Agnarr's claim to the throne as well. How can he effectively rule a kingdom, they'll ask, if he is in love with their number one enemy?"

"But that's ridiculous," I sputtered. "Northuldra are not the enemy! I've never seen even one of them in my entire time here! Whoever is behind the attacks is pretending to be them. Agnarr and I visit the mist twice every year. They're all still trapped!"

"I know that as well as you do," Peterssen assured me. "But it makes no difference. Fear will make them act without reason. And if Agnarr is found unfit to rule, the kingdom will fall into further chaos. There would be no clear heir to the throne. And with me gone as well, there would be no one to step in to lead. The neighboring kingdoms would certainly see an opportunity open up. The Southern Isles, for example, have always envied our position on Arenfjord. The Kingdom of Vassar is a valued trade partner, but they won't hesitate to move for an advantage if they see a chance to do so."

I squeezed my eyes shut. "I don't want to hear anymore," I said. I could accept responsibility for my own fate, but it seemed unfair to place the entire future of Arendelle on my shoulders. "I should have never agreed to any of this. You should have left me in that orphanage. Or better yet, had me arrested that first day and tried me as a traitor."

"No." Peterssen's expression was fierce. "I refuse to regret my decision to save an innocent child. You have been a wonderful gift to this kingdom. An asset, not a danger. The work you've done with the farmers and their windmills? Iduna, I couldn't be prouder of the young woman you've become. I just . . . wish things were different, that's all."

He rose to his feet. "I should get going. I have a meeting with the council to discuss this lie-detection test they want to use. I will do what I can to shelter you, as I always have. But you must stay on your guard. If you care about Agnarr like I think you do, say nothing. Trust no one. His security lies in your hands."

He headed out, his steps heavy and slow. I watched him go, feeling tears streaking down my face. I didn't bother to wipe them away. What was I going to do? I'd all but trapped myself in an impossible situation. A situation that would destroy not only me, but possibly the entire kingdom of Arendelle.

Not to mention Agnarr himself.

I sighed, feeling the weight of the world on my shoulders. I wandered back to the kitchen to drape some tea towels over the cooling bread loaves when I heard yet another knock on the door. Was Peterssen back? Or perhaps the guards with their lie test?

I walked over to the door, drawing in a shaky breath. Whatever it was, I could handle it, I told myself. Somehow. Some way . . .

I pulled open the door.

Agnarr stood on the other side.

CHAPTER TWENTY-SIX

Iduna

AGNARR STRODE INTO MY HOUSE. "WE NEED to talk," he declared.

I went and hastily shut the door behind him. "Aren't you supposed to be in the castle?" I asked, annoyance at his imperial tone mixed with the relief of seeing him again. He was dressed unusually, in a plain black shirt and matching pants. A large hat had been pulled low over his eyes. Not exactly his usual regal attire. "Also, what on earth are you wearing?"

"I'm in disguise, obviously."

"Obviously," I repeated, a hint of sarcasm to my tone. I knew I should tell him to go away. He was putting himself in danger by coming here. Not to mention I was still mad about our fight—his assumptions about the Northuldra, his bravado. But as much as I knew I should shove him back out the door, I found I didn't have the strength. It was too good to see him. I had missed him so much it hurt. And the ache that had settled in my stomach now felt both terrible and wonderful at the same time.

"What's wrong?" Agnarr asked, coming over to me, his green eyes glowing with concern. "Are you crying?"

"No!" I retorted just as a sob escaped my throat. He gave me a skeptical look. "Okay, fine. Maybe a little." I was so tired. So very tired.

Agnarr nodded. "This is my fault," he said. "I'm so sorry I haven't come sooner. I wanted to. You know that, right?" He searched my face for confirmation.

I nodded. "I do."

"Also, I'm sorry I was such a pig back at the castle. I should have never ordered you to stay. You are your own person, Iduna. You always have been. It's one of the million qualities I love about you. It was wrong of me to push that aside for my own self-interest." He gave me a pleading look. "I was just scared. People have been beaten in my name."

"By the evil Northuldra," I couldn't help muttering.

Agnarr stopped, looking at me carefully. "I don't think it's them, actually."

I looked up, surprised. "You don't? But you said—"

He waved his hand. "I know. I was panicking. Jumping to conclusions. But now that I've had time to think it through, it doesn't make sense. It's just like the evil spirits. People need someone to blame. But there's no evidence to support that it's them. I did some digging in the library, too. These attackers use swords. And nothing I've read ever claimed the Northuldra had swords. And their clothes! I don't know if you remember, but Northuldra dress similar to the ice harvesters. The attackers wore shirts with buttons on them." He raked a hand through his short hair. "It doesn't add up."

Relief flooded me at his words. I wanted to throw my arms around him. The fact that he hadn't given in to the fearmongering. That he'd done research and had come to his own conclusions based on actual evidence rather than fear or fantasy.

He was going to make a great king.

"Who do you think it is, then," I asked carefully, "if not the Northuldra?"

"I don't know," he answered. "It could be another kingdom wanting to weaken us. It could be someone here on the inside who wants to challenge my claim to the throne. Or even someone who just doesn't like me for personal reasons." He grinned crookedly. "Though who in their right mind wouldn't like *me*, right?"

"I've missed you," I admitted. "And I appreciate the apology. I'm sorry, too." I gave him a rueful smile. "Truthfully, it probably would have been safer for me to stay at the castle. I was being stubborn."

He bit his lower lip. "So, you forgive me?"

"I forgive you. And I will come to stay with you at the castle. If you'll still have me."

Agnarr's face brightened and I suddenly felt a little guilty for my ulterior motive.

If I was in the castle, the belly of the proverbial beast, I would more likely be spared from these lie-detecting interviews and all the fallout that would come from them. I could hide in plain sight.

"Really? Are you sure?" he asked, hope spreading over his face. "You don't have to. . . ."

"I know." I swallowed hard. He looked so happy, which made what I had to say next that much harder. But it needed to be said, painful as it was. Peterssen's earlier words had driven that point home.

"I will come," I repeated. "But I have one condition."

Agnarr grinned widely. His voice took on a jovial tone. "What is it, fair maiden? Be it half my kingdom, it shall be yours!" he declared in a grand voice, grabbing my hand and kissing it reverently. "In fact, all my kingdom, if you wish! Simply say the word."

With effort, I managed to pull my hand away. I cleared my throat. "We need to stop this, Agnarr. Whatever this is."

The smile fell from his lips. "What? What are you talking about?"

"This thing—between you and me. It can't go on. We must end it. Today."

Or you stand to lose more than you can imagine. . . .

He looked horrified. "You can't be serious. Iduna—"

"I am. We've gone too far with this whole thing. It was fun, but it needs to end."

Fun. The word tasted like sawdust on my tongue. It

had been so much more than fun. It had been everything. It had been life itself. And the last thing I wanted was to dismiss it so casually.

"You're the prince, Agnarr," I said, pushing on. "You have to marry a princess. We should have never started this to begin with. And the deeper we go, the harder it will be to crawl out. The more painful."

"Don't you love me?"

I hung my head. Part of me wanted to lie, say I never loved him, this was all a game. Push him away, hurt him so badly he'd stay away.

But I couldn't do that. Because I did love him. I loved him more than anything in the world.

"Of course I do, Agnarr," I said in a soft voice. "I love you with everything I have. But I also have to be realistic. We can never be together. The kingdom wouldn't accept it."

"Blast the kingdom."

"You don't mean that. I know you love your people. And they need you. Especially now. We can't be selfish."

He closed his eyes, clearly trying to wrest control of his emotions. I could hear the refrain ringing through his head clear as if he were shouting it at the top of his lungs. *Conceal, don't feel.* I hated that mantra of his. But right now, it was the only way.

He opened his eyes. His face took on a look of determination. "Fine. I will agree to your terms for now. But I do not agree that our love is hopeless. Our love is powerful. It can move glaciers. I will not let it simply wither and die. I will find a way for the council to accept this. For this to work between us."

He grabbed me then, pressing his lips against mine, cupping my face with his strong hands. A hard, desperate kiss. For a moment, I considered trying to pull away—but in the end, I found I couldn't.

Because this might be our last kiss for a long time.

Maybe forever.

CHAPTER TWENTY-SEVEN

Iduna

"YOU LOOK LOVELY, MY DEAR! LIKE A TRUE lady of the castle!"

Gerda clapped her hands in excitement as I slipped out from behind the dressing screen. I felt my cheeks heat up as I stepped in front of the full-length mirror and caught a glimpse of my reflection in the glass. The dress the castle steward had selected for me was a deep blue hue that matched my eyes. It clung to my waist and then fell loose to my feet in sweeping swaths of soft, rich silk. It was the most beautiful dress I'd ever worn, and I couldn't help wondering what Agnarr would think when he saw it.

Not that it mattered anymore.

I'd been at the castle for two weeks now, though it felt like an eternity. Though it was an immense structure, somehow it seemed that no matter where I chose to go,

I was always running into Agnarr. And while we tried to be pleasant to one another, there was an unbearable awkwardness growing between us. The way he looked at me with those hurt eyes. The way I forced myself to turn away, even though all I wanted to do was throw myself into his arms and never let him go.

But that wouldn't happen. That couldn't happen, especially not after tonight. The kingdom was throwing a huge ball to celebrate the arrival of Princess Runa and her father, King Nicholas of the kingdom of Vassar. I'd been dreading the visit since Agnarr first told me about Runa, and I'd thought up all sorts of excuses to get out of going to the ball. It was one thing to know they were meeting at last, yet quite another to watch it happen with my very own eyes.

But in the end, I decided to go. To prove to myself that I could. That I was strong enough to get through this.

"Are you all right, love?" Gerda asked, peering at me with concern. I realized, belatedly, I'd let a few tears slip down my cheeks. I'd cried a lot lately, hidden away in my small guestchamber at the far end of the castle. For I'd lost not only my true love, but also my best friend.

I didn't want it to hurt as much as it did.

"I'm fine," I said, resolvedly wiping at my tears. "I'm just overcome . . . the dress . . . thank you." I started to push off the shoulders to take it off. But Gerda stopped me, a stern look in her eye. I watched as she walked over to the door and turned the key in the lock, gesturing for me to sit. I groaned inwardly; I should have realized Gerda knew me too well to believe I would be moved to tears by a dress, no matter how beautiful.

"My sweet girl," she said, walking back over to me and leading me to the bed, "I've been the castle steward for years now. There's not much I don't see." She gave me a knowing look. "You and Agnarr. Did you have a fight?"

I shook my head, staring down at my lap. "Not exactly."

"But you're avoiding one another." I could feel Gerda's eyes on me. "Does this have something to do with our arriving guests?"

My head jerked in her direction before I could stop it. She gave me a kindly smile. "I'm not blind, sweetheart," she said, reaching over to clasp my hands in hers. "I know what's been going on between you two."

My heart pounded with fear. "Please don't say anything!" I begged. "It's over, anyway. We're not together anymore."

Gerda gave me a pitying look. "I'm so sorry to hear that, dear. We were all really rooting for you. You made such a great pair. And you were so good for our Agnarr."

The tears welled in my eyes again. This time I didn't bother to stop them. "He was good for me, too," I admitted. "But it was never going to work out. He has to marry a princess. And I am definitely not a princess," I added with emphasis.

Gerda's face slipped into a scowl. "Ah, yes. That rot again. I can't believe the council still abides by that nonsense. After it worked out *so well* for Runeard and Rita."

I cocked my head. "Rita?"

"Agnarr's mother," Gerda said with a wistful smile. "She was such a sweet soul. So smart, creative. When she laughed, you couldn't help but laugh with her." Her eyes grew distant as she remembered. "But as the years passed, her laughter began to fade. She was so sad. She missed her home so much. But Runeard never understood," she added. "He tried to give her everything, but she wanted nothing. Nothing except the one thing she could never have. Freedom."

My heart ached at her words. So what the trolls had said was true.

"Why does no one ever talk about her?" I asked.

Gerda's face darkened. "Runeard forbade it. When she ran away, he locked away all her things. Barred her bedroom door. No one was to speak her name again, under penalty of banishment."

"That's terrible," I said. "Poor Agnarr. It's bad enough he lost his mother. But to be denied all memories of her as well . . ."

Gerda rose to her feet and walked over to a small wardrobe. She reached into it, then pulled out a wooden chest. I watched, curious, as she brought it back over to me. Her voice lowered.

"I did manage to save one thing," she confided. "I don't think Runeard knew about it."

I watched, breathless, as she lifted the lid of the box.

Inside was a small stuffed puffin with one big button eye, wearing a light blue cape.

"Rita made him for Agnarr," Gerda explained. "When he was a baby. She called him Sir JörgenBjörgen. He always made Agnarr smile." Her eyes crinkled at the corners.

Warmth coursed through me as I pictured Agnarr as a small child, playing on the floor with this little puffin, his mother smiling down at him. I wondered if Agnarr would remember it.

"You should give this to him," I said. "And tell him about his mother. He deserves that at least."

"He does," Gerda agreed, looking suddenly far off again. "It's time he knows everything. And perhaps . . ." She trailed off.

"Perhaps what?"

She gave me a hard look. "Perhaps knowing what happened to his parents will prevent him from making the same mistakes."

CHAPTER TWENTY-EIGHT

Agnarr

"PRESENTING NICHOLAS, KING OF VASSAR, and his daughter Princess Runa."

The room erupted in applause as a tall, broad-shouldered man, dressed in a highly decorated military uniform, stepped into the Great Hall, which was masquerading as a ballroom for the evening. He was hand in hand with a petite-boned girl around my age, who was wearing a dramatic deep purple off-the-shoulder gown, trimmed with lace and finished with a matching bow at her chest. She had sparkling green eyes and a large mess of light blond hair, artfully piled on top of her head. She was pretty, graceful, walking into the ballroom as comfortably as someone would come to their kitchen table: like she'd been born to do it.

Unlike ... some guests.

I fought back a laugh as I caught sight of Iduna across

the room. She was attempting to sneak a piece of chocolate off of the treat table. She shoved it in her mouth,
trying to chew it without anyone noticing, but she must
have swallowed too quickly, because she began to cough
in a loud, sputtering fashion, causing several guests to
turn and give her bemused looks.

She looked so beautiful that night, wearing a gown
of the most searing blue that perfectly matched her eyes
and fell to the floor like a ripple of water from a crystal
clear stream. No jewelry, no fancy lace or embroidery for
my Iduna. She was a simple bluebird in a field of prancing peacocks. And yet the most stunning creature I'd ever
laid eyes on.

The past few weeks had been torturous. Iduna had
done as she'd promised, moved into a spare bedroom in
a vacant wing in the castle—about as far away from me
as was possible without climbing out a window. And
she had been resolute, determined to keep our relationship platonic. We could be friends, but not lovers. Now,
though, our friendship felt strained, our former ease
around one another replaced by a too-careful awkwardness, as though we feared either of us might shatter and
break if we said the wrong thing.

But still we kept on the charade, because that was
what she wanted. At least, that was what she *said* she
wanted. But on rare days, when she didn't realize I was
watching her, I could sometimes catch another look, deep
in her blue eyes. A secret weight, a sadness she couldn't
quite hide. And I knew in those moments that she still

loved me as much as I loved her. That being apart tore at her soul as much as it tore into mine.

"Your Majesty?"

I startled as I realized the princess—Runa—had made her way over to me and was holding out her hand. I took it awkwardly, bringing it to my lips as was custom, kissing the back of it. She curtsied before me. I gave her a stiff bow in return.

"Aw! I see the two of you have already become insep-arable!" cried her father, joining us. He placed a hand on the small of her back and pushed her a little closer to me. "Why, Prince Agnarr, it appears you can barely restrain yourself from asking my daughter to dance!" he added, giving me a wink.

Oh. Right. I cleared my throat, wanting to glance back at Iduna, but knowing I couldn't. I had promised Peterssen I'd be on my best behavior that night. "Would you . . . like to dance?" I asked Runa.

"My prince, there is nothing in the world I would like to do more," she replied politely, her cheeks coloring a little, her voice as sweet and clear as a bell.

The king slapped me hard on the back so that I nearly stumbled forward. "Well then! There's no time like the present! Get thee to a dance floor!"

I resisted the urge to roll my eyes. Instead, I took Runa's small, cool hand in my own and led her out to where the others were dancing. I could feel half the room's eyes on me as she tucked herself into my arms and began to sway. The band took note and launched into a beautiful waltz. But my legs felt like wood as I mechanically performed the steps. I flashed back to when I'd learned this particular waltz—with Iduna, back when we were kids, as part of our weekly lessons. And it was her I thought of now. Particularly the moment she'd accidentally stomped on my foot so hard I'd gotten a bruise.

We'd laughed heartily and our dance teacher had given up in a fit of annoyance, telling us he'd come back when we were ready to take this seriously. Once alone, we'd started making up new dances—better dances. Each one sillier than the last. There was a chicken dance, a prancing peacock dance, and my personal favorite, "the reindeer who had to pee really badly but was stuck inside a fancy ballroom" dance. Iduna had come up with that one, of course, and I'd laughed so hard my stomach ended up hurting more than my bruised toe.

Iduna. I stole a glance at the buffet. But she wasn't there anymore. I scanned the room, frantic. Had she run out, finding it too hard to watch me in the arms of someone else? I'd told her I didn't want to do this tonight. But she had insisted, telling me she'd be fine. That it was for the best. I should at least meet the girl, give her a chance. "Who knows, maybe she'll be really nice!" Iduna had said. "At the very least she'll be a better dance partner than me."

Suddenly I spotted her, dancing on the other side of the ballroom with a partner who I recognized as a few years older than her. Some random noble's son I barely knew. She was leading the dance, twirling him around as if he were the lady and she were the man. He was laughing heartily and her eyes twinkled with mischief.

Suddenly I realized what they were doing. It was the "reindeer who had to pee really badly but was stuck inside a fancy ballroom" dance! *Our* dance!

She'd taught it to a stranger. My stomach filled with lead.

"Well, that's certainly an *interesting* dance."

Startled, I turned back to my own dance partner. Runa had noticed me watching Iduna and the young man and had misinterpreted my expression of longing as one of disdain. I opened my mouth, wanting to tell her Iduna could dance circles around anyone here—and was it a crime, suddenly, to want to have fun?

But in the end, I just nodded and smiled thinly. I had to be polite.

Conceal, don't feel. . . .

Her expression faltered. "Is . . . something wrong, Your Majesty?" she asked.

"No." I swallowed hard. "It's nothing. It's just . . ." My mind whirled for an acceptable excuse. "Everyone's watching us," I finally confided in a low voice.

She looked around, her green eyes sparkling. "It seems you are right," she whispered mischievously. "Perhaps then we should give them a show!"

As though on cue, the band struck up a lively tune. I twirled Runa around, trying to play the good partner. Her skirts swirled gaily and her mouth lifted into a happy smile as she allowed me to spin her, dip her, then pull her back in. She was the perfect dancer, her steps pretty and poised, not a hair out of place.

She would never step on anyone's toes, never dance like a reindeer who had to pee.

"Shall we get a drink?" I asked her as soon as the song ended. Any excuse to get off the dance floor.

"That would be lovely, Your Majesty."

"You don't have to call me that," I told her as we headed over to the buffet. "Agnarr is just fine."

"Oh, I'm sorry," she said, blushing prettily. "Agnarr. You can call me Runa."

"Runa," I repeated, then smiled at her. "Let's get that drink."

We found Lord Peterssen and King Nicholas at the table, filling their glasses. When they saw us together, they beamed in tandem.

"Ah, Prince Agnarr. Princess Runa," Peterssen greeted us. "How was your dance?"

"It was lovely, sir," Runa gushed before I could reply. "You have such a beautiful ballroom here in Arendelle. And such a lovely castle, too. It puts our little manor house back home to shame."

"Castles! Bah! But you should see our military barracks," her father interrupted, looking a little annoyed. "Far more useful than some silly ballroom. No offense, of course."

There was a hardness to his voice. I was fairly sure he had meant offense. But I nodded politely anyway. The perfectly poised prince.

"Well, we're still working on building our military back up," Peterssen replied. "We lost so many good soldiers at the Battle of the Dam."

"Ah, yes! Such an unfortunate event!" the king of Vassar boomed. He made a great show of looking around the ballroom before speaking again, this time with a lowered voice. "Also, I heard a rumor that you've experienced multiple violent incidents around town recently." He shook his head, as if very disturbed by this fact. "Why, I was even told that up until today you've had the castle gates closed to protect your poor young prince here." He gave me a concerned look, but his eyes looked hungry for information.

Peterssen stiffened. "We have taken precautions, yes. But I am confident we have matters under control."

"Of *course* you do," agreed the king. "But then—who wants to live in fear of their lives? You must root out these traitors and nip this violence in the bud. Otherwise your kingdom will become ripe for takeover."

"We're doing just fine," I broke in brusquely, starting to get a little angry. We had hit a rough patch, surely, just as every kingdom did from time to time. But we were far from vulnerable.

Weren't we?

"As I mentioned before, we pride ourselves on our excellent military," the king added. "And if our kingdoms were to be united, well, we would certainly step in when our new family needed us." He gave me, then Runa a meaningful look. The picture of discretion, surely.

I waited for Peterssen to argue, but instead, he surprised me by nodding.

"Agreed," he said. "Our two kingdoms would complement one another nicely. You have the military. We have the port. And with no threats to our trade routes, both kingdoms would prosper."

"And these two would make some handsome babies," the king chortled. "Eh, Peterssen?"

I nearly spit out my drink. I needed to get away from here.

It was then that I spotted Iduna, standing by the hot chocolate bowl, filling her cup with a ladle. Or, more precisely, missing the cup completely and coating her arm in chocolate as she observed us in dismay, clearly having overheard everything. Our eyes locked and I tried to send her an impish look, like we were both in on the secret that this was all a farce, but she didn't smile back. Instead, her lips flattened. She gave me the most courteous nod—the kind you'd give to a complete stranger—then lifted her chin high.

It was then that she noticed her arm was getting a chocolate drizzle. She dropped the ladle back into the bowl as though it had burned her, accidentally splashing several ladies standing nearby. They gasped in dismay as big brown splotches of chocolate speckled their fancy gowns. Iduna stared at them, horrified, then fled the room, dripping a trail of liquid chocolate in her wake. The ladies clucked their tongues, scandalized. Several of the men started to laugh.

"What on earth?" Runa began. But I had already untangled myself from her arm.

"Excuse me," I said. "I need to . . . I mean, I . . . I'll be back!"

"Agnarr!" Behind Peterssen's jovial tone, there was steel. "Where are you going?"

I didn't answer. Instead, I ran from the Great Hall, following the trail of chocolate.

CHAPTER TWENTY-NINE

Iduna

IT WASN'T EASY TO CLIMB A TREE IN A BALL gown.

But then, that was my fault, I thought as I knotted the dress to free my legs, then swung myself up into the tree, to hide in the thick canopy of leaves. I was the one who had agreed to put on a ball gown, even if it was at Gerda's urging. To attend a ball I had no business attending in the first place.

I closed my eyes, trying to slow my racing heart. I'd known watching Agnarr move on was going to be hard, but I'd told myself it would be good for me. It had started out so well, too, with recruiting one of the other guests to dance with me while Agnarr entertained the princess. I felt strong and confident out on the dance floor, forcing myself to have fun and proving to myself that I could get past him—get past all of this.

But then I got a better glimpse of the girl in question.

The beautiful, graceful, perfect girl who looked exactly like what a princess should be—at least according to any Arendellian storybook. Regal, proper, dainty. Why, I bet she'd never climbed a tree in her life! And the way she danced! She was fluid, effortless, somehow managing to be both relaxed and precise in her movements at the same time.

But still, I'd managed to keep it together until I'd overheard that king, talking about babies. Runa and Agnarr's future babies. And suddenly my mind flashed back to the trolls talking about *our* daughters. I hadn't realized how much I'd held on to that idea until that very moment. The idea of two perfect little girls. Mine and Agnarr's.

But they wouldn't be mine. They would be hers.

It was too much.

Now here I was, covered in sticky chocolate, having embarrassed myself in front of a crowd of upper-class Arendellians, hiding in a tree, while the love of my life was inside, dancing the night away with his perfect princess. Yes, I was the one who had told him to do it. But I hadn't realized how hard it would be for me when he did.

What was I going to do? This was beyond torture. And it would only get worse. Agnarr might marry Runa. Or he might entertain a dozen girls at a dozen balls before he made his decision. But eventually he'd have to pick someone.

And it couldn't be me.

"I wish I'd never met you," I whispered, anger rising

inside me, my only defense against my anguish and fear. "I wish I'd been trapped in the mist like everyone else."

The tears came then. Big, fat tears, soon followed by loud choking sobs. An ugly cry, not like the dainty princess cry Runa probably had when something didn't go her way. Though what had ever not gone her way? This was the real thing—a stuffy-nosed, blotchy-faced, swollen-eyed kind of cry. My heart had been broken into a million pieces, then laid out on the dance floor to be stomped on over and over again.

"There you are!"

I looked down, startled. Agnarr had poked his head through the foliage, his eyes locking on me. A moment later, he boosted himself into the tree, crawling over to where I sat. I tried to hide my tearstained face, but it was no use. He reached into his pocket and pulled out a silk handkerchief. I blew my nose loudly, giving up on appearances. I was gross and snotty and covered in chocolate. But that was who I was.

"Iduna, why are you crying?" Agnarr asked, peering at me in the inky darkness. "What can I do to cheer you up?" A wicked grin spread over his face. "Maybe some more chocolate?" He nudged my shoulder with his.

I smiled despite myself and held out my dessert-covered arm. "I think I've had my fill of chocolate. Seeing as I've basically bathed in it tonight."

He smiled gently, then took my hand in his, dragging his finger down my arm. I tried not to shiver at the delicious feeling of his light touch against my skin. It had been too long since I'd felt his hands on my body, and I hadn't realized how much I missed them. I watched, breathless, as he brought his finger slowly to his mouth, making a great show of licking the chocolate away.

"Delicious," he whispered, his eyes never leaving mine. And suddenly I got the feeling he wasn't talking about chocolate anymore.

"Don't," I protested, but it came out sounding weak, even to me. "I can't."

His eyes turned ultraserious. "I'm sorry," he said. "Oh, Iduna, you have no idea how sorry I am."

"You have nothing to be sorry about, Your Majesty."

"That's not true and you know it! And don't call me that. It just doesn't seem right coming from you. I shouldn't have let them do this. I should have refused to go to the ball. To meet that girl. To dance with her."

"She was a lovely dancer."

"Who cares? She could be the best dancer in the world. She isn't you."

I stopped breathing at the fierceness I heard in his voice. The look on his face. The desperation in his eyes. He was going to break me. Right here, right now, in our favorite tree. But worse, if we kept doing this, I would break him, too.

No. I had to be strong.

"Please stop," I begged. "I can't. *We* can't. You know we can't."

He grabbed my hands, squeezing them so hard I was half afraid he'd break my bones. "We *can*," he whispered. "We have to. I can't be without you, Iduna."

"You have to be, Agnarr. It's for the good of the realm. You know that. We can't be selfish. Your people need a king and queen."

"Doesn't it matter at all what *I* need?" he asked in a quiet voice.

I had no answer. Instead, I watched as he rummaged through his satchel and produced a strange half-carved chunk of wood that mildly resembled a spoon. I frowned, puzzled.

He gave me a grave look. "It's a love spoon," he said. "Or . . . it will be, anyway."

Oh.

I tried to breathe, but it proved almost impossible to pull any air into my lungs. *A love spoon.* I knew what those were. I'd seen the fishmonger give one to the butcher. A love spoon was a traditional Arendellian gift for those wishing to join in marriage.

"It's for you," he said in almost a whisper. "It can only ever be for you."

It was too much. The desperate, hopeful look in his eyes was going to be my undoing. *Why can't you see?* I wanted to scream at him. *Why can't you understand this can't happen?*

Because you lied to him from the start, a bitter voice deep inside reminded me. *He has no idea who you really are.*

I could tell him now. But I knew deep down in my

heart it wouldn't change a thing. He wouldn't care that I had kept a secret. He wouldn't care that I had come from another place, even the home of Arendelle's supposed enemy. That I wasn't the Iduna he thought he knew and loved.

Because he loved me. The real me. All of me.

And with that love he would destroy a kingdom. Cause war. Destruction. Death.

No. I couldn't be that selfish. I *wouldn't* be.

I squared my shoulders. Lifted my chin. Forced a cold look to my face.

Conceal, don't feel.

He was strong. But I had to be stronger. Strong enough to put an end to this. "Agnarr, you need to stop this. Now." The harshness I heard in my voice was devastating even to me. But to see his face . . .

"Iduna, come on!" He tried to reach for me, but I pulled away. Only a few inches, and yet it was the hardest move I'd ever had to make.

"You should go back to the party." My voice was ice. "You should apologize to that poor girl."

"But—"

"Listen to me, Agnarr. We can't be around each other and just be friends. That's become clear to me after tonight." I softened my voice a little to deliver the next blow. "So I've decided that I am leaving Arendelle tomorrow, and you will never see me again." Unshed tears pulsed behind my eyelids, but I willed them away. "It is for the best."

He dropped the spoon. It clattered against the tree's branches as it fell, eventually hitting the ground with a whisper. Such a little noise. But it echoed in my ears like a thunderclap. And something inside me felt as if it had died forever.

Agnarr opened his mouth to speak. But I never got a chance to hear his words. For at that moment there was a thundering boom in the distance. Followed by a flash of white light.

We looked at each other, confused. Then we turned back toward the castle.

And saw the smoke.

CHAPTER THIRTY

Agnarr

THERE WAS CHAOS EVERYWHERE WHEN WE ran back inside the castle. Well-dressed guests, huddling together in the Great Hall, talking in urgent voices. It was hard, at first, to figure out what had happened. I smelled smoke but saw no fire.

"There you are!" Peterssen and a group of guards surrounded Iduna and me. The regent hugged me fiercely. "We thought they had you!"

"Who? What happened?" I asked.

King Nicholas answered, looking quite rattled. "There was an explosion in the Great Hall."

"An explosion?"

"By the dessert table. It was a miracle no one was hurt. Evidently someone had spilled chocolate on the floor earlier, so everyone was staying clear of the area until it could be wiped up."

At my side, Iduna gave a small squeak.

"I had men posted outside," added King Nicholas. "They informed me they saw a lone figure, dressed in black and wearing a sun mask, fleeing the castle, right before the explosion. They tried to follow him, but he slipped away into the shadows. Almost as if by magic."

I frowned, my mind racing. More attacks. This one far more brazen than the others. The culprit had snuck into the castle. Maybe disguised as one of the guests. Or maybe it *was* one of the guests.

"Do not worry, Your Grace," King Nicholas added, seeing the look on my face. "I have assigned men to posts around your castle. Others are sweeping each room for any additional incendiary devices. We will not stop until we can be sure your kingdom is safe."

I knew the right thing to do was express enthusiastic gratitude for the king's efforts, but I couldn't find the words. All I could think of was that there could be someone among us at this very moment who was a traitor to the kingdom.

"Thank you," Peterssen cut in smoothly, casting me a sharp glance. "That is very generous of you." He turned to me. "Agnarr, why don't you go check on Runa?" he said pointedly. "She seemed a bit shaken up by the sudden turn of events. I led her to the sitting room to spend some time in the quiet." He addressed Iduna. "Why don't you go see how you might help inside the Great Hall." His firm tone did not pose this as a choice.

Reluctantly, I left Iduna to her task, heading up the stairs to the sitting room. We'd have to deal with all that had transpired between us later; first the people needed our help. The next day I could go to Peterssen and state my case. Tell him all the reasons I needed to marry Iduna. And if he didn't want Iduna as my queen? Well, maybe *I* didn't want to be king.

"Your Majesty!" Runa cried, rising from her seat as I entered the sitting room. "You're all right!"

"Yes. I'm fine. I was ... outside the castle when it happened," I finished lamely. "And, uh . . . how are you? Are you all right?"

"Well, to be honest, I'm still a little shook up," she admitted. "I'd been standing quite close to the desserts. It was lucky my father had called me for a dance just before it happened."

"Wow," I said, a little taken aback. I'd been so distracted by everything, until this moment I hadn't thought all of this through. What if she'd been hurt—or killed? As much as I didn't want to marry her, I certainly didn't want her harmed.

But did someone else? Someone who didn't want *her* to marry *me*? My brows furrowed. Most of the attacks so far had been carried out against Arendelle. And now they'd tried to hurt the girl intended to be my bride. Who hated me enough to go to such great lengths? And how many more people would be put at risk if something wasn't done?

I realized Runa was still staring at me, an uncertain expression on her face. "I'm sorry," I said ruefully, walking over to her. "We're really not giving you the best first impression of our kingdom, are we? I promise you, it's usually a lot more peaceful. Almost boring, to be honest."

Maybe this would all be a blessing in disguise. She'd be too frightened to stay. Who would want to be queen of such a dangerous country? Between the recent attacks and now the explosion . . . To think once we were concerned about purple sheep . . .

"Don't worry," she said, giving me a shy smile. "I like what I've seen of Arendelle so far. All it needs is a little . . . discipline. Like my father says, you just have to set an example. Once people see what happens when you challenge the crown, they tend not to challenge you anymore."

"I guess," I said hesitantly, though the approach sounded a bit ruthless to me. Arendelle had always been a peaceful kingdom. I didn't want to see it turn into a military state. There had to be another way.

Runa lay a hand on my arm. "May I speak frankly?"

"Um, yes. Of course." Something inside me quivered, and not in a good way.

Her shoulders seemed to relax. "Look, I know this is hard, okay?" she said. "I just wanted you to know it's hard for me, too."

"What?" I was confused. "You mean . . . the explosion?"

She shook her head. "No," she said. "I'm not talking about the explosion." She turned for a moment, staring at the back of the room, as if thinking. Then she turned back to me, her expression resolute. "Agnarr, I know it can be intimidating to meet someone new, especially with such high stakes attached. I was scared to come here. To meet the future king of the mighty Arendelle. I was worried you might turn out to be a monster!" she added with a small laugh.

I felt my cheeks flush. "I was nervous about meeting you, too," I confessed.

"It's only natural," she agreed. "But I want you to know I am not worried anymore," she continued. "I can tell you are no monster. You are kind, smart. You care about people. Trust me, I've made the rounds to various kingdoms. I cannot say the same for all men in positions of power."

"I appreciate that," I said, unsure of where this was heading, and even more uncertain I wanted to stick around to find out.

She reached up, turning my chin gently so I was facing her again. Her green eyes met mine. There was no doubt in them. No fear. No confusion. She knew what she wanted. And she wasn't shy about asking for it.

"Forget about them," she said firmly. "You and I—we can do this our way. On our terms."

Then, to my shock, she rose up on her toes, pressing her lips against mine. They were soft and warm as they roamed my mouth, coaxing me to kiss her back. To show her I agreed. That we could find a way to make this work together.

But I couldn't do it. Her lips were full and pliant, but they were the lips of a stranger. There was no passion behind Runa's act—the kiss was not given in love, but out of duty and honor. She was doing what she was raised to do. Stepping into the role she was born to play.

But I didn't want to play anymore.

And while maybe someday we could learn to love one another—or at least live in a respectful partnership—there was always the chance we wouldn't. The chance I would end up like my mother—so sad she couldn't breathe, trapped in a life she never wanted to live.

But I had one thing my mother didn't have. A best friend. A true love. Someone worth fighting for. Someone worth risking everything for.

Iduna.

I broke away from Runa, stepping back from her arms. "I'm sorry," I said. "I can't. I just . . . I can't."

"Why not?" she asked, looking crestfallen. "I would be a good wife, Agnarr. I would be faithful to you. I would be a good mother to your children."

"I believe all that," I said. "I truly do. But I can't be a good husband to you. Not when I am in love with someone else." This was dangerous territory: one word from Runa, and King Nicholas could be tempted to pull back all of the help he had just offered, and more. I treaded carefully. "You deserve so much more, Runa. You deserve a man who will love you with all his heart. Who will marry you because he can't bear to wake up in the morning without you by his side—not because of some ridiculous idea of it being good for the kingdoms." I sighed. "Alliances can be built by other means. Partnerships, trade—all that can be worked out. But at the end of the day, what really matters is that you are happy. That you are loved. Whether it be by the richest prince or the son of the butcher."

Runa stared at me for a moment. I could practically see the gears turning in her head. For a moment, I wondered if she'd slap me. But instead, a slow, grateful smile began to spread across her face.

She reached out and gave me a tight hug. "I hope this girl knows how lucky she is to have someone like you," she whispered in my ear. "And I hope someday I'll be that lucky, too."

CHAPTER THIRTY-ONE

Iduna

I RAN INTO THE SECRET ROOM IN THE library, slamming the door shut behind me. Leaning against the stone shelves, I sucked in a shaky breath. I could feel the tears streaming down my cheeks, but I didn't bother to swipe them away.

Agnarr and Runa, all alone, in the sitting room.

Kissing.

I'd slipped out of the Great Hall earlier, sneaking past Peterssen to go check on Agnarr. I'd told myself I was just making sure he was all right. But if I was being honest with myself, I was worried about him and Runa being alone together, despite my brave words in the tree.

As it turned out, my worries were well founded.

I closed my eyes and saw Runa's dainty hand snaking behind Agnarr's neck, pulling him close. His strong hands at her waist.

Bile rose to my throat.

"This is what you wanted," I reminded myself. "He's just doing what you told him. He tried to ask you to marry him. And you turned him down before he could even manage to get the words out. You told him you were leaving. What was he supposed to do?"

But none of that logic could squash the pain searing in my soul. Bearing witness to Agnarr taking that next step. Leaving me behind forever.

And so quickly, too. He was literally begging me to stay—he'd carved me a love spoon, for goodness' sake— when the explosion hit. And not twenty minutes later, he'd already moved on to another.

I reached into the bodice of my gown and pulled out the half-carved spoon. I ran my fingers along its still-rough edges. Unbeknownst to Agnarr, I'd picked it up off the ground as we'd run back inside the castle. Maybe I should leave it here for him. Maybe he could finish it and present it to Runa instead.

Despair rose inside me. What was I going to do? I'd told Agnarr I was leaving, but where was I supposed to go? My life was here, in Arendelle. And even if I did manage to find some other safe haven, I knew the memories would follow me like restless ghosts. Anywhere I went, Agnarr would remain there, in my heart.

Anger rose inside me, displacing my fear. I kicked a nearby chair, only succeeding in hurting my foot. I gritted my teeth, hopping up and down in pain a few times, managing to knock over a stack of papers in the process.

Typical clumsy Iduna. I bet Runa had never knocked anything over accidentally in her life.

When I reached down to scoop them back up, I realized a map sat on top of the pile.

Not just any map. The map to the mountain trolls.

I stared down it, my heart thumping as a thought began to take form in my mind. Could this be the answer I was looking for? The one sure way to absolve me of my pain?

The trolls had wiped the ice harvester's memory, to give her peace. And Agnarr's mother's memory, too.

Could they do the same for me?

A thread of hope wound through me. Was it possible? Could the trolls really help me forget my love for the prince? If so, I could stay in Arendelle, keep working with the farmers. Maybe make some new friends.

Maybe even find someone new.

Part of me hated the idea. Part of me wanted to jealously hold on to the time spent with Agnarr, painful as it was. But another part of me, the more sensible part, told me that until the pain was gone, I would never be able to move forward with my life. And I had so much more to live for. So much more to do.

Memories faded eventually. I would just be . . . speeding up the process a bit.

I grabbed the map and rolled it up in my hands. My

whole body was trembling as I slipped out from behind the bookcase again, leaving the secret room behind. Next time I was here, I wouldn't remember it at all.

And the pain would be gone for good.

CHAPTER THIRTY-TWO

Agnarr

"ANY SIGN OF HER?"

Kai closed the door to my chambers behind him, shaking his head. "I'm sorry, sir. I checked the entire castle. Lady Iduna is not here."

I scowled, wanting to slam my fist against the wall. Where had she gone? I'd returned to the Great Hall right after parting with Runa, but Iduna was nowhere to be seen. I'd questioned all the guards, but in the chaos of the incident at the ball, no one had seen her go.

Had she made good on her threat to leave Arendelle forever?

Despair rose inside me. I sat down in the chair next to my bed, scrubbing my face with my hands.

"Are you all right, sire?" Kai asked, his voice sounding troubled. "Are you worried about her? Shall I send the guards out to track her down?"

I shook my head slowly. "Don't bother. She's gone. She's probably never coming back."

"That would be a real shame, sire." Kai pressed his lips together. "We all love Lady Iduna. She brings so much life to this castle."

"Yeah, well, I don't blame her for leaving," I muttered. "Though I wish she had at least come to say goodbye."

Kai came over and put a warm hand on my shoulder. "Agnarr—" he started, but was interrupted by a knock at the door.

For a moment I had a wild idea it might be Iduna, coming back to say that she could never leave me—that she loved me too much for us to be apart. But instead, it was Gerda who poked her head inside. "Would Your Majesty like some supper?" she asked. "I brought you a sandwich." She entered and set a tray on the table. Then she looked from Kai to me.

"Is everything all right?" she asked.

"Iduna's gone," Kai told her when I didn't immediately answer. "The prince is . . . concerned."

"Do you think she's not safe?" Gerda asked, her face turning pale.

"No!" I practically shouted. "She just doesn't want to be with me!"

Gerda was at my side in an instant, pulling me into a tight hug as she used to do when I was a boy. "That is not true," she said firmly. "I know for a fact Iduna loves you."

"A blind man would know that," Kai added with a chuckle.

I struggled out of the hug. "You don't understand. I was about to ask her to marry me. I carved a love spoon for her and everything! But she says I'm supposed to marry a princess. Like Runa." My hands curled into fists. "I'm so sick of people telling me what I should do. Whom I should marry. Sometimes I wish I could renounce my crown altogether. So I could marry the person I love."

Gerda exchanged looks with Kai. "But you can," she told me, her voice low and careful. "I don't mean renouncing your birthright," she clarified quickly. "But marrying the person you love? That's your choice in the end."

I frowned at her words. "You don't understand. The council said—"

Kai waved a hand dismissively. "The council likes to say many things. But there's nothing in the Arendelle lawbooks that says you must marry someone of royal blood."

I stared at him in disbelief. "How do you know that?"

Guilty smiles crept to their lips. "We may have done a little research," Gerda confessed, "when we saw you two suffering so much from that ridiculous council trying to force you into a marriage you didn't want, to a girl who was completely wrong for you."

"We spent hours in the library," Kai added. "Scoured all the books we could find on the subject."

"And we found nothing!" Gerda exclaimed, excitedly

clapping her hands together. "There is no Arendelle law—now or ever—that says the prince must marry into another royal family."

"Are you serious?" I asked, astounded at the news and more than a little surprised that Gerda and Kai had gone to such lengths on my behalf. I'd had no idea that they cared so much. That they had been rooting for Iduna and me from the sidelines all this time.

Kai grinned. "The council may not like it. But you, as their monarch, have the final say. You can marry whoever you want. A princess, an orphan—it's your choice."

"I think that choice has already been made," Gerda added with a teasing smile.

I felt a lump rise in my throat. "Thank you," I said sincerely.

Gerda gave me a soft look. "Agnarr, we both care about you greatly." She took a deep breath. "And we don't want to see you end up like your mother. That would be the worst thing in the world."

My mother. I nodded slowly, thinking back to the trolls' story. I had been so close to the same thing happening to me.

If not for Iduna . . .

Gerda reached into her bag and pulled out a small stuffed puffin with a blue cape and a button eye. For a moment, I didn't recognize it. Then, slowly, a warm memory floated to the surface.

"Sir JörgenBjörgen!" I cried, grabbing it from her and

just staring. "I forgot all about him! Where's he been all these years?"

"Your father packed away everything that reminded him of your mother after she left. And we have no idea where he put it. He also forbade anyone to speak of her," Gerda explained. "But I saved this—because he was your favorite. I'm sorry I kept him hidden from you all these years. But it's high time you had him back."

Tears misted my eyes as I gazed down at the raggedy stuffed animal, memories now pouring back into me as if a dam had burst. All those years I'd kept locked away after being shamed by my father for weeping when my mother left.

But now I remembered.

The way she'd get on the floor and play with me, even if it was unbecoming of a queen.

The way she'd tickle me until I couldn't stop laughing.

The great games of hide-and-go-seek through the castle.

Happy memories of our time together. Before it had all screeched to a halt.

What would she think if she saw me now, at the crossroads of the same decision she'd once been forced to make? She wouldn't want me to marry a princess for the good of the realm. She'd want me to marry Iduna.

Because I loved Iduna. Iduna made me happy. Iduna made me whole.

With Iduna I would be a better man. A better king.

And now nothing was standing in my way.

CHAPTER THIRTY-THREE

Iduna

"SERIOUSLY, COULD IT BE ANY COLDER?" I muttered as I trudged through the falling snow, map still clutched in my hand. It had been almost balmy when I slipped out of Arendelle Castle through the secret passage early that morning. I knew I was taking a risk, but I had run home to grab a few hours of sleep, change clothes, and grab a few supplies. And with the harsh turn the weather had taken, I was glad I did. The wind howled through the trees, and snow fell in thick clumps. It was only a dusting at first, but now it was at least a foot deep. With no signs of stopping anytime soon.

I knew I should probably turn around. Go back to the village and wait it out. But I was on a mission. And I was afraid if I abandoned it now, I would never get the courage to try again.

I pushed on, through what was now looking to be a very intense blizzard. Worse still, I was on foot. Last time we'd journeyed here, Agnarr and I had ridden horses up the steep, winding trails. But I hadn't dared ask anyone to loan me one, afraid it would bring up too many questions, and I didn't want to risk being caught borrowing one without permission.

"Argh!"

I stumbled over a boulder that was completely obscured by the snow. Flailing, I tried to keep my balance but ended up falling face-first into a large drift. I scrambled to my feet, attempting to brush the snow away, but the flakes were heavy, wet, clinging to my neck and cloak and soaking me to the bone.

I shivered, beginning to get scared. This storm was no joke, and even with my outdoor skills, I was no match for its power. Looking back the way I'd come, I realized I'd already traveled too far to turn around. In fact, Arendelle Castle was so far below at this point that it looked like a toy. The ships in the fjord's harbor were ant-sized. Would I even make it back down the hill in these icy conditions?

My teeth chattered. Looking at my hands, I realized they had a strange blue tinge. The wind whipped at my cloak, snapping it against my legs so hard it hurt.

I needed to get under cover—fast. Or I wouldn't make it through the day.

I drew in a breath, my Northuldra instincts kicking in as I scanned the mountainside for shelter. I could try to build one out of fallen trees, but that would take too long. What I really needed was a small cave or at least an outcropping of some sort to protect me from the wind and snow.

Nothing but whiteness surrounded me.

My heart pounded with fear. What was I doing out here? All alone, not having told anyone where I'd gone. If I died out here, which seemed more likely by the moment, no one would ever find my body. It would be impossible before spring. And the wolves would have taken care of me long before that.

Once someone noticed I was gone, they'd probably assume I'd fled the kingdom. Or maybe they'd wonder if one of the masked attackers had kidnapped me. In any case, I'd never be heard from again.

What would Agnarr think when he realized I was gone? I had told him I was leaving and never coming back. But he'd lost so many people in his life . . . I hated the idea of him suffering over the loss of yet another.

The wind whipped up in a large gust, almost knocking me backward with its force. I grabbed on to a nearby tree for support, hugging it with all my might until the blast faded. I could feel tears leak from my eyes only to instantly turn into tiny particles of ice on my cheeks.

On a last impulse, I lifted my voice in song. That was what I told the children I did when I was scared, after all, and I couldn't remember ever being as scared as this—except maybe the day of the dam celebration when the spirits rose up in anger. But I had sung that day, too, calling Gale to my side to help me. Gale had always helped me when I was a child, to get out of whatever scrape I'd gotten myself into.

Of course, I hadn't seen Gale in years; for all I knew, the spirit had been trapped in the mist like everyone else.

But something inside me still told me to try.

"*Ah ah ah ah . . .*" I called, putting my hand to my mouth. But the wind greedily ripped the notes from my mouth as soon as I sung them. Stealing them and carrying them away.

"*Ah ah ah ah.*"

And yet, still I sang. What choice did I have? What else could I do?

"*Ah ah ah ah.*"

I collapsed into the snow, unable to move. A great tiredness came over me. Maybe I could rest here. Just for a moment . . .

I closed my eyes and let the darkness in.

Ah ah ah ah . . .

What was that?

My eyes flew open at the sudden sound. I scrambled to my feet, weak and confused. I looked around, suddenly spotting a strange little whirlwind a few feet away. Leaves were dancing above the snow. Where had they come from? The trees were bare and the ground was covered with snow.

I rubbed my eyes, thinking at first it must be a hallucination. But no, the leaves were still dancing when I pulled my hands away. I opened my mouth, senseless hope rising in my chest.

"Gale?" I whispered.

The leaves whipped away, up the mountain. They stopped for a moment, swirling in a circle, as if waiting for me to follow, before moving onward.

With a surge of adrenaline, I started to climb. I didn't know if it was really Gale or merely an illusion brought on by the cold. But a moment later I stumbled across a small rocky cave cut into the hillside. My heart lifted.

I rushed into the cave, ducking under the low-hanging entrance. The storm howled angrily outside, but inside, the cave was dry. I drew a shaky breath, still shivering like crazy and soaking wet, but it was better than being out there. If I was smart, I might have a chance.

Forcing my stiffened limbs onto hands and knees, I searched the cave for wood. There wasn't a lot, but I did find a few stray pieces. Pulling my flint from my pocket, I shakily tried to light a fire, near the entrance to ensure proper ventilation. I missed the first few tries, my hands too freezing to properly strike the stones together. My despair rose.

Then an idea struck me. I looked out the mouth of the cave. "Bruni?" I called softly for the Fire Spirit. If Gale had found its way here, maybe Bruni could, too. "I could use a little help."

I hadn't asked the spirits for anything in years. I'd tried to do it all on my own. And I'd been successful for the most part. For years I'd stood on my own two feet. Made my own way. But, I realized, it wasn't shameful to ask for help when you truly needed it.

And I needed it that day.

I struck the flint once more. This time, I was able to make a spark. I didn't know whether it was by my own hands or if Bruni had intervened, but the leaves caught the spark, igniting. I blew on them gently until those flames spread to the wood.

I held my hands over the small fire gratefully, warming them until my skin felt as though it were covered in small pinpricks, a sign the cold was retreating.

My eyelids felt heavy, and I no longer struggled to keep my eyes open as I had one last thought: *maybe, just maybe, I would live through this day after all.*

CHAPTER THIRTY-FOUR

Iduna

I AM A NEWBORN BABY.

My father cradles me in his arms in our small tent. My mother is near; I can smell her warm, earthy scent. She's carefully finishing up knitting a berry-colored shawl while humming the familiar Ahtohallan lullaby. She will give me this shawl when she is finished.

It will change the course of my life, forever.

The entrance to our tent parts. A village elder ducks inside and sits down with my parents. He is old, the oldest of our family, and he has lived long and seen many things. My father smiles at him and greets him with respect. The elder nods solemnly and lays a hand on my forehead. His fingers are rough, calloused, but gentle.

"You may be small," he says in a deep voice, "but you are already one of us. A blessed child of the sun. As such, the spirits will always be with you. They will protect you. They will keep you safe."

My mother and father exchange warm smiles.

"But you must do your part," he adds, "to be worthy of the spirits' gifts. To respect the land we walk on. To listen to nature and heed her call. To seek out peace whenever possible. To love even when it might be easier to hate."

Then he smiles, his watery blue eyes crinkling at the corners. "But for now, little one, all you have to be is yourself. Your very adorable self," he adds, winking at my mother. My parents beam with pride.

The elder says goodbye, exiting the hut. My mother sets down her knitting. The shawl that has taken her weeks is finally done. She inches closer to my father and me, cuddling up against us. She takes the shawl that she has filled with love at every stitch and wraps it carefully around my body until I feel warm and snug and secure.

"My sweet girl," she murmurs, gently stroking my nose with her finger. It tickles a little but also makes me sleepy. "May the spirits always protect you. And may you grow to do great things."

I am a small child. No more than five years old.

I'm huddled in my family's tent, now terrified and alone, hiding under the same berry-colored shawl my mother made for me when I was a newborn. My mother and father instructed me to stay here, hidden, as they led would-be invaders from our encampment. They would come back, they promised.

They haven't come back.

Light suddenly pours in from outside. I shrink in fear, trying to make myself as small as possible under the cover of the shawl, as a stranger steps into the tent. She looks around, her eyes searching. I can't help emitting a small squeak of terror as she inches closer.

She freezes at the sound. I cower in fear as she reaches down, lifts up the shawl, and discovers me hiding underneath. She gasps in surprise; then her face softens. She drops to her knees and pulls me into her arms. I should be frightened, but her touch is gentle, kind. She smells a little like my mother.

"Sweet little girl," she whispers, "are you here all alone?"

I let out a small sob. The first one I've dared since my parents disappeared. "They told me to hide," I explain in a wobbly voice, pulling the shawl around me and hugging it tight. "They said bad men were coming. But that I would be safe."

"You are safe," she assures me.

She carries me out of the tent. More people are outside, milling about. They are dressed like my family—but they are all strangers to me. Still, they look kind. My fear begins to fade.

"She was hiding in the tent," the woman explains when they turn to look at me. "I think she's the only one left."

Fear once again grips my heart with icy fingers. "Where's my mother?" I cry. "Where's my father? I want to see them—now!"

The woman sets me gently on the ground, then kneels before me. She takes my hands in hers. They are coarse, hardened, but her touch is somehow soft. "I am sorry," she says, seeming genuinely distraught. "I am afraid they are not coming back."

I stare at her in horror. "No!" I shake my head. "You're wrong! My mother would never leave me! She promised never to leave me." I clutch the shawl around my body. It still smells like her. It still feels like her.

"Sometimes we make promises we cannot keep," the woman says slowly. "But do not fear. You are not alone, little one. You may have lost your family today, but you have also found a new one."

"How?"

"The Northuldra are made up of many groups, but in the end, we are one family. One people under the sun." She smiles at me. "What's your name?"

I am around nine years old. I'm wandering through our camp, weaving my way through the huts as Gale sweeps in behind me, tickling me under my arms. I screech, erupting in giggles.

"Go pick on someone your own size!" I scold the Wind Spirit playfully.

Gale obliges, sweeping over to tease a young woman as she cooks by the fire. When she shoos it away, it heads over to an older man, stealing the carrot he's about to feed to his reindeer. Then it sweeps under Yelana, who's busy knitting a shawl. The Wind Spirit steals the nearly finished project straight from her hands and drops it on her head. She starts scolding the spirit in a loud voice, but I can tell she's not really mad.

My heart swells as I watch them all. My family. Maybe not the one I was born to, but the ones who now hold my heart. I still miss my mother and father, but the pain has dulled over time to a slow ache.

"May the spirits protect you," I remember my mother saying each night as she'd tuck me in. "May you grow to do great things."

I don't know if I'll do great things. But I have done this thing. Made a new life, found a new family to call my own. Not of blood this time, but of love, friendship, and respect. I hug the shawl my mother made me close to my chest. I think she would be proud of me if she saw me now. I think she would be happy that I found a new peace.

Gale swirls around me again, tossing me into the air. This time I don't scold it or send it away. Instead, I let it take me high into the sky, then look down at my family below. My heart soars.

I am home.

The peaceful scene in the village shatters. The forest has erupted in violence. Wind, fire, smoke. The ground is buckling under my feet.

I am twelve. Agnarr is fourteen. And he's lying on the ground, bleeding.

I stare down at him, feeling the conflict rise inside of me. I should leave him here. Go back to my family. The longer I stay, the more I risk not being able to go back. The fires are fierce. I may get cut off, trapped.

I turn to leave. But not before I catch his face again. Pale, anguished, eyes fluttering. A soft moan escapes his lips. He's clearly in pain. And no one else is around to help.

Only me.

My mother's words once again echo through my head. "May you grow to do great things."

I don't know if this is a great thing. This could be a stupid thing. A terrible thing. The worst thing I could do.

But then I remember how I felt back in that tent, the day my family was killed. How scared I was. How alone. If I hadn't been found, I would never have survived.

Found by someone who didn't know me. But saved me anyway.

As I will save this boy.

I call out to Gale. The Wind Spirit sweeps in, taking Agnarr and me, cradling us gently in its breezy embrace. As it carries us away, I just want to make sure he gets to his people safely.

I don't know if I'll ever do great things.

But I will do this thing.

Hopefully it will be enough.

I awoke in the cave later that evening. The storm had vanished and the setting sun was painting its last pictures before dipping below the horizon. I sat up groggily, examining myself for any injuries. But the spirits had protected me.

And maybe spoken to me, through my strange dreams.

I thought over the dreams as I took stock of my surroundings, noticed the still-smoking heap of ash that had been my blazing fire, acknowledged the hunger roiling deep in my belly. Something inside told me that I should pay attention to what I'd seen. That these long-ago fragments of the past could be pieces of a puzzle meant to be linked together to help me determine my future.

My mind flashed back to the village elder's mandate when I was just a newborn baby. To seek out peace whenever possible. To love even when it might be easier to hate.

I thought of Agnarr lying on the forest floor. Me, calling out to Gale.

A simple act of love, powerful enough to change the very course of the world.

May you grow to do great things.

"Iduna!"

I looked up, startled by the sudden voice. To my surprise, I was no longer alone.

The mountain trolls I'd been seeking.

They'd found me.

CHAPTER THIRTY-FIVE

Iduna

BULDA RUSHED OVER TO ME, CHECKING ME out carefully for any injuries. Grand Pabbie looked at me solemnly. "You are awake," he said.

I scrunched up my face, confused. "What are you doing here? How did you find me?"

"We trolls have our ways."

"Are you all right, dear?" Bulda asked, grabbing my arm and sniffing it. "It's too cold for a human to be outdoors, even if you are in a cave. Where is your husband, dear Agnarr? Does he know you're out here?"

"Do you have any daughters yet?" added the younger female troll curiously.

My heart ached at their words. *Husband, daughters . . .*

"He is not my husband, and there will be no daughters," I corrected them wearily. "Agnarr is to marry a princess of another kingdom. She will have his daughters, not me."

"But the vision said—"

"I guess the vision was wrong. Agnarr must marry a princess." I walked over to a nearby rock and brushed off the snow to settle on its unforgiving surface. "And I am no princess."

"Bah!" Bulda blurted out in disdain. "What is a princess, anyway? Some silly title made up at birth? Because their great-great-ancestor was good with a sword? Royal or common, your blood runs red. And it has nothing to do with one's ability to help one's people."

"Yeah, well, tell that to the Arendellian council," I muttered. "They are very set on Agnarr being married for the good of the kingdom."

"And you don't think you'd be good for the kingdom?" Bulda pressed.

I opened my mouth to argue the point, then closed it. I thought of my years in Arendelle. Inventing the turning blades on the windmill to help the farmers with their output and better feed their families. Reading to the children. Baking for the elders. They weren't the grand acts of a king or queen, but they had the potential to be life-changing all the same. To bring people together. To make them feel safe and cared for. Loved. Respected.

But it wasn't enough.

I shook my head sadly. "They want to create an alliance between two nations."

"And would not your marriage do that?" Grand Pabbie suddenly broke in. He gave me a knowing look.

"I know where you come from, Iduna. And I know what you did that day to save Agnarr. An act of love, saving one's enemy. Don't you think the spirits know the same?"

I stared at him, unable to speak. He wasn't wrong. I had saved Agnarr in an act of love—even before I fell in love with him. In that moment in the forest, there had been no Northuldra, no Arendelle—just two people who needed one another coming together.

Forming an alliance all our own.

And even though the spirits had been angry that day, raging through the forest, Gale had still seen fit to help me save Agnarr's life. That had to mean something, right?

"Also, this may not be written in the Northern Lights or all that," Bulda added, "but the guy clearly loves you. Though he's a bit of a fixer-upper. That mustache! What is going on with that half-grown mustache?"

I giggled. I couldn't help it.

Grand Pabbie's eyes settled on me. They were kind and knowing. "Iduna, do not sell yourself short. You are one of the people of the sun. You are more than worthy of an Arendellian prince." He smiled, his eyes crinkling at the corners. "You have saved his life. You have won his heart. All that's left now is for you to take his hand."

Tears streamed down my cheeks as I gazed at the trolls. "It's funny," I said. "I came up here to ask you to help me forget. Instead, you helped me remember." I drew in a breath. "Thank you."

"The pleasure is all ours," Grand Pabbie assured me. "Now go, Iduna. Go back to Arendelle. And forget about the council. Agnarr is the only one who matters in the end."

"And get that boy to grow out his mustache!" Bulda added. "Tell him Bulda said he'll look utterly dashing with it!"

And with that, the trolls popped back into boulder shape and rolled up the hill to return to the Valley of the Living Rock. I watched them go, feeling a warmth rise inside me, despite the cold weather outside. It was an almost giddy happiness I could barely contain.

For so long I'd lived in fear. Not sure who I was. But now I realized that what really mattered was who I *could* be.

And there was only one way to defeat that fear for good.

We didn't need an army to bring peace to Arendelle. We only needed love.

And what could be stronger than my love for Agnarr?

CHAPTER THIRTY-SIX

Iduna

I PRACTICALLY RACED DOWN THE MOUNTAIN, the exhilaration inside me thrumming through my body, propelling me forward. Down the pathway, to the lower altitudes, where the snow had already melted except in small, random clumps. It was hard to believe I'd almost frozen to death on my way up.

When I neared the town, I looked out over the hillside, smiling at all the windmills spinning contently in the morning breeze. There were so many now; each farm had wanted their own. And grain production had been up so much this year, we were able to send some by ship to neighboring kingdoms that weren't so lucky.

"Iduna!" a farmer called, waving to me. I waved back, a feeling of joy washing over me.

"Hey, Mr. Hansen!" I greeted him. "How's everything going?"

"Wonderful!" he declared. "My farm has never produced so much. And now that we're not reliant on horses to do all the heavy work in the mill, we've started breeding them instead. We'll have a whole new stable of foals soon, ready to be sold."

As he spoke, a small white colt skittered across the field on spindly legs. I laughed as he darted toward me, then stopped in front of me, nuzzling my hand. I reached into my satchel, digging out a carrot. Fortunately, I'd traveled prepared.

"Here you go, boy," I said, stroking him softly. As he chomped down on the treat, I looked up at the farmer. "What's his name?"

"We called him Havski," the farmer replied. "It means handsome."

"He certainly is a handsome boy," I agreed. "When he's ready to be sold, will you come to me first? I've never had my own horse before. Maybe it's time."

"Iduna, you can have him for nothing!" Mr. Hansen exclaimed. "After all you've done for us, it's the least I could do."

I grinned, happiness washing over me. "Thank you," I said. I knelt down in front of the colt, who was already sniffing my satchel for another carrot. "I'll see you soon, Kjekk," I whispered. "And I promise, you'll have all the carrots you can eat."

I rose and headed down the hill toward Arendelle, feeling proud and content. Like the trolls said, what was a princess, anyway? Someone who was born lucky. But I had made my own luck over the years. That had to count for something, right?

Agnarr didn't want to marry Runa. He'd made that perfectly clear. He was only trying to do what was right, what was expected of him as king. Now all I had to do was prove that we could be right together, too. Just in an unexpected way. It might not be easy to convince the council. But between the two of us, our love had the power to move mountains. Surely we could move a few minds to our side as well.

And King Nicholas and his daughter could go back home where they belonged.

Speaking of King Nicholas . . . I stopped, realizing I was not far from the Vassar encampment just outside of town, colorful pavilions dotting the clearing, their country's flags waving from the tops. I knew King Nicholas had refused Peterssen's offer to stay within the city walls, saying as soldiers they were used to fresh air, not the confines of city life. At the moment, the place looked half abandoned; most of the men were likely out on patrols, keeping Arendelle safe from new attacks.

I frowned. That was the only downside to all of this. Agnarr would have to publicly reject Runa if he were to marry me. That would be an insult to King Nicholas. Would he withdraw his patrols? Would that lead to an escalation of attacks? Would it put people's lives in danger? We had been so fortunate Vassar had come to town with their army just as things were getting bad. . . .

Fortunate. Or . . .

I frowned, a sudden disturbing thought prickling at the back of my brain. I glanced over at the camp, my eyes locking on a clothesline just outside the perimeter, filled with Vassar cloaks, hanging out to dry . . . just like I had found cloaks at the Arendelle camp that fateful day in the Enchanted Forest.

I shook my head. No. This was crazy. Absolutely crazy. And likely dangerous, too.

But then . . .

I set my jaw, tiptoeing over to the clothesline.

"For Arendelle," I whispered to myself.

CHAPTER THIRTY-SEVEN

Agnarr

"YOUR MAJESTY! THE PEOPLE ARE WAITING for you. You're not even dressed?" Kai clucked disapprovingly. "Why, it's almost noon!"

I groaned, yanking the covers over my head, wishing he'd go away. The last thing I wanted that day was to face the council, as well as the people of Arendelle at the weekly petitioner session. Not to mention have to look at the smug face of King Nicholas and have him try to foist his daughter on me once again.

Ever since learning from Kai and Gerda that there was no official rule requiring me to marry a princess, I'd been trying to figure out a way to get Runa and her father to go home. Once they were out of the way, I could make my case for Iduna. It was going to be difficult, seeing as I had no idea where Iduna had gone.

No one had seen her since the night of the explosion. To make matters worse, King Nicholas wouldn't take the hint to go home. If anything, he'd dug in even deeper since the night of the ball, assigning his soldiers to patrol the streets and guard the castle. And Peterssen had let him get away with it all, because it meant Arendelle would be safer. That was the number one priority, he liked to keep reminding me.

In other words, my love life would have to wait.

"Your Majesty—"

"I'm up, I'm up!" I grumbled, forcing myself out of bed. Kai helped me with my green suit, then assisted with flattening my bed head hair. I usually protested that I could do this myself, but today I didn't have the energy to argue.

"Your Majesty seems out of sorts," Kai remarked casually, though his eyes held a knowing look. He escorted me to the mirror and had me sit down on a stool in front of it as he worked a brush through my hair.

I sighed. "Arendelle has become like a prison, thanks to King Nicholas. Did you know he even canceled the annual holiday ringing of the yule bell?"

"Yes. I was sorry to hear that. I always enjoyed that tradition," Kai agreed politely, dabbing sticky goop onto my hair to smooth any unruly flyaways into place. "But if it is for Arendelle's safety, I suppose it is for the best."

"I suppose," I muttered, sick of hearing that line. It wasn't as if I didn't care about keeping Arendelle safe. I did. It was just something about the way King Nicholas went about it all. . . .

Suddenly, Gerda burst into the room so abruptly that I jumped and Kai dropped his brush.

"Now see here, Gerda!" he scolded. "You really need to learn to knock before—"

"She's back!" Gerda interrupted, a huge grin on her face.

I stood up, knocking over my stool. "Who?" I asked, hardly daring to breathe. But even as I asked the question, I knew there was only one person whose reappearance could get Gerda this excited.

Her eyes gleamed with happiness. "Lady Iduna," she said, clutching her hands to her chest. "She's here. In the Great Hall. The First Great Hall. Not the Second Great Hall. I saw her waiting with the other petitioners."

My heart thumped. Kai reached down for his comb, but I waved him away. "My hair's fine," I told him. "I've got to go!"

I dashed to the door. When I reached it, I turned around, catching Kai and Gerda exchanging fond looks. My heart melted a little at the sight. Because of them, I might actually have a chance at happiness. My throat tightened.

"Thank you," I said simply, even though I wanted to say so much more.

Gerda shooed me away with her hands. "Are you still here?" she scolded. "Go and get that girl of yours!"

"And this time," Kai added with a toothy grin, "don't let her go."

I bolted from my bedroom and ran down the hall, down the stairs, toward the Great Hall, where the meeting would be taking place. When I arrived, there was already a line out the door. Not surprising, I supposed, given the recent attacks. I wondered how many of them knew about the ballroom explosion. News traveled fast in our kingdom.

"Those monsters!" a short, thin woman in an embroidered gray dress was saying to King Nicholas as I made my way to the front of the room, trying to scan it for a glimpse of Iduna. The woman thrust a half-eaten cabbage at the regent. "Is there no low they will not stoop to? They came to my house! Ate half my vegetable garden!"

"Terrible!" King Nicholas declared. He had evidently found a nice comfy spot right next to Peterssen himself, and his daughter Runa was standing by his side, obedient as ever. "But not surprising. The Northuldra are simply notorious for vegetable stealing!"

"As are rabbits," Peterssen interjected, looking weary. "Did you witness the Northuldra doing this, by any chance, Miss Nillson?"

"Well, no!" she sputtered. "But of course it was them! They are everywhere. I am quite afraid to close my eyes at night for fear I might be murdered in my sleep!"

"And my sheep are now *pink*!" added Aksel, the shepherd, from the back of the room. He held up a colorfully dyed lamb. "Pink, I tell you! Will this brutality never end?"

Gunnar stepped forward, crossing his arms over his chest. "Forget the sheep and the vegetables. The rest of us want to know about the explosion," he declared. "What are you doing about these attacks? How will you stop them? If the monarchy can't keep its own castle safe, how can we expect it to protect its people?"

A roar of agreement rolled through the crowd. Everyone started talking at once. I caught King Nicholas giving his guard a small smirk. He seemed to be enjoying this way too much for someone who had gone to the trouble of posting his own army around the castle for our protection.

I stepped onto the dais, turning to face the crowd. "Silence!" I demanded in my loudest voice. "I will not have this chaos in my court! If you cannot be respectful, then I will dismiss you all."

The crowd grumbled a little but eventually settled. Peterssen gave me an encouraging nod. I cleared my throat and continued. "Now, has anyone actually seen an individual or group committing these crimes?" I asked, still half scanning the room for Iduna. Where was she? "Does anyone have a real idea of who might be behind them?" I held up my hand to stop them before they could speak. "I'm talking facts. Firsthand accounts. I don't wish to hear suspicious stories of monsters hiding under children's beds. We're better than that."

I waited. Everyone was glancing uneasily at each other. But no one stepped forward. Until a lone voice came from the back of the room.

"I do."

Everyone wore a look of surprise—me included—as Iduna finally stepped out from the crowd. She was wearing a simple woolen dress, with half of her beautiful glossy hair up in a braid, while the rest cascaded down her back. Iduna wove her way to the front of the room and stopped before the dais. She was carrying a sack, whose contents she proceeded to dump out onto the table. To my surprise, nails, chunks of metal, and what looked like fertilizer spilled out from it.

"What is the meaning of this?" King Nicholas sputtered. "This is a castle of high regard, young lady! Not your garbage dump!"

"You asked for evidence of criminal activity," she explained. "I have found supplies used for making explosive devices. Likely the same type that were used in the castle the night of the ball."

King Nicholas frowned, suddenly looking uneasy. "What did I tell you?" He turned to the crowd. "This is why you need a strong army to protect Arendelle! The Northuldra will stop at nothing to destroy your way of life!"

Iduna's eyes locked on to the king's face. There was a fierceness in her gaze that I recognized all too well. What was she doing?

"I didn't say they were from the Northuldra," she said.

"But who else could they be from?" King Nicholas sputtered. "We all know the Northuldra have been attacking your people for months now!"

"Have they, though?" Iduna asked, her voice calm. "Or could it be someone else?" She arched an eyebrow at the king. "Someone with a vested interest in Arendelle needing an army to protect it, perhaps?" Her tone was neutral, but her eyes blazed.

"What are you saying, Iduna?" Peterssen demanded.

Iduna looked at me. "Your Majesty, I found these in the tents of the Vassar soldiers," she said. "Along with these." She reached into the sack again and pulled out several all-too-familiar-looking sun masks.

CHAPTER THIRTY-EIGHT

Agnarr

THE CROWD GASPED. EVERYONE STARTED talking at once. King Nicholas looked down at the masks, then up at Iduna, his face red and his eyes furious.

"What is this?" he responded. "What are you trying to say? Who is this girl, anyway? Some peasant? Maybe *she's* Northuldra herself! Trying to shift the blame from her people to ours!"

"Enough!" I boomed, stepping to Iduna's side. I reached out and grabbed her hand in mine, squeezing it tight. It was then that I realized she was trembling. This had taken all her courage, opening herself to risk like this.

But she had done it. And maybe saved us all in the process.

"You will not speak to Lady Iduna like that," I declared. "And you will be taken under custody until we can determine the truth. Lord Peterssen, please call Sorenson with his lie test. We will be in need of his services."

"There's no need for that."

Suddenly, Runa stepped forward. Her face was pale and her voice was shaking, but her posture was rigid and determined. "You don't have to interrogate," she said in a low voice. "Because I can tell you for a fact: what Lady Iduna says is true."

Another gasp went through the crowd. The king's face turned purple. "What are you saying, Runa?" he demanded. "Clearly my daughter does not feel well at the moment and—"

"I'm not going to lie for you anymore, Father," Runa spit out. "This is your doing, not mine. You didn't trust me enough to win the prince on my own merits. You had to have insurance—to make Arendelle appear weak so that you could look strong. Ready to step in and help. Too bad it was *you* they needed protection from all along." She looked at me, her eyes sorrowful. "I apologize, Agnarr. I should not have gone along with any of it. But then, I have met such terrible men in my rounds of courting princes. Greedy men, desperate for power. I thought it was the normal way of things to achieve one's desired ends." She sighed. "But then I met you. And you were a genuinely good person. And I thought—I hoped—that maybe it could work out between us. That this act of my father's—evil as it was—could have a positive outcome."

She hung her head. "But I know better now. You deserve to be happy. To marry for love. As do I."

King Nicholas's face twisted in rage. "Why, you traitor!" He lunged for his daughter. But the Arendelle guards jumped in, quickly blocking his path.

"Take him away," I ordered.

The guards began dragging him to the exit while the people of Arendelle booed and hissed at him.

"You need me!" he cried, trying to fight off the guards, to no avail. "You are making a big mistake!"

Mistake or not, King Nicholas was soon gone.

I turned to Runa, who was still standing there, shoulders back, head held high. A regal princess to the very end. When she caught me watching her, she gave me a sad smile.

"You may have them take me away as well," she said. "I won't put up a fight."

The remaining guards started to move in her direction. But I stepped forward. "No," I said. "Runa, I won't make you pay for your father's crimes. You stood up to him and told me the truth. You are free to go home. Once things have calmed down, let's meet again." I lowered my voice so only she could hear me. "Not as suitors this time, but as rulers of our respective kingdoms. Surely we can come to a mutual trade agreement—without muddying the waters with the whole messy marriage thing."

Runa beamed up at me. "I'm sure we can work something out."

And with that, she headed from the throne room. I watched her go, thinking of my mother. Hopefully now, with her father gone, Runa would be able to find her own happiness. Her own true love.

I turned to the people of Arendelle, who were watching the scene unfold with utter bemusement and fascination. I knew it would be all over town the second they left the castle.

"Thank you all for your patience," I said. "We will continue to work on this new . . . development. But I believe it is safe to say we won't have to worry about men in sun masks again."

"What about pink sheep?" demanded Aksel, holding up his lamb.

I groaned. "Let's table that till next week, shall we?"

"Or . . ." Iduna suddenly interjected, a wicked gleam in her sky-blue eyes, "we could all start wearing pink shawls? I mean, who here would love a beautiful bright pink shawl?"

The hands of pretty much all the women in the room shot up at once. Aksel's eyes lit up. He hugged the pink lamb tight to his chest, looking proud. "Pink shawls it is!" he cried. "Purple, too! I'll start taking orders immediately."

The crowd surrounded him, everyone talking at once.

Iduna smiled triumphantly.

I watched her, my heart in my throat. She hadn't been gone long, but I'd missed her with my entire being. And there was no way I was letting her go ever again.

"We should talk," I whispered.

She nodded. "We should."

"Library or tree?"

"Tree." She grinned mischievously, as though she had something up her sleeve. My heart skipped a beat.

"Now?"

She glanced over at Peterssen, who was watching from a few feet away. "No," she said. "You're needed here. Finish up and find me tonight. Eight o'clock sharp." She briefly touched her hand to mine on her way out the door. "Don't be late."

CHAPTER THIRTY-NINE

Agnarr

"PRINCE AGNARR!"

Iduna's voice rang out right as I heard the clocks chiming 8:00 p.m. on the dot. I walked into the courtyard, toward our favorite tree. It'd been a long day, full of council meetings where everyone tried to figure out what to do with the disgraced King Nicholas. But in the back of my mind, I hadn't been able to stop thinking of Iduna. Was she going to give me the second chance I'd prayed for?

I stopped short, doing a double take.

She wasn't in the tree.

Instead, she was standing on our bench.

Flanked by two . . . reindeer?

As I watched, dumbfounded, the reindeer on the ground at her right pressed his hoof down on a small wooden box, setting free a swarm of purple butterflies. At the same time, the reindeer on the ground at her left released a cloud of those little helicopter seeds, which whirled through the air like brown smoke. Iduna lifted her chin, standing tall and proud as she addressed me in a clear voice.

"Prince Agnarr of Arendelle. My kind, handsome, fearless love . . ." The butterflies swarmed around her, creating a halo around her head. Her eyes met mine. "Will you marry me?" she asked in a soft voice.

I stared at her in disbelief. Iduna grinned sheepishly, a giggle escaping her lips. She jumped off the bench and approached me, reaching into her pocket and pulling out something small. It took me a moment before I realized what it was.

The love spoon. The one I thought I'd lost forever.

"You finished it," I whispered.

"Yup." She beamed. "Though I had a little help. Who knew Olina was a master woodworker as well as a master chef?"

I ran to her and pulled her into my arms. The reindeer surrounded us, snorting and huffing, but I shooed them away, holding her close, until her face was inches from mine. She looked at me with those big blue eyes of hers. Eyes I could lose myself in.

And find myself in, too.

"I love you," I whispered.

"I love you, too," she replied, her eyes teeming with affection. Then she added, "Look, Agnarr, I've been giving this a lot of thought. You were right all along. We love each other. That's all that matters in the end. We can go to the council and make our case. Or go to the people, even. What can Peterssen say if everyone in Arendelle is behind us? They're the ones who matter, right? Not just the council." She smiled bravely at me. "You said our love was worth fighting for. Well, I'm ready to fight. I want you to marry me."

I raised my hand, brushing her soft cheek with my fingers. "And I definitely *can* marry you—no council fight required," I told her.

"What?" Her eyes clouded with confusion. "I don't understand."

"You'll never believe this, but it turns out there's no official rule in the Arendelle lawbooks saying I have to marry royalty." I grinned broadly. "You can thank Kai and Gerda for that."

"Really?" Her eyes grew wide. "There's no rule?"

My hand snaked around her neck. "None at all," I whispered.

Our lips met. My hands dropped to her hips and pulled her flush against me. I could feel every curve of her body as her mouth moved hungrily against mine. I pulled away for a moment to rest my forehead against hers. "Are you sure this is what you want?" I asked in a low voice. "You've seen what my life is like—and I'm not even king yet."

"I know," she said solemnly. "And I don't expect it to be easy. Don't get me wrong; there's a part of me that wants to ask you to just run away with me. To live a simple life of farmers in a field. But Arendelle needs you as much as I do. So I'm okay with sharing."

"I think Arendelle needs *you*," I corrected her with a laugh. "But I guess I'm okay with sharing, too. You are the most amazing person I have ever met," I whispered. "Will you ever stop surprising me?"

Her blue eyes sparkled. "Seems unlikely, Your Majesty."

"I am glad to hear it, my queen."

CHAPTER FORTY

Iduna

"IDUNA? MAY I SPEAK WITH YOU FOR A moment?"

Peterssen's voice cut through the happy daze I was in as I gazed out at the royal gardens turning colors in the waning light of early dusk. Agnarr had been pulled away by another group of well-wishers, and I had been basking in the glow of our love and all that had happened over the past two days to cement it.

When Agnarr had stated his case to the council the day following my proposal, they didn't put up much of a fight. I think they were embarrassed by the publicity of the botched courtship with Runa and her scheming father. And when we soon after announced our betrothal to the people of Arendelle, they were thrilled at the idea.

"The castle may have its head in the sand," declared Halima as Agnarr and I shared the good news over a cup of tea at Hudson's Hearth. "But we have all been paying attention. And I can't think of anyone who would be better for our prince—and our people—than our sweet, talented Iduna. Mattias would be so proud if he was here." Agnarr had beamed in pride.

Mattias might well have been. But the look on Peterssen's face now told me perhaps the sentiment was not universal.

I followed him to a quiet alcove, a small feeling of unease gnawing at my stomach. When we were out of earshot, he turned to face me, a grim look on his face. "I am happy you and the prince have found each other," Peterssen began. "I truly am. And I know you will make a wonderful pair. You will make a wonderful queen. But, Iduna, if you go through with this, I must warn you: it's more important than ever for you to keep your past a secret—at least for now."

"But why?" I asked, aggrieved. I had actually been planning to come clean to Agnarr about everything later that evening, when it was just the two of us. I wanted to move forward with him with no more secrets between us, only openness and truth.

Peterssen looked troubled. "You just implicated the king of Vassar in violent acts against Arendelle while basically vindicating the Northuldra. If the people ever learn that you're secretly Northuldra, don't you think they might wonder if you and Runa worked together and schemed to plant the evidence in the Vassar tents in order to exonerate your own people and win the prince for yourself?"

I stared at him, crushed by his words. I knew what he said made sense. But why did I also have to keep it from Agnarr? Surely he wouldn't jump to such conclusions.

"Agnarr loves me," I insisted. "He would keep my secret."

"Are you so sure?" Peterssen asked quietly. "For I never knew anyone who hated secrets as much as our prince. And if the truth were to come out—whether by his own mouth, in a misguided attempt to defend your honor, or by some other means—it would be disastrous to his rule. People learning he willingly married you, knowing you were the daughter of Arendelle's enemy, might cost him the throne. Better he does not know. Then if something were to happen, he could use his ignorance as a shield.

"Vassar is gone," he continued. "But there are plenty of others who watch carefully for an opportunity to gain such a rich trade route. To discover weakness, to plant seeds of discontent and fear. We need a strong king. A king whose rule will never fall under question. If you care about Arendelle, you will keep silent—at least a bit longer."

Ah, yes. There it was, the duty to country that was now my obligation as much as it was Agnarr's. I would not be keeping the secret for myself, or even for the sake of my and Agnarr's relationship.

It would be for Arendelle.

And for the Northuldra, too.

As queen I would have the power to protect the Northuldra, to finally put to bed the rumors of their supposed magic and misdeeds once and for all. And if the mist ever were to part, my family and the others could emerge protected, their lands safe.

My voice might seem silent. But it would be strong, persistent, and persuasive. It would be a powerful one.

"Iduna! Come over here!"

I turned my head, my eyes locking on Agnarr, who was beckoning me back to our well-wishers. Mrs. Blodget was standing next to him, holding the most enormous block of chocolate I had ever seen and grinning happily. I gave them a small smile and waved, then turned back to Peterssen.

"Very well," I said, lifting my chin as I fought to keep the tremble from my voice. "I will do as you ask. At least for now. But someday I will tell my story. Agnarr will know the whole truth."

And with that, I walked back to the celebration, not waiting for his response. Shoulders back, head held high. A perfectly poised soon-to-be Arendellian queen.

Conceal, don't feel. Don't let it show.

CHAPTER FORTY-ONE

Iduna
Six Months Later

I STARED AT MYSELF IN THE MIRROR AS Gerda affixed the jeweled silver wedding crown to my head. I was not yet a queen, of course, but the Arendelle wedding tradition sure made me feel like one, along with this sweeping silver gown that cinched at my waist, then billowed out around me like a cloud.

Me, Iduna, Northuldra orphan. Soon-to-be queen of Arendelle.

It was the stuff of those fairy tales I had read about in the books the Arendellians had brought to the dam. Now come to life.

Who would have thought it?

"Are you ready, my dear?" Gerda asked, her eyes shining. "I think it's time."

I drew in a breath, my heart pounding, as Gerda led me to the chapel inside the castle. The place was packed, but instead of inviting dignitaries from neighboring

kingdoms, we'd filled the vast space with all the townspeople of Arendelle. They cheered as I entered the room,
and I felt my cheeks heat in a blush.

The music swelled. I started down the aisle. As I
walked, I saw Agnarr standing at the end, dressed in his
formal Arendelle military uniform with its gold epau-
lets and shiny medals. He'd finally grown his mustache
out, which did indeed make him look especially dashing.
Bulda would be so proud.

But it wasn't his outfit or his new facial hair that had
my heart pumping madly. It was the nervous smile on
his face.

"Well, hello, you," I whispered as I stepped to his side.

"Hello yourself," he whispered back. "You look . . .
incredible, Iduna."

I beamed. "You clean up pretty nice yourself."

He blushed, holding out his arm. "You ready?" he
asked softly.

My heart brimmed over with the look I saw in his
eyes.

No doubt. No fear.

Just love.

"So ready," I declared.

The reception was held in the streets of Arendelle. The
musicians played merry tunes and we danced every
dance under the sun, including "the reindeer who had to
pee really badly but was stuck in a ballroom"—which had

turned out to be a crowd favorite. We feasted on an endless array of delicacies, including a traditional wedding kransekake—a tower of sweet bread topped with cheese, cream, and syrup. As a special touch, Mrs. Blodget had added two little figures to the top of the tower—to represent Agnarr and me. They were made of solid chocolate.

We couldn't stop smiling through it all, our giddy grins disappearing only for the space of a kiss. We were so ridiculously happy to finally be together, out in the open, without fear of getting caught. After years of stolen glances and secret moments, we no longer had to hide our love.

"You look so beautiful," Agnarr told me for probably the fiftieth time since the reception began, taking me into his arms for yet another dance. I could feel the crowd watching us in delight, but I kept my eyes on my prince . . . my husband.

"I think you might have mentioned that already," I teased.

"Are you sick of hearing it?"

"Not at all, Your Majesty."

"Good. Because I plan to repeat it every day of your life from this point on . . . *Your Majesty*," he added, his eyes twinkling.

I groaned. "Are you really going to start calling me that?"

"Absolutely," he declared. "If only to get back at you for all the times you've *Your Majesty*'d me over the years."

I sighed in mock dismay. "Great. I've created a monster."

"No." His eyes grew soft. "You've created a king."

He reached up, cupping my face in his hands, meeting my eyes with that green gaze I would never in a million years tire of. "I could never have done this without you, Iduna," he whispered. "And I want you to continue to be a part of it. You're to be Arendelle's queen now. And I want you to rule with me. Equally. Side by side."

"I love you," I whispered, feeling a little overwhelmed by his words. Me, a wife, a queen. I'd been preparing for this moment for a long time now, but it still seemed so crazy to have it actually come to pass.

Olina bustled toward us then, clapping her hands briskly. "What are you waiting for, Your Majesties?" she asked with a twinkle in her eyes. "It's time for the kransekake!"

I smiled shyly at Agnarr, remembering how the chef had explained the Arendellian wedding tradition to me. Together, we'd lift up the top ring of the kransekake, and however many lower rings were lifted with it would predict how many children we'd have together.

"Are you ready?" Agnarr asked, giving me a wink.

I giggled, suddenly a little nervous. "I think so?"

Together we reached down and slowly lifted the top ring of the cake as pretty much all of Arendelle watched, holding their collective breath.

The top ring rose. Two lower rings came right along

with it. The crowd burst into cheers and applause. Olina clapped her hands and jumped up and down. Kai and Gerda hugged each other enthusiastically. I thought I caught tears in Gerda's eyes.

"Two rings!" Olina declared. "That means two blessed royal children!"

I turned back to Agnarr. "Wow," I said in a low voice, meant only for him. "Guess Grand Pabbie was right."

He nodded, looking like a proud papa already. "Two children," he said, his voice hushed with awe.

"Two *daughters*," I corrected him with a smile.

And somehow, at that moment, I knew it to be true.

CHAPTER FORTY-TWO

Iduna
Three Years Later

"AND NOW, LADIES AND GENTLEMEN, MAY I present to you your new princess, Elsa of Arendelle!"

The roar from the crowd below was almost deafening as I stepped out onto the balcony, cradling my newborn daughter in my arms, her tiny form swathed in a soft blue nightgown that matched her crystal blue eyes. I knew the people were almost as impatient to meet her as I had been.

Agnarr stood beside me, placing a hand at the small of my back. He looked down at me, an adoring smile on his face. "Are you ready, my love?" he asked.

I nodded, stretching out my arms and passing Elsa to Agnarr. He fumbled for a moment—we were both still getting used to handling such a small package—then took her into his arms, holding her up for the crowd to see.

"Long live the princess!" shouted Gunnar, the florist. Everyone laughed and cheered. In fact, they were so loud and excited they must have given little Elsa a start, as she began to wail loudly, shaking her tiny fists in dismay. I quickly took her back from Agnarr, surprised to find that for some reason, her skin was suddenly ice cold. My heart stirred with concern. Was she getting sick?

"I'm going to take her back inside."

Agnarr nodded and planted a kiss on my forehead before turning to the crowd. He clapped his hands. "Please help yourself to food and beverages. There is plenty for all. Musicians, will you give us a tune?"

The band burst into a merry song while the crowd dashed toward the food and drink stations. Some started to dance. All were still excitedly chattering about the beautiful baby. Her sweet mama. Her doting papa. The perfect royal family for Arendelle.

But I shut out all the noise, concentrating on getting Elsa wrapped back up in my shawl. She was still wailing, near inconsolable. Not sure what to do, I gently placed her back in her crib, twirling her little mobile in an attempt to distract her. Gerda had made it for her and it featured the most adorable white-painted stars that swirled in a circle when spun.

Elsa's eyes began to track the motion of the spinning stars. For a moment, she watched them as though mesmerized, her sobs fortunately subsiding. I let out a breath of relief. But when the mobile began to slow, she grew angry again, her tiny face scrunching up with rage. I watched, amused, as she reached up as if to try to grab the mobile and spin it herself.

Instead, to my shock, a streak of what looked like ice shot from her fingers, blasting the mobile straight on.

What on earth?

The mobile started spinning again, but it now appeared to be crusted in ice. I reached out with shaky fingers to touch it. Sure enough, it was freezing cold.

Elsa giggled, happy again. I stared down at her, my pulse skittering. Had she really done that? Shot ice from her fingertips? But that was impossible.

Unless...

Magic.

"How are my girls?" Agnarr asked, leaving the balcony to come up beside me. He stopped as he caught the look of fear that must have been written on my face. "What's wrong?" he asked. "Is she all right?"

I swallowed hard. "Watch," I said, reaching out to stop the mobile. I held my breath, waiting to see if she'd do it again.

Elsa stared up at the mobile, her nose wrinkling in frustration. As the two of us watched, she reached her finger up and pointed. Another blast of ice shot through the air and the mobile began to twirl again.

I looked up at Agnarr. His eyes were like saucers. "How is this possible?" he whispered.

"I don't know," I answered helplessly. And I didn't. Sure, she was half Northuldra, like me, but contrary to popular belief, we didn't possess any magic.

Except Elsa somehow did.

Agnarr stood as though frozen himself. I could

practically see the thoughts whirling through his brain. Even after all this time, was he still fearful of magic because of his father's influence?

Frustration rose inside me. I scooped Elsa from her crib into my arms. Then I went to Agnarr, holding her out toward him.

"Look at her, Agnarr," I commanded, my voice leaving no room for argument. "She's our daughter. We created her, you and I. Whatever powers she might possess, they were born out of love. Which makes them a gift, not a curse."

As my heart beat furiously in my chest, Agnarr said nothing. Then he looked down at Elsa. I could see his whole body was shaking. "*I* know that," he replied softly. "I do. But the people out there. What will they say if they learn of her power? They haven't been taught by you, like I have, that we shouldn't be afraid of what we don't know. We shouldn't be scared of magic."

"They will *say* she is amazing," I answered in as firm a voice as I could muster. "And maybe she will help them finally get over their fears." I sighed. "Agnarr, fear has been the true enemy of Arendelle all along. And maybe—just maybe—if they see their beautiful little princess using her magic for good, they can finally stop being afraid."

For a moment, Agnarr did nothing. Then he slowly reached out, his hands still unsteady, gently brushing the fuzz of Elsa's white-blonde hair on top of her head. She looked up at her papa with wide blue eyes and smiled sweetly at him.

Agnarr's face crumpled. He took her from me and cradled her close. Elsa snuggled against his chest, cooing contentedly as Agnarr gently stroked her head.

My heart melted as I watched the two of them. Maybe this would be all right after all.

Agnarr looked up at me then, his expression solemn. "Look," he said. "We have to be smart here. And cautious. Until we understand what's going on, and the extent of these powers, we must keep this quiet. For Elsa's own safety."

I nodded slowly, my heart sinking once again. I knew he was right. And I would do anything to keep our daughter safe.

But how could I bear keeping yet another secret?

Especially one as big as this?

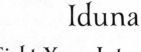

CHAPTER FORTY-THREE

Iduna
Eight Years Later

"AND THEY ALL GOT MARRIED!"

Agnarr shot me an amused smile, then cleared his throat, making our presence known to the girls, who were playing on the floor in their nightgowns just before bed. He stepped further into the room.

"What are you playing?" he asked, observing the small pile of snow and the ice figurines eight-year-old Elsa had whipped up for their game. Anna was always begging her older sister to conjure up ice-skating rinks and snowmen and other forms of icy entertainment for her enjoyment—sometimes being rather persistent about it, as five-year-olds could be. But to her credit, Elsa always obliged. She liked nothing better than making her little sister smile.

We only let her do it indoors, of course. Within the safety of the castle walls, on days when we had no visitors. Even after eight years, Agnarr held firm to the belief that we should keep her powers a secret—which I understood, even if it made me a little sad. I hated the idea that Elsa would have to grow up thinking her beautiful gift was something to be kept hidden. I knew all too well what it felt like not to be able to be yourself.

At least she had her sister's full adoration.

"Enchanted Forest!" Anna crowed, answering her father's question with her usual exuberance. Though Anna did not have magic like Elsa's, her special nature came through in her boundless energy, insatiable curiosity, and genuine love for all things fun. Meanwhile, Elsa had always been a cautious, careful child, almost guarded at times. She reminded me of the man her father had become, whereas Anna was more like the child I had been.

Different as the summer and winter—but close as could be.

"That doesn't look like any enchanted forest I've ever seen," Agnarr teased them, sitting down on the bed. Immediately, he had their attention.

"You've seen an enchanted forest?" Anna asked, looking up at him in awe.

I frowned, something stirring deep inside me. Agnarr loved telling his girls bedtime stories. But I wasn't sure it was wise to tread where this story went. They were still so young. Especially little Anna.

"Are you sure about this?" I asked Agnarr, shooting him a concerned look.

He gave me a slight nod. "It's time they knew."

I sighed. I supposed he was right. It was part of

Arendelle's story, painful as it was for me. They'd hear it someday, from someone. Might as well be from their father, who had actually been there to see it firsthand.

Well, some of it, anyway.

The girls and I sat down on the bed. Anna leaned toward her sister, whispering something in her ear. Typical of Anna's attention span: she'd probably already forgotten about the forest.

Agnarr raised an eyebrow. "*If* they can settle down and listen."

I stifled a laugh as they both immediately snapped their mouths shut.

"Far away," he began, "as far north as we could go . . ."

And so he began to tell the tale, his storyteller voice soft but dramatic as both girls listened with rapt attention, wide-eyed. I leaned back on the bed, closing my own eyes, trying to stay focused on his words. But soon an all-too-familiar storm began to swirl inside me, stirring up long-ago, almost forgotten memories of that fateful day.

It had been years since Agnarr and I talked about the forest. Even longer since we'd traveled out to the mist itself to check on it. Now we were busy, ruling a kingdom, parenting two little girls. We did still send a patrol to the mists every six months, but they always came back with the same news.

The mist still held.

I turned my attention back to the story, realizing Agnarr was almost done.

"And someone saved me," he explained. "I'm told that

the spirits then vanished and a powerful mist came over the forest, locking everyone else out and keeping others in." He looked solemnly at the girls. "And that night, I came home king of Arendelle."

I smiled a little at the hyperbole, remembering all the intervening years he'd been the crown prince, not yet anointed, rolling his eyes through every council meeting and running off to our tree every chance he got. But that didn't make for a good story.

"Whoa, Papa!" Anna breathed. "That was epic! Whoever saved you, I love them!" She fell back into my lap in a dramatic swoon. I couldn't help a small smile. If only she knew. . . .

My smile faded as Agnarr responded seriously, "I wish I knew who it was."

If only *he* knew. . . .

My heart ached. All these years had passed between us. A loving marriage, two beautiful girls, a peaceful kingdom. And I'd still never found the right moment to tell him everything, still bound by the night Peterssen had pulled me aside and bidden me to keep my secret.

I set my resolve. Maybe tonight. After we got the girls to sleep.

"What happened to the spirits? What's in the forest now?" Elsa piped up, looking quite concerned. I sighed. I'd known this story was going to upset them. They were still so young.

"I don't know. The mist still stands. No one can get in. And no one has since come out," Agnarr responded.

"So we're safe," I added, shooting him a stern look.

"Yes," he said. "But the forest could wake again. And we must be prepared for whatever danger we might face."

"And on that note, how about we say good night to your father?" I interrupted, laying a gentle hand on Agnarr's arm—even though at this point I wanted to shove him off the bed. Why did he think getting his children all riled up right before bedtime with his stories was always such a good idea?

"Aw, but I still have so many questions!" Anna pouted.

"Save them for another night, Anna," Agnarr teased, tugging on her toe. He rose and headed out the door, leaving me alone with the girls. I sighed. Time for damage control if I wanted them to get *any* sleep that night.

"You know I don't have that kind of patience!" Anna said, scowling after her father. Then she turned to me. "Why did the Northuldra attack us, anyway? Who attacks people who give them gifts?"

"Do you think the forest will wake again?" Elsa added, still looking concerned.

"Only Ahtohallan knows," I murmured before I could stop myself.

"Ah-to-who-what?" Anna asked, her big eyes growing even wider.

I startled a little. Had I just said that out loud? And here I hadn't wanted Agnarr to tell his story. Was I really about to tell them mine?

"When I was little," I said slowly, unsure of the best way to start, "my mother would sing a song about a special river called Ahtohallan that was said to hold all the answers about the past and what we are a part of."

"Whoa!" Anna breathed.

"Can you sing it to us?" Elsa asked.

My breath caught. Could I?

But then I looked down at them, their sweet faces, their large eyes. Anna curious, Elsa a little more reserved. And something inside me gave, for the first time in many years. Maybe it *was* time. Not for the whole story—not yet. But maybe just a song. After all, it was part of who they were, even if didn't know it. And maybe it would comfort them somehow. It had always comforted me when I was a child.

"Okay," I said, gathering them into my arms. "Cuddle close, scooch in," I urged them, as I used to say to their father many years before.

Just as my mother used to say to me.

And then I began to sing.

CHAPTER FORTY-FOUR

Agnarr

"WOW. WE HAVEN'T BEEN IN HERE FOR AGES!"

I stifled a sneeze as I slipped into the now very dusty secret library, memories flooding through me as I looked around, everything still in its place. I thought back to all the hours Iduna and I had spent in here, hiding out from the world. As I glanced back at her now, closing the door behind me, an impulsive urge rose over me. I grabbed her and swung her around, kissing her hard on the mouth.

She kissed me back, laughing. "Wow. This place really does it for you," she teased.

"*You* really do it for me," I corrected her, smiling wickedly at her. I kissed her again, deeply, my body warming at her touch. Even after all these years, Iduna still made my heart race like when I was just a young boy.

"You'd better watch it," she said, pushing me away gently. "After that story you told? The girls are bound to be up all night, worried about monsters in the mist. We'll find them both in our bed when we get back, I bet."

I groaned. "Too much?"

"*Epically* too much," she replied, mimicking Anna's words. She sat down on a nearby chair, scrubbing her face with her hands. "But then, I guess they had to find out someday."

"Yes," I agreed. "They need to know the truth, even when its unpleasant. I don't want them growing up as I did. With all those secrets."

I watched the playful smile disappear from Iduna's face as she visibly paled. I cocked my head in question. "Are you all right?" Iduna shook her head, blue eyes welling with tears.

"What's wrong?" I asked, reaching down to clasp her hands in mine.

"Agnarr. There's something—"

"*Mama! Papa!*"

The sharp cry roared through the room, as if it came from right outside. Loud screeching, hysterical. Iduna turned stark white.

"Elsa!" she whispered.

We dove out of the room, following the sound of her voice. We headed past the girls' now empty bedroom, down the stairs, to the Great Hall. I could hear sobbing coming from behind the closed doors and my heart seized with panic. What were they doing down here? They were supposed to be in bed! I threw open the doors wide, then stopped short, horrified at what I saw.

Mountains of snow, piled high. The walls crawling with ice.

Elsa cradling her sister in her arms.

No!

My heart leapt in my chest. "Elsa!" I cried. "What have you done? This is getting out of hand!"

The second I spoke the words, I regretted them. Especially when I caught the agonized look on my eldest daughter's face.

"It was an accident!" Elsa wailed, looking down at her sister. "I'm sorry, Anna."

Iduna dropped to her knees, pulling Anna away from Elsa and into her own arms. Anna lay so still. Was she even breathing? Iduna looked up at me, her eyes wide and frightened. "She's ice cold," she whispered.

I did everything in my power to keep it together, even though all I wanted to do was fall apart. This was too much. And if anything happened to my Anna . . . my sweet, silly Anna . . .

I shook my head. Those thoughts didn't help. Right now my family needed me. I needed to stay strong. For them.

I froze, an idea suddenly forming in my mind. *The trolls.* Grand Pabbie. He'd proven he could do magic. Could he help Anna somehow? And if so, could we reach him in time?

We had no choice but to try.

"I know where we have to go," I said. "Take the girls

to the stable. Have them saddle up two horses. I will meet you there."

Tears slipped down Iduna's cheeks. "All right. But hurry. . . ."

I rose to my feet. Iduna lifted Anna, cradling her like a baby. Elsa was still crying hard, clinging to her mother's skirt. I gave them one last look and then ran straight to the library, heading back into the secret room.

Where I'd hidden the map.

With trembling hands, I reached up to a high shelf, pulled the old folklore book down, and paged through it until I found the map, tucked away. I smoothed it out on the table, refreshing the route in my mind. Then I stuffed it in my satchel and ran to meet my girls at the stable.

We rode out into the night. Iduna was white-faced and quiet, cradling the still-motionless Anna in her arms. Elsa was with me on my horse, sobbing her eyes out. She kept glancing over at her sister longingly. My heart ached at the pain I saw her on face.

"I'm really sorry, Papa," she whimpered. "I'm so, so sorry!"

"It's not your fault," I said wearily. "I'm sorry I shouted. I was scared, that's all."

"I'm scared, too."

I reached out to touch Elsa's shoulder, wanting to comfort her. But she recoiled from me. A sob escaped her throat. "Please don't! I don't want to hurt you, too."

Pain shot through my heart at the anguish I saw on

her face. As angry as I was, my rage was never directed at my daughter. It wasn't her fault. She was a good girl. She loved her sister. She would never willingly hurt her.

"Don't worry," I said, trying to make my voice sound reassuring. "I'm taking you to someone who can help. We're going to fix this. I promise. Anna will be okay."

But even as I said the words, I wondered. Would anything be okay, ever again?

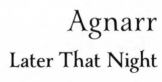

CHAPTER FORTY-FIVE

Agnarr
Later That Night

"WHAT DO I DO, PAPA? WHAT IF I CAN'T control it?"

"Shhh, sweet girl," I whispered, tucking Elsa into her bed, pulling the blanket over her shivering frame. Iduna was doing the same with Anna a few rooms away. Though Anna had not yet woken, she was breathing easier, and her skin was once again flushed with warmth. The only lasting effect of the incident seemed to be a strange streak of white in her auburn hair. Something she would likely keep, the trolls said. But it was not dangerous.

She would be okay.

This time.

"Just try to get some sleep," I said. "We can talk more in the morning. Form a plan."

"Will Anna be okay?" Elsa whimpered.

"She will," I assured her. "And you will be, too." I

forced the words past the lump in my throat, hoping that if I said them with enough conviction, I could convince myself of their truth, too.

Her face crumpled. "I wish I never had magic!"

I stroked her forehead. "I know," I told her gently. "Unfortunately, we can't simply wish away who we are. But, sweetheart, you are not alone in this. We will work together, as a family, to help get your power under control. Whatever it takes. You are strong. You are a princess of Arendelle, after all."

She nodded her little head resolutely. I rose to my feet and started toward the door.

"Papa!" she called out after me.

I stopped. "Yes, Elsa?"

"Please! I don't want to be alone!"

For a moment, I just stood there, not sure what to do. Then a sudden thought struck me. I turned to my daughter. "Hang on," I said. "I'll be right back."

I left her room and raced down the hall to my chambers. I reached to the back of the wardrobe and pulled out a wooden chest. After opening it, I reached in and unwrapped the small object I'd placed on top.

Then I returned to Elsa's room.

"Hello!" I said, making my voice as silly as possible. "Allow me to introduce myself! I am Sir JörgenBjörgen. And I am a protector puffin!" I waved the little stuffed animal in front of me, as if it were waddling in her direction.

Elsa stared at the puffin. "Nice to meet you . . .

JörgenBjörgen?" she said, her voice still no more than a whisper. But I could see the childish interest piqued in her wide blue eyes and it gave me hope.

"That's *Sir* JörgenBjörgen to you, madam!" I corrected haughtily. "I am a royal member of the Arendelle guard. Once I was tasked to keep your father safe. But now, I have been reassigned to you! Which I'm very excited about, because I love ice," I added.

I tossed the puffin in her direction. She caught it in her arms and cuddled it to her chest. "Thank you, Sir JörgenBjörgen," she said softly, stroking his fur. "Now I don't have to be alone."

I crept toward the doorway. "Try to get some sleep," I said again. "We'll talk more in the morning."

I closed the door gently behind me, finding Iduna standing in the hallway. She gave me a sad smile. "That was a good idea," she said. "Giving her your stuffed animal."

"Sir JörgenBjörgen got me through some tough times," I admitted. "Hopefully he can help Elsa, too."

Iduna's shoulders slumped. With the adrenaline of the evening fading, exhaustion was setting in. I pulled her into my arms and held her close. I could feel her heartbeat against my chest as she snuggled into the crook of my shoulder.

"Do you think we're doing the right thing?" she whispered. "Separating them like this? I mean, they're sisters! They're so close."

"Which is part of the problem," I said. "From what we've seen, joy seems to bring out Elsa's powers as much as fear. Which makes it dangerous for us to keep them together. At least for right now." I shuddered, thinking back to Anna's pale face. Her little body, so cold. If we had lost her . . .

I felt Iduna's reluctant nod. It wasn't what she wanted, but she knew it was for the best.

"It won't be forever," I said, trying to soothe her. "I'll work with Elsa every day. We'll figure out a way for her to control her power. Once she does, there will no longer be any reason to keep them apart."

Iduna pulled away from my embrace, meeting my eyes with her own. "And Arendelle? Did you mean what you said to Grand Pabbie about closing the gates? Shutting the people out, too?"

I flinched at the note of accusation I heard in her voice. But I had to do what was best for Elsa, what would keep her safe. "Just temporarily," I assured her. "To protect Elsa. You know how the people of Arendelle react to magic. If they learned what her magic did to Anna, they'd think her a monster. They'd never allow her to become queen. We can't let that happen. We must protect Elsa and her right to the throne. Unless you can think of any other way . . ."

She hung her head. I knew she didn't like it, but she also saw no alternative. We needed to protect our family. Our girls.

"I love you," she whispered.

"I love you, too," I murmured back, stroking her hair with my hand. "And I know this is hard. Probably the hardest thing we've ever had to face. But I promise you, we *will* get through this—together."

And until then?

Conceal, don't feel.

CHAPTER FORTY-SIX

Iduna

Ten Years Later

"NO! NO! NO!"

Elsa's anguished cry rang through the hall. Heart in my throat, I ran to her door and pushed it open after making sure no one was standing nearby. I ducked in, then quickly shut the door and locked it before turning to my daughter. Elsa was standing at her window. Ice seeped from her fingers, crusting the sill. The entire room was freezing cold and I fought back a shiver. Usually I wore my coat to visit her. But she had sounded so distraught I didn't know if she could wait.

"Elsa," I called quietly, not wanting to frighten her. She lost control when she was scared. And that was when things got worse. As long as we could keep her calm, quiet, she could sometimes regain her composure.

She turned to me, icy tears crusting her eyelashes. The sorrow that surrounded her was unbearable.

"Sweetheart," I begged, stepping toward her.

She held up a trembling hand. "No!" she cried. "Please don't come any closer! I don't want to hurt you!" I could see the icicles forming at her fingertips and took a hasty step backward, though it killed me to do so. She was my daughter!

But she had grown into something else, too. Something so powerful it scared me half to death.

I thought back to Grand Pabbie's words.

Your power will only grow, he had warned. *You must learn to control it.*

Since then, Agnarr had tried to help her do just that—control her emotions, control her magic.

Conceal, don't feel. Don't let it show.

It hadn't worked. In fact, things had only gotten worse.

It was as though the castle had been put under a storybook curse: Anna wandering the halls like a ghost, not understanding why her sister had shut her out, her memories of her sister's magic, and the night she was injured, erased. Elsa, too frightened to leave her room. I used to try to talk her into coming out to play a game or eat dinner with the family. Surely she could handle that! Her powers only manifested when her emotions were strong. We could keep things calm. Peaceful. She'd be safe. Anna would be safe.

But she always refused. Too afraid she'd hurt her sister again. Even after all these years, I still saw the guilt of what she'd done to Anna swimming in her eyes. It broke me every time.

As for Agnarr, he'd retreated into his work, throwing himself into the affairs of state and holding endless meetings. I felt like I hardly saw him these days, except at night when he finally crawled into bed, so exhausted he barely spoke before falling asleep. When I pressed him, he assured me everything was fine. He was just busy. But I could see the torment deep in his eyes. He knew, deep down, that his plan hadn't worked, would never work. And our family, our happiness, was being torn apart, day by day.

I spent most of my days in the secret room in the library. But instead of painting stars on the ceiling, or sharing hopes and dreams, I now dove into research, translating old books and scrolls. Taking notes, trying to piece together clues.

"Why?" I asked the spirits in frustration after a particularly grueling translation of an old folklore book. "Why did you do this to her? Why must she suffer so? If this is a gift, let her use it! And if it is a curse, take it away!"

But the spirits didn't answer. For they were still locked away behind the mist.

"Mama," Elsa whimpered now, her voice drawing me back to the present. But when I tried to step closer, she backed away again, until she was flush against the wall, with ice crawling up the sides of it. I remembered, sadly, how she used to cuddle up to me as a child, allowing me to sing her to sleep. I wondered if she even slept these days at all.

"It's okay, dear one," I told her, forcing myself to stop

in my tracks. "I won't come any closer if that's what you want."

Her face twisted in agony. "Conceal, don't feel," I heard her whisper. "Don't let it show." My heart panged.

"I know that's what your father has told you," I said slowly. "And maybe it does help, for a time. But squashing down your emotions can only work for so long. Before you feel like a powder keg. Ready to explode."

I cringed at the idea of the coming explosion, which at this point seemed unavoidable. It could be devastating not only to her, but perhaps to the entire kingdom. That was why we had her here, tucked away, I tried to remind myself. But all the rationality in the world couldn't quash the guilt. It was cruel to keep her here in this cramped room. The kind of thing villains did in the storybooks— not heroes.

"Elsa, please," I begged. "You can do this. I know you can. Just try a little harder."

"I've *been* trying, Mother! I've been trying so hard and it's only getting worse. I don't know how much more I can take!" Her sobs echoed through the frigid room. "I don't want to hurt anyone. Not you, not Father. Not . . . Anna."

She looked like a broken doll. A shell of the person she'd been meant to be. All these years, we'd tried to protect her. We'd tried to keep her safe. Instead, we'd broken her spirit. This beautiful, wild, magical girl should not be trapped in a cage of our making. She should be free to spread her wings and fly like the wind.

Like the spirits themselves . . .

Was this destined to go on forever?

Only Ahtohallan knows.

Ahtohallan. The one spirit still out there. Somewhere. If only there was a way to find her.

"I understand, sweetheart," I said at last. "Just . . . hang on a little longer, okay? My brave girl." My voice cracked on the last part and I felt a tear fall from my eye, sliding slowly down my cheek. Elsa saw it, and to my surprise, she suddenly stepped forward, closing the distance between us. I watched, breathless, as she reached out with a shaky hand and swiped the tear from my cheek. It froze on her fingertip—a perfect crystal trapped in time. Then she flicked it away, looking at me with her great, deep, sorrowful eyes.

"I love you, Mama," she said slowly. "And I trust you. I know you will help me."

I nodded woodenly, wanting to grab her, to pull her close and squeeze her tight. Never let her go. But such a move could cause her to hurt me. And I knew if she did—however unintentional—it would destroy her.

I gave a fleeting smile and a wave, even though inside I felt like dying. "I'll be back," I assured her. "Soon."

I unlocked the door and headed through it, back into the warmth of the castle.

Back to the library. This time I wasn't leaving until I figured it out.

CHAPTER FORTY-SEVEN

Iduna

"I NEED TO TALK TO YOU."

I burst into Agnarr's study, not bothering to knock. Agnarr looked up from behind the great oak desk, where he was going over his papers. "Can it wait?" he asked, looking a little stressed, which these days was nothing new.

"No." I shook my head, excitement coursing through me, mixed with quite a bit of fear. "It can't."

To his credit, he set down his papers, then rose to his feet to face me. "What is it?"

"Not here," I said. "Meet me in the secret library."

I dashed out of the study and down the hall, not waiting for his reply. I'd been practically living in the secret library for weeks now, barely bothering to eat or sleep, never mind bathe. I probably looked like a castle ghost at this point. Kai and Gerda were constantly asking me if I was all right. Encouraging me to get some rest. To eat.

But I couldn't. Not until I found what I was looking for.

And now, maybe, I had.

Maybe.

And now I had to share it with Agnarr.

I had to share *everything.*

It shouldn't be so terrifying to talk openly with my own husband. But it had been too long. There were too many secrets. And I was fully aware that coming clean now might finally cause the house of cards we'd been building for years to topple over for good.

But I had no choice. Elsa's life depended on it.

I stepped into the library, still remembering that first day in the castle, when Agnarr had proudly showed it off to me. I recalled my surprise as I looked up from floor to ceiling at the seemingly endless rows of books lining the shelves. Before then, I'd only seen a few books in my life; most Northuldra stories came from song and oral tales. It had been quite a shock, back then, to see so much written down.

But now I walked past the shelves, hardly noticing them as I headed directly to the back of the room, where the statue of the Water Nokk stood, guarding our secret chamber. With a quick, practiced motion, I activated the door, and it opened with a loud creaking sound. I stepped inside, with Agnarr on my heels. It was embarrassingly messy—a result of my desperate studies—and I paced the room nervously, sitting down one moment, standing the next.

After this conversation, everything would change. Forever. And I wasn't sure I was ready for it.

Agnarr joined me after closing the passageway door behind him. I thought back to all the time we'd spent here when we were young, hiding our love from the world. Had my whole life just been a series of secrets, each more dangerous than the last? Was that why we were cursed now, by a secret so awful it was destroying my child's very life?

It's a gift, not a curse, I scolded myself. But it was getting harder to believe each day. Each time I gazed upon Elsa's tortured face.

Conceal, don't feel. . . .

No. We were done with that. I swallowed hard, turning to Agnarr.

"There's something I have to tell you," I said, surprised at how strong my voice rang out. "Something about my past."

Agnarr stepped toward me, grasping my hands and pulling them to his chest. His eyes met mine. His were troubled but focused.

"I'm listening," he said softly.

It was more than I could take. Tears streamed down my cheeks like rain. Agnarr pulled me into his arms, stroking my back with his hands. Hands as gentle and strong as they'd always been. I almost gave in right there—almost melted into his embrace and pushed down the truth for another day.

But in the end, I pulled away, angrily wiping at the

tears. I couldn't fall apart now. I had to get through this.
For Elsa. My sweet Elsa. And for Anna as well. My two
daughters. I had to be strong for them.

I had to tell the truth at last.

Only, I didn't know where to start. How would I
even begin to explain? But then a single moment rose to
my consciousness, blooming in my heart. The first spark
that had grown into this inferno.

"That . . . day in the forest," I managed to say. "The
battle by the dam."

"Yes?"

"The person who saved you. That was . . . me."

His eyes widened. I could feel his hands trembling
against my body, but he stood tall and still, only tighten-
ing his grip, not letting me go.

"It was you?" he whispered, but I could see the recognition begin to dawn in his eyes. "It *was* you," he said
again, this time in a sure and certain tone.

I nodded, emotions flying through me too hard and
fast to catalog. "Me," I continued. "And my friend Gale,
the Wind Spirit."

He stared at me, for a moment, not comprehending.
"Wind spirit? But . . ."

He dropped his hands to his sides. Fear thrummed in
my heart as I searched his face.

There was no going back.

"I am Northuldra," I blurted out. "I was trapped outside the mist because I saved your life. I was discovered
in Arendelle and Peterssen felt bad for me and protected

me, saying my Arendellian parents died in the fight. In truth, my parents were already dead." My cheeks felt as if they were on fire as I stumbled on.

Agnarr staggered backward. But I had to get it all out there now if there was any chance to save Elsa.

"I'm sorry," I said simply. "I know people have kept secrets from you your entire life. The last thing I wanted was to be one of them. I wanted to tell you, Agnarr—so much. I was going to right after the proposal. But that night, Peterssen told me to keep my secret close, for the good of Arendelle. I was told I would be responsible for Arendelle's fall if people were to learn the truth. And your fall, too." My voice broke. "I was told you could lose everything—your crown, maybe even your life—if I revealed my secret. And even when he said it, I knew it was true."

"What?" Agnarr's face twisted. "But that's not fair! You were just a girl! To force you to keep silent about who you are? To make you think your truth could take down a kingdom?"

His anger on my behalf brought tears to my eyes. His willingness to put the blame on others—not me. But though Peterssen had indeed pushed me to keep my secret safe, in the end it had been my decision to stay silent. Not out of shame of who I was.

But out of fear.

Fear was the only true enemy.

And it was still hurting us now.

"I did what I thought I had to do," I said. "I regret it

now, but I cannot change it. I do believe Peterssen, for all his faults, was trying to protect Arendelle—the only way he knew how." I gave a sour laugh. "And who could blame him? It's practically the castle's motto, right? 'Conceal, don't feel'?" I paused, meeting his eyes with my own. "And before you judge Peterssen, haven't we, ourselves, been guilty of demanding the same from Elsa? Asking her to hide who she truly is?"

Agnarr's face went stark white. I stood there, waiting for him to digest this truth. I knew it was harsh—for he, like Peterssen, had only wanted to do the right thing.

But sometimes even the best intentions can lead to disastrous ends.

"My whole life I was told to hide," I said after a pause. "I don't want Elsa to have to grow up doing the same."

Agnarr bit his lower lip. "Do you . . . have magic?" he asked slowly. "Is that why . . . Elsa . . . ?"

"No." I shook my head firmly. "Like the rest of the Northuldra, I lived in harmony with the spirits and used their gifts. But I have no magic running through my veins. I never have. And yet . . ." I trailed off, not knowing how to continue.

He reached out, brushing my cheek with gentle fingers. "And yet?" he asked. So calm, so quiet, considering the storm I'd stirred up with my truth. He had to be screaming inside. But somehow, he didn't look angry. And not because he was concealing it; I knew that look by now. But rather because he wasn't angry. He was just sad. And not sad for himself, either.

But sad for me. For all those years I'd suffered in silence.

Sad for Elsa, too.

I pushed on, suddenly feeling brave. "I believe Elsa is a gift from the spirits," I told him. "A daughter of Arendellian and Northuldra blood. A union of our people, born out of love instead of fear. I believe Elsa was born with her powers for a reason."

For the longest time, Agnarr stood stock-still. Then he nodded slowly. I could tell he was struggling to take it in. It was too much, far too much to lay on him all at once after so many years of keeping him in the dark. I tried to imagine if the tables were turned, how I would feel if I learned everything he'd told me had been a lie. It wasn't a comfortable thought.

But Agnarr, I realized, was strong. His love for me was strong. I had never doubted that. And I couldn't doubt it now.

Drawing in a breath, I dared to slip my hands back into his.

"Look, Agnarr, you need to know. Though I may have hidden where I came from, I never once hid who I am. The girl you grew up with, the woman you married? She was always me. The real me. And my love for you? That's always been real, too. I love you more than anything in the world, and I always will." My voice hitched. "Though I would understand if you wanted to—"

His hands tightened around mine. "I love you, too," he said firmly, without doubt or hesitation. "And there is no need to hide anything anymore. From anyone—ever again." He looked down at me, an expression on his face so earnest it made me think of the boy he once was. "And we'll tell the girls, too. They're going to think it's so great. Maybe you can even teach us some of the Northuldra traditions. Your songs, your stories." He paused, a look of realization washing over his face. "Your crazy reindeer marriage proposal," he added, as if it had just come to him. "Was that . . . ?"

My mouth spread in a bashful grin. "It was," I confirmed. "After all, you had the Arendellian love spoon. If we were truly coming together, I wanted to include something from my family's traditions, too. However ridiculous that particular one might be," I added with a small laugh.

"I think the word you're looking for is 'amazing,'" he corrected me, looking down at me with so much love it took my breath away. He pulled me into an embrace and held me tight. Tears of sharp relief rolled down my cheeks as I cradled my head in his solid chest, listening to his heartbeat. Strong, steady. Just like Agnarr himself.

For a moment, we just stood there, wrapped in one another's arms in the tiny secret room just off the library. How many times had we been here before? How many kisses had been shared? Declarations of love made? But this time felt different. For now he knew the truth. And all the guilt and fear I'd pushed down deep inside was finally gone.

For the first time in forever, I was free.

But we still had to talk about Elsa.

Agnarr cleared his throat. "You said you think Elsa was a gift from the spirits," he said slowly. "And you also said since you're Northuldra, you know the spirits. Can you . . . maybe . . . ask them about her? Maybe they would know what we could do to help her?"

I practically gasped. In all the emotion of telling him, I'd almost forgotten why I'd started to do so.

"The spirits are still locked away in the mist," I explained. "At least as far as I can tell. I have not been able to talk to them for years. I thought once they might have come, when I was out in the blizzard the day I left Arendelle. But it must have been a hallucination. For I have called them every day since and they have never returned."

"I see," Agnarr said, his face ashen, the hope gone.

I drew in a breath. "However, there is still . . . something . . . that might be out there. Who might be able to give us the answers we seek."

His head cocked in question.

"Ahtohallan," I explained. "My mother used to sing me a song about her when I was small. It's a Northuldra song about a spirit—the mother of all the other spirits—who knows everything about the past. A river of memories. I always thought if I could only find her, she could provide answers about Elsa and what we are a part of."

"Well, then let's find Ahtohallan," Agnarr declared, his voice fierce. I always loved when he decided on a plan of action. He committed fully and immediately, no matter the challenges.

I reached down and pulled the old, faded map off the table. "I think I already have," I said slowly. "That's why I've been in here every day. Puzzling over all these maps. The song says, 'Where the north wind meets the sea,' but I could never find a river there that fit that description. Until now."

I placed my finger over the dark block on the top of the map.

"Ahtohallan," I declared.

"But that's not a river."

"No." My eyes shone as I looked up at him. "It's a glacier. Glaciers are rivers of ice."

"Ahtohallan is . . . frozen?" he asked, eyes wide.

I shrugged. "It's the only thing that makes sense."

He stared down at the map. I could practically see the gears turning in his head. Then he looked up at me. "And you think if we were to go there, to this spirit, it would be able to provide us answers about Elsa?"

"I think so," I said, my voice hardly more than a whisper. "It's worth a try, right?"

"Yes," he said. And I was relieved to hear not a drop of doubt his voice. "I would go to the ends of the earth to help her."

My shoulders slumped in relief. Hope rose in my chest.

Agnarr rolled up the map. "We will travel there. As soon as it can be arranged." He gave me a hesitant smile. "One last, last adventure. You and me."

CHAPTER FORTY-EIGHT

Iduna

"DO YOU HAVE TO GO?"

Things had moved quickly from the night I had told Agnarr the truth in our secret room. Our story was simple: we were going on a two-week trip, to attend the wedding of a faraway princess by route of the Southern Sea. We would trust only the captain of the ship and his skeleton crew with the truth—and even then, not until after we'd set sail.

No one wanted us to go, of course, the seas being notoriously dangerous at this time of year. But no one was more adamant about this than Elsa.

"You'll be fine, Elsa," Agnarr said to her sympathetically. I knew he was trying to build up her confidence, but it ended up sounding a little patronizing. I could see her chin wobble. Her lips tremble. I could practically hear the thoughts whirling through her head.

Conceal, don't feel.

Ignoring the danger of my daughter's emotions, I grabbed her in a tight hug. "We will be back soon," I promised her. "You'll barely notice we're gone."

And if all works out, you'll never have to conceal your feelings again.

She was stiff in my arms, and when I released her, she looked a hair's breadth from breaking down in tears. My heart tore and suddenly it was all I could do not to back down, beg to stay home. Send Agnarr alone on our quest so I didn't have to leave my baby girl behind. Elsa had no one but us, not even her sister. She would be truly alone.

But I had to stay strong. We needed answers. And this was the only way to find them.

To help Elsa once and for all.

"Come on," Agnarr said firmly, placing a hand at the small of my back and leading me away. I went with him, almost reaching the front door before I turned around again for one last look.

Elsa stood there alone. Her shoulders pushed back. Her head held high. Trying so desperately to be brave. And suddenly my mind flashed back to that day I'd first arrived in Arendelle so long ago. I had stood there, too, at the entrance of the orphanage, alone in a new world filled only with strangers. I still remembered how badly I wanted to give up at that moment. To crumble and fall apart and let it all go. But instead I managed to hold my head high. To force myself to go on, even when all seemed lost.

And I had. I'd built a life here in Arendelle. I'd found

friends. Built a family with my true love. A beautiful life, blooming out of ashes. It hadn't always been easy, but I wouldn't change it for the world.

And Elsa would find her way, too, I told myself as the lump formed in my throat again. For all her pain, she was stronger than anyone I knew. Far stronger than I had ever been. And no matter what happened, she would find a way to keep going. To forge a path into the unknown.

A little while later we were at the harbor, crossing the gangplank and boarding the ship. Everything in me cried out to turn around, to run back to the shelter of the castle, to my daughters.

But this was Elsa's one hope. I had to be brave. I had to do this. For her.

I just hoped it wouldn't all be in vain.

EPILOGUE

Iduna

THE WIND PICKS UP AGAIN, SENDING A FIERCE swell slamming into the side of our ship, nearly causing me to fall out of bed. My vision is blurry and it takes me a moment to realize why. Then it hits me.

I'm crying.

I'm sobbing, actually.

I turn to Agnarr, reaching for his hands. He clasps them in his own, his face troubled, trying to take it all in. I would give anything to know his thoughts. Everything has happened so fast. We haven't had a chance to really talk until now.

"I'm sorry for not telling you everything from the start," I say, my voice barely audible over the raging storm.

Agnarr pushes back the bedcovers, rises to his feet. His eyes meet mine and I am surprised to see the fierceness they reflect. "Don't apologize again," he said. "You did what you needed to do to survive. And because of it,

I got to spend my life by your side. There is no other life on earth I would have rather lived."

I don't like the past tense he's already started to use. But I know in my heart he's not wrong. The storm is raging, growing worse with every passing moment. Whatever I want to say, it has to be now. Even still, so much has been left unspoken.

But *I love you* is all I say. They're the only words I can get past my trembling lips.

"I love you, too," he murmurs. "So much." He pulls me into his arms. "And I promise you, there's no secret in the world big enough to tear that love apart."

I lean against him, absorbing his strength. He is as warm and strong as always. But still, I'm not at peace. "Our girls," I murmur. "What will they do?"

When we're gone, is the part I leave unspoken.

"They will do what they will have to do," Agnarr says gently. "As we once did."

I know he's right. But I don't want to accept it. I don't want my daughters suffering, all alone.

"At least they have each other," Agnarr reminds me.

"They *don't,* though!" I cry, suddenly angry. "They barely know each other." My voice cracks. "Maybe we made a mistake separating them. Maybe we should have—"

"We did what we thought was best," Agnarr says firmly. "For our children. Only time will tell if it was right or wrong. But I have faith in them. They are young. But they are already so strong. And if anyone can help

Elsa, it's Anna." He smiles softly. "There's not much that girl can't do."

"You're right about that," I reply, shaking my head as I think lovingly about my youngest daughter. "Her love could hold up the world."

Agnarr nods. "When the time comes, I truly believe they will do the right thing."

"For Arendelle?"

"No." He shakes his head. "For each other."

The thought about breaks me. My mind flashes to Elsa, standing at the bottom of the stairs, fear running through her eyes. I think of Anna, waiting endlessly, hopefully, at her sister's bedroom door.

Will they ever have the chance to become the sisters they once were, before we tore them apart? And could it be possible that someday they will find happiness and love as Agnarr and I did?

I can't bear the thoughts swirling through my head any longer. I walk to the door and start up the stairs to the top deck of the ship. I won't spend what may be my last minutes below deck—all darkness and stale air. I am Northuldra. We are the people of the sun.

I may never see another sunrise. But I refuse to die in the darkness.

I hear Agnarr follow me on the stairs and am relieved. I'd never force him to follow me. But I am glad he has chosen to.

I step out onto the deck. The ship is rocking furiously and I have to grab on to a mast to keep upright. Sailors are running half-heartedly, checking the sails, but I can tell from their faces they've already lost hope. The end is coming. There will be no last-minute salvation.

And if all we have left is this moment, I don't want to waste it.

I walk to the side of the boat, staring down into the angry sea. The waves are huge and the water is swirling in immense, twisting shapes. It makes me think of the Water Nokk—the Water Spirit from my childhood long ago. A sharp pain of regret stabs at my stomach.

I never did get back home.

I stare down at the water, my vision blurry from the driving rain. To my surprise, a wavering image seems to float up from the depths of the sea.

A girl, laughing and dancing in the wind.

Is it me? But no . . . it looks more like . . .

I turn and ask Agnarr, "Are you seeing this?" But he's gone off to confer with the captain.

I turn back to the water, desperate for another look. But the girl is now gone, too. In her place stand two women. One dressed in a glowing white gown with white-blond hair tumbling down her back. The other—a redhead—clothed in rich greens and blacks and purples, with a familiar-looking crown atop her head. Both women are smiling.

Smiling at each other.

My breath hitches. Tears well in my eyes. Could it be? Could these two beautiful women really be my daughters? Not as they are now . . . but as they will be?

Only Ahtohallan knows . . . a voice seems to whisper in my ear.

The waters churn again and the vision vanishes. I cry out in alarm, causing Agnarr to rush to my side. "What is it?" he asks urgently.

I shake my head. "Nothing," I say. "I just . . . I thought I saw something in the water."

Was it a vision from Ahtohallan? Or simply a mother's heartfelt wish on a wave? I will never know for certain. But still, I draw that image of my beautiful girls deep into my soul. Their wide smiles. The joyous looks in their eyes. It seems an impossible future.

And yet . . .

Why couldn't it be? They are strong; they are smart. They will be able to shape their own destinies. Make their ways as Agnarr and I once did. Find their own hap-pily ever afters.

I just hope they find them together.

Agnarr puts his arms around me. I cuddle in close to him, feeling a strange sense of peace wash over me at last as the sea rages on. We won't survive this night. But it doesn't matter in the end. For our love has created a legacy. A true magic all its own that will live on in our daughters. And hopefully their daughters and sons.

Arendelle and Northuldra, united again and again, in every heartbeat to come.

I lift my face to the wind. My voice rises in song.

"Ah ah ah ah . . ."

ACKNOWLEDGMENTS

AS A LIFELONG DISNEY NERD AND HUGE Frozen superfan, I felt like being asked to write this book was like someone telling me I'd won the lottery–only better! Even now, I'm still pinching myself!

All the gratitude and thanks to my dream editor, Heather Knowles, who is so fun to work with it doesn't even feel like work! I loved brainstorming with you and diving down deep into the Frozen 'verse. (But not too deep, to avoid the whole messy drowning bit . . .) I hope we do a million books together in the future!

Of course, these books also take an Arendelle-size village. Thank you to all the hardworking people at Team Disney, including Elana Cohen, Monica Vasquez, Alison Giordano, Al Giuliani, Susan Gerber, Anne Peters, Megan Speer, Warren Meislin, and Jennifer Black. Also, Grace Lee for the amazing cover artwork and Winnie Ho for the gorgeous overall design.

On the film side of things, thank you to Heather Blodget and Peter Del Vecho for their tireless answering of questions on Frozen lore—and for their openness to my little twists on it.

And thank you to the incredible filmmakers, Jennifer Lee and Christopher Beck, for creating such an amazing world and wonderful characters to play with. (Is this the spot where I beg you for a part three?)

Thank you also to my agent, Mandy Hubbard, and to editor Kieran Viola, who knew how much a book like this would mean to me. We Disney girls have to stick together!

And to my husband, Jacob, for supporting me and cooking for me and becoming a legit "dance dad" when I was under tight deadline. I couldn't do any of this without you. And to my sweet daughter, Avalon—you are a total Anna and I am so proud of the girl you have become. Smart, creative, talented. But most importantly, your love could hold up the world.

Lastly, to all the Frozen superfans out there—you make this all possible. Thank you for continuing to support and embrace this world and all its inhabitants and for allowing us to keep telling their stories. Some people are truly worth melting for!